Legion

-Hell on Earth Book 2-

by Iain Rob Wright

SalGad Publishing Group

Worcestshire, United Kingdom

Legion

Hell on Earth Book 2

Copyright © 2016 by Iain Rob Wright

ISBN-13: 978-1533587978
ISBN-10: 1533587973

Cover art by Stuart Bache
Edited by Autumn Speckhardt
Interior design by Iain Rob Wright

www.iainrobwright.com

Give feedback on the book at:
iain.robert.wright@hotmail.co.uk

Twitter: @iainrobwright

First Edition

Printed in the U.S.A

For my readers. You rule.

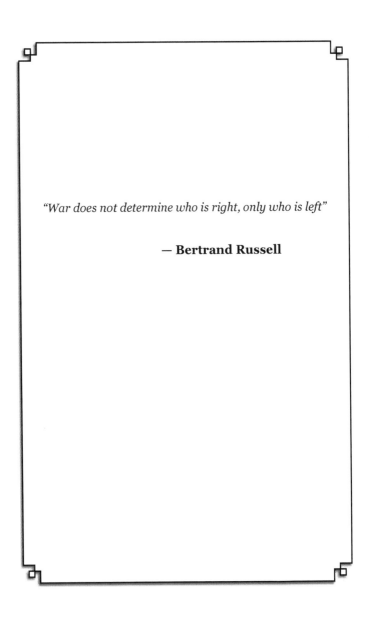

"War does not determine who is right, only who is left"

— Bertrand Russell

John Windsor

THE ROOM STANK of death. A syrupy sweet odour melding with a brown, noxious rot. Sweat, blood, piss, and filth. It was all there. The blanket stench of the infirm.

Hospitals. If ever there was a place John Windsor loathed, it was the hospital. Prime Ministerial obligation was the only reason he inhabited one now, and the last time he had entered one voluntarily, his granny Margaret gave in to the smoker's curse and let lung cancer take her. He'd been twenty years old, but he remembered it as being the very last time he had cried. His Law degree completed not long after, he had begun his journey to the courtrooms, where emotion was a hindrance. Now, twenty years later, he was the youngest Prime Minister of the 21st Century, the prospects of his own hospital stay still many years distant. Being faced with other people's impending death was an unwelcome task, even if it was a necessary part of the job, and he was counting the minutes until he could leave.

A sycophantic nurse waddled over, a proud grin on her chubby face. No doubt she felt important, getting the job of shaking the PM's hand, but the truth was she would be forgotten the moment he turned his back. Some people held such small ambition, yet he did not deny her the small moment of victory. Leaning forward, he paired the hearty handshake with a peck on the cheek that sent the woman giddy. He fought the urge to wipe his mouth on his sleeve afterwards.

The plump woman gushed. "We're so glad to have you here, Prime Minister."

John smiled, certain he could taste the woman's sweat on his lips. "It's my pleasure, Joan." Good spot on the name badge. Plebs love it when you use their names. "It's a wonderful job you're doing here."

"We do what we can. It's a hard job, but so vital. We had our funding cut last—"

"Shall we take the tour?" said John, waving a hand towards the ward. Cramped tent cubicles filled it, and likely housed various dying occupants. So much money just to park the nearly dead. So inefficient.

"Oh yes, of course, the tour." The nurse nodded. "This is the oncology ward where we care for stage 4 patients. I would introduce you to our guests, but most will be sleeping. Best not to disturb them."

John nodded gravely, although it was great news. He had held little desire to look upon the diseased. "Of course, Joan. You are an angel to these people."

"Me? Oh no, I'm just one woman doing what she—"

"Shall we move on?"

"Yes, Prime Minister, of course. There is lots to see."

And lots to see there was—a dreadful amount in fact. John endured over an hour of sweaty handshakes and prattling small talk. In the children's ward, he had to go so far as to kiss a collection of clammy foreheads (his PR Secretary's idea, not his). By the time John looped back around to where he had begun, exhaustion had set in. Two bodyguards accompanied him the entire time and looked just as bored as he was.

It was time to go.

John turned and gave the chubby nurse one last sweaty handshake. This time he was powerless not to wipe his palm on the pocket of his blazer. Thankfully, the woman didn't seem to notice, although Barry—one of his bodyguards—had to stifle a laugh. John gave his man a wry smile as he spoke out the corner of his mouth. "Thank you so much for having me, Joan. I will check in and see how you are doing again very soon, you can count on it. Give my love to your husband, David."

The woman beamed. Simple tactic, asking about her family during the tour, and reciting it back to her now was enough to make her love him. People would eat shit with a smile if they thought you were feeding it only to them.

John's bodyguards opened the fire door at the side of the hospital and stepped out before him. Their hands rested in their blazers, fingers on their guns. Not that they had ever needed to wield them—this was England, not Baghdad. All the same, his two burly men of action broke into panic now.

Something hit John in the chest, just over his heart, and when he looked down he saw a mess. Barry barrelled into him and covered him with his wide bulk. Meanwhile, Jeff launched himself forward at a stranger who John didn't even realise was out there.

The scowling stranger yelled. "You're a disgrace!"

John realised he was covered in egg just as another one hit him. This time it hit square in the face, hurting John's ego more than his flesh. So incensed was he that he released a bellowing war cry and threw himself at the egg-pitcher. Barry grabbed him and held him in place as if he were a twig—which wasn't far from the truth. John's strength came from his dark brown eyes, his precise words, and his booming voice, not his slender body and willowy limbs.

Jeff grabbed the stranger around the neck and dragged him away, but the crazed buffoon continued his tirade. "You'll ruin this country," he yelled. "The NHS will be in tatters by the time you finish stripping it for parts. My sister's in there because she couldn't get the help she needed a year ago. She's dying because of you and your fucking government."

Barry barked into his radio, alerting Special Branch. John shouted over him, putting his powerful voice into action. "You pathetic creature. You think throwing eggs will change things for your sister? Maybe if you had done something worthwhile with your life, you might have earned enough money to pay for the operation yourself. Why should other people pay for it? Blame yourself."

"I blame you!"

John regained a hold of himself and lowered his voice. Anger withdrew from his eyes. Just in time, too, as people had begun wandering into the backstreet to witness the kerfuffle. This would already be bad press, but him berating a member of the public in front of witnesses would be a disaster. He quickly grabbed a handkerchief from his pocket and wiped away the egg on his lapel.

Time for a little damage control.

John looked upon the furious stranger and smiled compassionately. "I'm sorry for what you are going through, sir. My dear old grandmother died in hospital of cancer too. I vowed that very day, as a young man of twenty, that I would see an end to such a dreadful disease. You have my pledge that I will do everything within my power to have the NHS restored to its former glory. Your passion is to be admired, sir, and I understand your frustrations completely. Leave your details with my assistant, and we will talk later."

The egg thrower opened his mouth to speak, but was utterly confused. "Y-you're a liar."

John chuckled. "You caught me quite by surprise, but your concerns matter greatly to me, sir. I wish to help."

"You can help my sister by—"

"I really must be going," said John. He moved towards the black Mercedes that had suddenly appeared. The black Range Rover behind would be full of Special Branch ready to break this idiots arms if John ordered it, but there were too many spectators now. The true pleasure anyway was in spinning this fool's attack into good press. It would be on the news within the hour, spun to portray him as the calm, passionate man his party worked so hard to make him. Idiots.

John waved quickly to the growing crowd of spectators, then allowed Barry to hustle him towards the car—as if it wasn't his choice at all but something he fought against. The face he pulled suggested he would happily stay and greet people all day if he weren't so frightfully busy.

Inside the Mercedes, the air conditioning was running, and a glass of gin sat in the alcove beside the handle. John took the drink and waited for his bodyguards to get in beside him. Jeff slid in earnestly, but Barry let out a chuckle as soon as the doors were closed, and they were on their way. "What a morning, aye, boss?"

John sipped his drink. "Just another day at the races. Bloody fools. What point did the idiot think he would make throwing eggs at me? At least do it somewhere there's a crowd. Not a single person even saw him do it."

"They saw your recovery though. You deserve an Oscar."

"An Oscar?" He waved a hand. "Pah, anything American isn't worth having." He fiddled with his silver cufflinks as he expressed other concerns. "Hopefully there were no cameras on us that caught the whole thing. You never bloody know these days."

Barry eased back in the seat as if there was nothing to worry about. "I doubt it. Even if there were, they wouldn't have sound. You got a bit red faced, but what man wouldn't when pelted by eggs?"

A beeping sound invaded the car's interior, making them look at one another. Jeff pulled out his phone and glanced at the screen. "They have the egg-thrower in custody. Shall I tell them to let him go?"

John gave his bodyguard a stare that made the bigger man shrink. "You must be joking. The man assaulted the leader of his country. You'd be shot for doing such a thing in some countries. No, I want the man charged to the full extent. Prison time if possible. Community service if not. The man believes things come for free, so let's see how he likes giving his time away for nothing. You have to love irony."

Jeff frowned.

"Is there a problem, Jeff?"

"No, it's just... the man was just upset about his sister. Maybe you could—"

John leaned forwards. "Throw him a bone, perhaps?"

"Well, yes."

John glared at the man, letting him know he'd overstepped his boundaries. Jeff was new, but he would learn. "Okay, I'll show some compassion. Barry, please tell my secretary to find out the name of the man's sister and send a bouquet of flowers." He looked at Jeff. "Good enough? No? Okay... Barry, make it a really big bouquet."

Barry broke into hysterics. "Right-o, boss."

Jeff stayed quiet for the remainder of the journey.

John was glad to get back to Downing Street an hour or so later. He had meetings all day, but most were with lackeys who would do little to annoy him. He would keep one eye on the news—to see if anything came of his morning altercation with the egg-thrower—but the day would fly by. Tomorrow morning, he had a meeting with an American healthcare provider vying to pick the final morsels from the NHS's corpse. They were welcome to it, so long as their pockets were deep enough. The time of free healthcare was over. It hadn't been sustainable since the population boom in the sixties. People needed to take responsibility for their own lives in today's world. The free lunches were finished. No tyrant ruled over them—they all had the chance to make something of their lives. No more excuses.

John went into his office and sat down in his high-backed leather chair—a kind gift from the Italian PM. He liked its size—tall, like he was. An imposing, yet sophisticated piece to cement his position at the head of an empire—his throne. And make no mistake, Britain was still an empire—albeit it financially now rather than martial.

John had just pulled a sheath of papers from his in-tray when the buzzer rang on his intercom. He accepted the call. "Yes?"

No answer. Only a crackling hiss.

"Stephanie, are you there? Stephanie, you best not be interrupting me for no reason."

The line went dead. John leaned across his desk and prodded a finger at the black, plastic intercom. It hissed at him. "Chinese piece of crap!"

"I believe it was made in the USA," said a voice in the room.

John shot back in his seat. "What the...?"

A well-dressed gentleman smiled politely at him from the back of the room. Donning an old-fashioned, yet impeccable suit, the stranger's aquiline face was indifferent. Pointing to the intercom, he nodded. "Motorola, see? I believe they are based in the United States."

"Who the Hell?"

The man grinned. "Who the Hell, indeed. My name is Oscar Boruta. They call me the Toy Maker, but that's of no consequence. My time is short, and I am here only as emissary."

"Emissary for whom? How did you get past security? If you're another of those bloody imbeciles from the anti-fracking commission I will—"

"Silence! I am not here to discuss trifling matters. My intention is to present to you an offer."

John was unnerved, and he realised that it had led to him humouring this intruder when he should have been slinging him out. He sat up straight in his chair and pointed a finger to his door. "You can bloody well make an appointment like everybody else. You do not barge into the office of the Prime Minister. I am this country's leader."

"You lead nothing—a shepard of sickly sheep and mewing lambs."

John stood up, fists clenched. "How dare you! I'll have you—"

"Hear my offer," said the gentleman. "And then I'll leave you to your impotent bluster."

John wondered how the man could be so brazen, to walk in here and talk to the PM in such a manner. He seemed to possess utter conviction about being there and that he should be listened to. But his eyes' cold, grey flare betrayed his calm expression. The old man was dangerous.

"You have thirty-seconds, Mr Boruta."

"I need only one." With that the elderly man lunged forwards and gripped John's skull between his bony fingers, squeezing so hard that he saw stars.

Boruta glared into John's eyes. "Take a look at what is coming."

And John did see.

He saw it all—what was coming, and what would be.

The end.

When Boruta finally let go of his skull, John was sweating and panting. It seemed like he had been trapped in a nightmare for days, but he knew it had been mere seconds. He gawped at the old man standing before him and realised the truth—this was no man at all. His cold, grey eyes were devoid of life—of anything that made a man human.

"Well," said Boruta. "What is your answer?"

John was too shaken to speak at first. After a long swallow, he was able to say, "Yes, yes, I will serve him."

Vamps

VAMPS DIDN'T KNOW what made him grab his grandfather's old Browning pistol from the safe beneath his bed, but something in his gut told him he might need it today. The city was on edge. Born and raised on the streets of London, Vamps felt the energy of its people in his veins. Just as an investment banker knew where the next trendy wine bar would pop up, Vamps knew where the next pocket of unrest would be. He had known which areas would get hit worst in the 2011 riots and where the pigs were most likely to pinch you. The City of London was an organism, its brain in the financial centre, heart in the tourist districts, and a diseased liver in the poorer areas that dealt with all the filth produced.

Today, Vamps experienced a feeling uncommon to him. He'd lived in Brixton his entire life, so danger was an everyday part of life, but this was different. Standing on the balcony outside his fifth floor flat and clutching his grandfather's pistol in the pocket of his hoodie, he felt truly afraid for the first time since he was a child. The city was humming, from the rough areas to the posh. Trouble was brewing.

And it's all because of those weird black stones.

Vamps had watched the news for most of the morning after awakening with a whiskey-hangover. The breaking reports told of a strange black stone in the centre of Oxford Street. A bus crashed into it, and when the driver got out to inspect the damage, he fell down dead in the middle of the street. He had touched the strange black stone moments before.

There were more strange stones all over the country. An old lady died near the coast next to one, and a stone in the middle of a Scottish football ground killed the groundsman. Anyone who touched the stones died. Simple as.

But it was the one in London—Vamps' home—that concerned him.

So what the hell were they? And where had they come from? Nobody knew the answers, which was why everybody was afraid. London was afraid. Vamps was afraid.

The gunpowder was primed and ready to ignite.

Vamps needed to get out on the streets—his streets. He couldn't be a bystander if things were about to go bad. He had a duty to look after his home. They all did. Brixton was a tough place, but there was a code they all stuck to. You didn't tolerate shit coming in from the outside.

The elevators to Vamp's low rise had been out of order for over a year, so he hurtled down the piss-stained steps instead. On his way, he hopped a sleeping junkie on the third floor without so much as a second glance—local wildlife. When he reached the pavement outside, he struggled to breathe for a moment. It was a warm day, but it was more than simple mugginess. The air tasted thick and ominous.

The newsagents on the other side of Tanners road was chock-a-block, people seemingly having gathered there to gossip about what was going on. Everywhere else was quiet though—no kids on bikes, and no gangs hanging around on the brick walls that lined the car parks surrounding the low rises. Vamps knew where they would all be—glued to a television set somewhere.

One person stood out in the open though. The nearest car park contained the usual mix of barely running Escorts and Golfs, as well as one or two newer—although not by much—motors. Vamps himself did not drive, but it still annoyed him whenever someone's ride got messed with. Why should someone pay all that money to tax and fuel a car only to have some dickhead slash the tyres or key the bodywork? It was that kind of shit that kept them all in the gutter. That was why, when Vamps saw the lad in the luminous green beanie cap trying to shove a metal coat hanger down the window of an old Corsa, he marched right on over.

"The fuck you think you're doing, blud?"

The lad flinched, the beanie cap almost flying off his head. When he recovered from the fright, he put on a scowl and thrust out his chin. "This your motor?"

"No."

"Then what the fuck you care, innit?"

Vamps stepped up to the lad. "I care because you're shitting on my doorstep. You vandalise this car and the owner has to pay to fix it. That means he struggles to buy his kid new clothes, which means they go to school and get bullied. Then they grow up with a big, angry chip on their shoulder that makes them go round robbing cars like the fucking low life you are. You're victimising people who have had to deal with the same shit as you, yo. We should be helping each other, not keeping each other down."

"The fuck you talking about, man? Just piss off, innit. Some guy is stupid enough to leave his sat nav on display, he deserves to get it pinched."

"And you deserve to get rolled if someone catches you."

The lad lifted his chin higher. "You ain't man enough, blud, trust me."

Vamps grinned wide, letting his gold fangs show. "You is a toddler, blud. Don't run before you can walk, you get me?"

Just as Vamps could feel the vibe of the city, he felt the vibe of the lad, which was why he saw the punch coming in plenty of time. He stepped aside, and the lad's swing became a miss, but a line had been crossed. Rep was now at stake. Vamps had no choice but to deliver a vicious hook to the lad's unguarded ribs. The blow produced a meaty thud, and its recipient dropped to the ground like a bag of bricks, gasping. The lad's green beanie cap fell off his head, and Vamps retrieved it. Instead of giving it back, he put it on his own head.

"Don't throw your fists unless you know how to use them, blud." He said it with more pity in his voice than malice. "I understand what it's like living on these streets, yo, but you don't have to be what they tell you. There's no cred in hurting the people you live with. You want to be a criminal, then go down Canary Wharf and rob some rich-ass business man that deserves it. Only cowards sneak around and prey on the weak."

The lad lay on his side, clutching his ribs and wheezing. Vamps didn't know whether his words had been heard, but was satisfied that the lad would not be robbing any of the cars on this estate today. Just a pity it had needed to devolve into violence. So many things in this part of the city did.

2

Gingerbread had texted to say the boys were all down at the snooker hall, so that's where Vamps headed. He found them at one of the tables, but they weren't playing. Instead, they were propped against the cushion and staring up at one of the televisions. The volume was off, but someone had switched on subtitles.

Vamps moved up beside Mass and Ravy, but only Ginge noticed him. "Hey Vamps, nice cap," he said with a worried look on his podgy face. He was wearing his gingerbread man t-shirt that Vamps swore had gone months now without a wash.

Vamps forgot he was wearing the bright green beanie cap, and he fingered the brim to make sure it was still sitting right. "How's it going, Ginge?"

Ravy and Mass noticed him, nodding hello. Mass sniffed and said, "This shit is messed up, buster."

Vamps glanced up at the television, mildly sick of the news by now. What mattered now was the news on the streets, not the BBC. "What's the latest?"

"That stone in Oxford Street just started glowing," said Ravy, his eyes wide and white against his dark brown skin. "Shit's about to go down."

Vamps nodded. "I've been thinking the same thing all morning. We should get down there."

Ravy frowned. "Down Oxford Street?"

"If something's gunna happen, it's gunna happen there."

Ginge scoffed. "Which is why we should be anywhere but Oxford Street."

"No," said Vamps. "This is our city, yo. I'm tired of being told about it on the news. I want to see with my own eyes. If something is happening I don't want to be a spectator."

Mass, rarely concerned by anything, shrugged his massive shoulders. His confidence came from the fact he could choke a person out in ten seconds or break an arm in half that. When you fought as well as Mass did, very little could make you anxious. "I'm up for heading out," he said, "if you want."

"You lot are tripping," said Ginge, running both hands through his greasy, copper hair. When he saw that their minds could not be changed, he sighed. "Fine. Let me grab a snickers from the bar, and we'll get going. But only because I don't wanna hang around here on my own."

And that's what they did. Ginge grabbed a snickers bar—as well as two bags of paprika crisps and an energy drink—and they headed out onto the street. The first thing they noticed as they neared the Thames was how many pigs were about. The police assembled everywhere, moving from shop to shop, or sat in squad cars. There hadn't been this much presence even during the riots, and the only thing that brought this many pigs from their sties all at once was terrorism. It was exactly what Vamps had been afraid of—that the stones were some kind of weapon put there by someone with a grudge. The way the police were eyeing everybody up and inserting themselves into people's business was not a good sign. People hung off the balconies of the nearby low rises heckling the pigs, but they would not be deterred from their presence.

"Shit man, I don't like this," said Ravy, fidgeting with himself.

"Me either," said Vamps.

Ravy shook his head. "Nah, I mean I'm carrying."

Vamps stared at his friend. "On today of all days? You muppet, what you holding?"

Ravy swallowed and looked embarrassed. "An ounce."

"Shit man, what you carrying an ounce of weed on you for?"

"Not weed, man. Charlie."

Vamps stopped walking and let his jaw drop. "The fuck? Where you even get that from?"

"Limpy Laz sold it me cheap down at the Boiler House. I got a bargain. Thought we could go sell it in Angell Town."

Mass shook his head and chuckled. "Laz must have known you're the only mug who would hold an ounce of cocaine today with all these pigs about. Not to mention all the robbing that's gonna get under way."

"Well, I can't dump it, can I? Cost me six-hundred quid. Money I was meant to put on rent. If I'm late again, the council are gunna kick me out."

Vamps glanced across the road at the police. They were chatting to everyone, and he knew that they would see Vamps and his boys coming a mile away. They couldn't risk getting patted down. "We need to offload it to some other mug. You'll get your money back if you're lucky."

Ravy looked relieved. It was a big time move to grab an ounce of C, and Vamps was a little impressed, but today was not the day. On top of that, he wasn't a fan of Class A dealing. It did too much damage as far as he was concerned and put a massive target on your head.

"I know a guy nearby," said Mass. "Can't vouch for him that well, but I've had a few games of pool with him down Clapham way. Think he deals out of the Grey Goose over by the Evangelical."

Vamps itched at the back of his neck—the hairs standing up. "We'll have to risk it. Would rather get caught with our pants down by some a-hole dealer than the pigs."

"Me too," said Ravy. "Cheers, Mass. You got me out of the shit, yo."

They got going, heading west. The Grey Goose was a rough boozer at the northern end of Brixton. Vamps and the boys preferred the snooker hall on the east boundary in Moorlands Estate. It was better to stick to places you knew and the people who knew you, which was why Vamps was uneasy at the prospect of visiting another gang's manor. Still, it was the middle of the day and things were not as they usually were. All bets were off.

They took twenty minutes to reach the Grey Goose. It was a run-down old boozer with rotting boards running below its roof. They may once have been painted white, but were now grey and peeling. One window had a board over it, and the double doors did not hang evenly. In that respect, it wasn't dissimilar to the snooker hall where Vamps and the boys hung around. Many of the pubs in London were in similar shape. The spiralling cost of a pint made bar tending a dying trade.

"I'll go in on my own first," said Mass. "We go bowling in all together, they'll think we're looking for a scrap."

Vamps nodded. It made sense, so he stood and watched as Mass headed off alone. It would take a brave soul to pick a fight with him, but that didn't mean there wouldn't be someone stupid enough to do it. Vamps didn't like letting him go in without backup, but his friend could handle himself.

Ginge was staring at his phone. Vamps asked him if there was any news.

"Nah, man. That stone is still just sitting there glowing. The front of Selfridges is trashed because of how many people are outside."

Vamps pictured the scene. The more people flooded into Oxford Street, the more tempers would fray and nerves wear. Eventually, the massive crowd would provide cover for thieves to pinch anything not tied down. You could swipe a person's phone and melt away into the crowd before the victim even noticed. That person would then turn around and accuse the wrong person which meant a fight would break out, inciting others to join in. One of London's poshest streets was a firework waiting to go off. Yet, Vamps was still adamant they should make it there. They couldn't just sit back.

It took five minutes for Mass to come swaggering back out of the pub. He had a smile on his face that put them at ease. No one was hanging around outside, but it had still been nerve wracking standing exposed in a street they weren't known in.

Mass grinned. "He said he'll take it off our hands."

Ravy waved his fist in the air. "Great! How much?"

"Five-hundred quid."

"What? I paid six-hundred."

Vamps patted Ravy on the back. "And that's what happens when you make a stupid decision. A hundred quid to get rid of the risk you put on yourself. Call it a life lesson."

Ravy let his head drop. "Man, this fucking sucks. Fine, okay. Here!" He went to hand the coke over to Mass.

Mass put his hands out. "Hey, hey, keep that shit inside your jacket. Don't go flashing it around out here. He said we can all go inside and do business in the back room. He's waiting for us."

"All right, let's get this over with," said Vamps. "What's this guy's name, anyway?"

"Pusher," said Mass.

Gingerbread folded his arms. "You sure everything's cool, Mass?"

"Yeah, Ginge. Guy's sound."

Vamps led the way, wanting to be first in the firing line if anything went down. While Mass could handle himself better than anyone, Ginge and Ravy were less handy. Ravy had grown up in a strict Muslim family that had erased most of his confidence by the time he was ten. Ginge was the son of two alcoholic parents and had turned to food early on as a way to drown out their constant arguments. Mass lived alone, after a fall out with his single father, a burly builder from Lambeth. Vamps... Well, Vamps had no one and never had. No one except his brothers here with him now.

Entering the pub, Vamps was immediately hit by the sticky-sweet odour of spilled lager. He felt hardened stains underfoot as he traversed the threadbare carpet, but he kept his eyes forward, not looking anyone in the eye. Like everywhere else, the news was playing on the television above the bar.

A gang stood at the back of the room watching him approach. The men were in their twenties, but the young girls draped over them looked much younger. One girl even wore a school uniform. No one said a word to Vamps, but one guy—an idiot with tribal art on his face like Mike Tyson—nodded his head towards a door at the side of the room. Vamps nodded respectfully, not wanting to cause a scene, and headed through the door.

A dance floor lay inside, with an empty bar and chairs piled up on top of the tables. Looked like no one had danced there for a while. Only three men stood present, and it was obvious who was in charge.

"You Vamps?" said a skinhead with wiry arms and legs. A long scar ran alongside the left side of his face, giving him a villainous look that cemented him as the group's leader. Underlings didn't have disfiguring scars unless they really went out of their way to make themselves a target.

"Yeah, I'm Vamps. Heard we can do a bit of quick business. You Pusher?"

"Maybe I am."

Vamps tilted his head but kept his stare on the other guy. "Maybe?"

"Let me see what you got, boy. Then we'll talk business."

Vamps looked at Ravy, and nodded to let his friend know to go along. Nervously, Ravy slid out the packet of Charlie and moved across the dance floor with it. The silence broke only by the awkward clip-clops of his Timberlands on the floorboards.

When Ravy offered out the packet of product, Pusher didn't re-spond. He left Ravy standing there looking stupid with his arm out-stretched. It was a power play—and it irritated Vamps immensely. He had to fight to keep his cool. While Vamps had no qualms with taking out the three guys in this room, there was at least another six guys in the bar and perhaps more who would keep them from ever making it out of the area in one piece.

Things couldn't come to blows.

Before things got too tense, Pusher finally took the packet from Ravy and popped open the seal. He dipped his thumb into the powder and rubbed it over his gums. Lips puckered, he nodded. "Not the best I've had, but it'll fly. Give you two-hundred for it."

"What the fuck?" Ravy spluttered. "You told Mass five-hundred."

"Yeah, you did," Mass confirmed. "Thought we were sound about it."

Pusher shrugged, as if it were of little consequence to him. "That was before I tasted it. It ain't that good. Plus, there's bacon everywhere right now. Not a good time to be holdin'."

Ravy looked at Vamps with desperation in his eyes. Vamps wished his boy could keep things a little cooler, but the situation was in play now. They needed to get rid of the gear, and they needed to do it now. Two-hundred quid was better than five years in the nick.

But Vamps wasn't about to let this wannabe Tony Montana take them for a bunch of mugs. This might be his manor, but Vamps was no victim. He clapped his hands together loudly, making the two thugs either side of Pusher flinch. "Sorry we couldn't do business. Thanks for the time though, blud. Respect, yeah?"

Pusher didn't react. His eyes shifted to Vamps and stayed there. It was some time before he spoke. "You fuckin' me around, blud?"

"Nah, man." Vamps opened his arms out to the side, trying to keep things light and non-threatening. "Just didn't meet our price. Business, yeah?"

"This is my fuckin' manor. I name the price, and you fucking take it."

Damn it. Shit is about to go down. This fucker is looking for a fight.

If Vamps showed the slightest bit of nerve, the situation was lost. Respect was a cold war, and the moment the other guy thought you were weaker, the violence started. Vamps took a step forward, chest out, chin up. "Hand me back the product, yo. You want it, the price is five-hundred."

Pusher glared at him, the slash on the side of his face quivering as his jaw locked. A standoff ensued, and it was some time before the other guy eventually moved towards Vamps. He offered out the packet, but when Vamps went to take it, he pulled it back again.

"Actually," said Pusher. "Think I have a new price for you. I'm going to take this off your hands for free, and you mugs are gunna fuck off out of my patch before you get your skulls caved in."

Vamps realised that the boys from the bar had entered behind him. They were boxed in by at least nine guys. A couple brandished snooker cues. Mass started hulking up, bunching his muscles and preparing to fight, and Vamps figured his big friend could take out at least three by himself. Maybe Vamps could take another three. But Ravy and Ginge would get hurt.

Vamps moved his hand into his pocket and gripped his grandfather's Browning. The pistol would shift the power back to them, but it wasn't a move to make lightly. If just one of the other men in the room had a gun of their own hidden, things would turn into a shootout—and you couldn't predict what would happen when bullets flew. Also, aside from Pusher, who deserved a bullet, Vamps didn't know a thing about any of the other guys. For all he knew, they were decent lads just showing some front.

No, too risky. Vamps moved his hand back out of his pocket. If it were only him, then he might escalate things, but he didn't want to take risks with his friend's lives. They all walked here in one piece, and that was how they would leave.

"All right, we're leaving," said Vamps. It hurt him to lose so much face, but it would be stupid to fight when they were at a disadvantage. He'd lost count of the number of guys he'd seen go down because of their egos. Backing down was smart, even if the taste it left was piss and shit.

Pusher grinned like a ghoul. "Smart boy. I see you round here again, I won't let you leave."

Ravy sucked at his teeth. "Man, this is fuck—"

Vamps snapped his fingers. "I said we're leaving, yo, so let's bounce."

Everyone was silent as they left, boys on both sides. Eyeballs screwed into Vamps and his friends as they headed back out into the pub and towards the exit.

"Pleasure doing business with you," Pusher shouted after them to an audience of laughter.

Vamps paused, stopped walking and clenched his fists.

The laughter stopped. The air froze.

"Come on, man," Ginge whispered to him. "This ain't worth it."

"It's my fault," said Mass. "The guy mugged me off!"

"It's just money," said Ravy. "Let's go."

"You lads got something to say?" Pusher shouted after them.

Vamps looked at the door in front of him, took a deep breath, and left. But he would be back.

3

The street outside bustled. When they entered the pub less than fifteen minutes ago, the roads and paths were deserted, but now people were everywhere, spilling out of local businesses and flats. Many people headed for their cars if they owned one.

Vamps grabbed a kid who should've been at school as he tried to rush past. "Hey, blud, what's going on?"

"It's the freaking end of the world!" came the kid's reply. "We're under attack!"

The kid tried to rush off again, but Vamps held him in place. "What do you mean? Under attack by who?"

"By monsters. They came out of the gate."

"The gate?"

"The stone," he cried. "The stone on Oxford Street. It opened. We all need to get the hell away from here."

Oxford Street was not far away, which was obviously why the streets had erupted into panic. Car horns blared like a chorus of angry ducks. A dickhead in a Mini Cooper sideswiped a battered Mazda as he went up on the pavement to get around. The Mazda gave chase, its driver hanging out his window and shaking a fist. A black Cocker Spaniel ran around without an owner, stopping briefly to cock its leg over a steel bike railing. A cat perched atop a wall and hissed at it.

"This ain't good," said Ginge. When Vamps turned to him, he was holding up his phone which was now playing a video. It was a news report from Oxford Street—and it was live.

Vamps, Mass, and Ravy gathered around Ginge's phone as scenes of chaos played out. Above the strange black stone in the middle of

Oxford Street, a strange, shimmering gate had appeared. Things piled out of it in a steady stream. Monsters. They looked like men but horribly burned. Some hunched over with vicious talons at the end of their arms, but most were smouldering corpses. As soon as the creatures landed on the tarmac though, they set about the nearest person and tore them to shreds. Blood filled the air like mist from a sprinkler. Even the camera lens filming was red-hazed. It was hard to get a good look at the invaders, for they moved so quickly, but eventually one came towards the camera. Its eyes swirled with black oil. Blood stained its broken teeth.

Then the camera clattered to the ground, settling on a skewed view of the curb with a hundred feet fleeing.

"We need to get out of here," said Ravy.

A window broke nearby as if to punctuate his point.

"And go where?" asked Vamps. "Those stones are everywhere. If the one in Oxford Street opened up some kind of gate, I bet the other ones did too. The news this morning said hundreds had been identified."

Ravy hopped from foot to foot anxiously. "So what are you saying?"

"I'm saying there might not be anywhere to run."

Even Mass looked nervous now. A thick vein bulged in his trunk of a neck "You really want to stick around?"

Vamps thought about it and shook his head. "Nah, man. I ain't crazy. Just feels wrong running from our home, you know? If we don't defend it, who will?"

The sound of a door slamming spun them around. When Vamps saw who was coming out of the pub, he grabbed his boys and pulled them behind a nearby bus stop. The bricks stank of piss.

"It's that prick," said Mass. "We should go do him while he hasn't got all his backup."

Vamps watched Pusher barrel out of the Grey Goose with only two of his meat heads. It would be a good opportunity to roll the fucker, but... No. It wasn't enough.

"That bitch has something that belongs to us," said Vamps with a snarl.

Ravy raised an eyebrow. "The coke?"

"Nah, man. Five-hundred quid. I walked out of there with the intention of getting it back later, and this might be our chance. Everything is about to turn to shit. The law ain't gonna care about us rolling a low life dealer for half-a-grand."

Mass smacked his fist into his palm. "Let's go get it done."

Vamps held back his muscled friend. "Not yet. Let's see where he's going first."

Mass frowned. "Why?"

"Because it ain't enough to just take what he owes us. The piece of shit needs to learn a lesson. If there's a chance to take him down a peg, we do it."

"You're stone cold," said Mass with a grin.

"Nah, man. I never wronged no one who didn't wrong me first, you know that. We gave him a chance to get a bargain, but he was too greedy to take it. Got no time for people who only think about themselves. We're going to show him where that attitude gets you."

"Let's show him we ain't a bunch of fuckin' mugs," said Mass.

Ravy nodded. "I really need my money back, so yeah, let's do it."

Ginge sighed. "Ah, man, this is gunna suck. Fine, okay, but only because I don't want to see Ravy get shafted. I just need to get something to eat first."

"Fuck sake, buster," said Mass. "You never stop filling your gob."

"I have a thyroid problem."

"Like hell you do."

"He does," said Ravy. "I went the doctors with him once."

"Come on," said Vamps, ushering them in the direction Pusher had gone. The dealer was hurrying along the pavement towards one of the low rises that housed people together like ants in a nest. Vamps knew because he lived in one exactly the same. They had been built recently as part of a refurb of the estate, but the way the buildings all faced in on one another made the whole area isolated from the outside.

"You reckon this is where his gaff is?" Ravy asked in a whisper, even though they were outside and there was noise coming from everywhere. Police cars and fire engines blared in every direction.

"Maybe," said Vamps. "Let's keep back so he doesn't spot us."

But there was little chance of Pusher spotting them because he was talking loudly on a mobile phone and hurrying along at a jog. His two meat heads stuck close enough that all they could hear was him.

Vamps and the boys followed at a distance, but were forced to get closer once Pusher headed into the stairwells. It would be easy to lose the dealer if he slipped onto one of the floors and into a flat, and it was only his frantic voice on the phone that gave any chance of staying on his trail.

"He's panicking about something," said Mass. "Having a right flap."

"He's probably been screwing people over a little too often," said Ravy. "Maybe someone's coming for him."

Mass nodded. "Yeah, us."

"Maybe someone he knows is in Oxford Street," said Vamps, sympathetic at the thought. The guy was a crook, but it was hard not to be in a place like Brixton. Not every scumbag started out as one, but living in shit turned as many men to fungus as it did to flowers.

The sound of a fire door opening—squeaking hinges—made Vamps shove out an arm. "Hold up. I think he headed in. Next floor up."

Mass smacked his fist again. "We got the prick. There can only be three or four flats to a floor. Nowhere he can run once we find him."

Vamps peered down the centre column of the stairwell, eyed the concrete below. He hadn't been counting, but he figured they were six or seven floors up. Pusher really would have nowhere to run.

Vamps kept his voice low. "All right. Mass and me will handle things, but Ginge and Ravy, you got our backs, yeah?"

"Of course," said Ravy.

"Then let's go give this guy an education."

Vamps took the next flight of steps two at a time, fists clenched. Mass was right behind him, and Ravy a step behind that. Ginge was halfway down, panting and wheezing. They opened the fire door and spilled into the landing. They knew which flat to go to because Pusher's meat heads were standing right outside it. Maybe they weren't trusted enough to come inside. They saw Vamps and Mass coming towards them, and at first didn't seem to recognise or understand, but once they realized they were about to get rolled, they panicked and started throwing punches.

Mass ducked the first punch and whipped around behind the guy. He locked in a rear naked choke and pulled back so hard that the guy's feet dangled off the ground. Vamps took care of the other guy, raising his left forearm to block a punch and landing a vicious right hand of his own. The guy dropped to his knees, blood gushing between his fingers from a broken nose. The sound he made was like a cat in heat. Mass let go of his man, who slumped to the floor unconscious. The calm expression on his face made it seem like he had just dropped off a bag of rubbish. Knocking guys unconscious was no big thing to Mass.

The door to the flat was ajar. Vamps put a finger to his lips, and they all kept quiet—the only sound the rattling wheeze of Ginge's chest.

Vamps nudged open the door with his shoulder and crept into the hallway. A bout of screaming caused him to stop, but he realised it was coming from a floor below and carried on. The floor was cheap laminate—badly laid—and it squeaked with every step. If it were not for the sound of the television blaring in the next room, it would have been obvious that someone was inside the flat, but as Vamps made it into the living room, Pusher was still shouting into his phone, oblivious. With his free hand, he rooted around inside a chest of drawers.

Vamps stepped into the middle of the room, cutting off the dealer's escape. "Hey, motherfucker."

Pusher spun, but Vamps had already pulled out his grandfather's Browning and pointed it at his face.

"The fuck you doing in my gaff?"

"Come to take back what's ours, blud. You screwed with the wrong gangsters."

It was obvious Pusher was concerned—in Brixton, a gun in your face was not an empty threat—but he remained calm, and even smiled. "Just the way of the street, innit? You want your drugs back, fair dos, but know that it don't end here, boy. You don't crash my fucking gaff and get away with it. Where are Dwayne and Goldy?"

"Sleeping," said Mass. "You bout to take a big long nap of your own if you don't hand over the cash."

"You want the money? For that bag of crap you tried to sell me? I've snorted better washing powder."

Ravy stepped around the coffee table in the centre of the small room. "What you talking about?"

"I mean you should leave the drug game to people who know what the fuck they're doing. Shit you tried to sell me was so cut down it wouldn't get a baby high. I did you a favour."

"You're a liar. Limpy Laz and me go way back."

Pusher let out a spluttering laugh. "Limpy Laz? You'd have to be a right mug to buy off him."

"Enough!" said Vamps, waving the pistol to get Pusher's focus. "I ain't here to debate the quality of the product. It was good enough for you to steal, so I think you're full of shit. You're going to stand here like a good little boy while we turn your gaff over for whatever's worth taking. You think you can rob us? Well, guess what—your ass is about to get robbed."

"You'll regret this. You won't be able to show you face on the entire fucking estate! I'll have you fucking shot, blud, you get me? I'll have you buried in Max Roach Park."

"You ain't the one with the gun, blud." Vamps took a step closer, showing he wasn't afraid. "I should plug you right now and be done with it. I'm tired of your fucking noise."

Sirens blared outside. The possible sound of an explosion across the Thames.

Pusher was panting. However tough he was acting, part of him must have expected Vamps to pull the trigger. Vamps had never pulled the trigger before—and he didn't want to now—but this was Brixton. Shit happened in Brixton.

Mass tossed the room, shoving aside sofa cushions and checking down the sides. Ginge and Ravy took his lead and started rooting around too.

Vamps headed to the chest of drawers that Scarface had been rifling through. "Step away. I wanna see what had you in such a panic."

Pusher's eyes narrowed. "Don't do this, blud. Last warning."

"Shut the fuck up." Vamps pulled open one of the drawers, far enough that it almost fell out of the unit. Inside was mostly junk letters, but at the bottom was a white envelope—a fat envelope. "Looky what we have here."

Pusher had stopped talking—probably realised it was doing him no good—and only stood and glared at Vamps now as he opened the envelope and peered inside at the cash. There must have been a few grand, easy.

Mass had stopped searching the sofa and looked up to see what Vamps had found. "Nice! Guess we call that interest."

"The fuck you do," said Pusher. "You take your five-hundred and piss off!"

Vamps grinned. "No need to be sore. Just business, blud. Way of the street, innit?"

"Daddy? What's happening outside?"

A little boy entered the room, rubbing sleep from his eyes. When Pusher saw him, his face dropped in horror. He looked at Vamps, almost pleadingly. "Everything's okay, sweetheart. Daddy's just talking to his friends about something."

Vamps lowered his gun. It might have been foolish, but seeing a child made him do so instinctively. The streets were tough, but there were still rules. He moved the pistol behind his thigh where the little boy wouldn't see it. "Hey, little man. My name is Vamps. I'm a friend of your daddy's."

The little boy looked like his father—same dark brown eyes and shaved head. When he looked at Vamps, he didn't seem afraid—a Brixton boy in the making. "Why is your name that?"

"Because of my teeth. See?" Vamps bared his golden fangs—an up-grade required after a couple of Angell town boys had smashed his head against a curb.

The little boy giggled. "Cool."

"Come on, man," said Mass. "Let's take the envelope and bounce. We done here."

Vamps nodded, eyeballed Pusher. "Yeah, man, we done."

"Can we all go and get ice cream, daddy?" the little boy asked. "I want to see what's happening outside."

Pusher smiled at his son. "Yeah, sweetheart, but just you and me. These guys are leaving." He nodded at Vamps and whispered, "Just go, man."

Vamps remained rooted to the spot for a moment. His guts churned with what he supposed might be guilt.

Ah, for fuck sake.

He dug into the envelope and thumbed at the cash inside. He pulled out five-hundred quid in twenties and threw the rest down on the chest of drawers. "Let's bounce."

Mass frowned at him. "Seriously?"

"Yeah, seriously. Move it."

They got out of there. Mass gave one of the meat heads outside a swift kick to the ribs as they passed back towards the stairwell. On the way down, he struggled to understand what Vamps had done. "What the fuck, man? Why did you leave the cash?"

"Because we didn't need it. We got what we were owed. I ain't tak-ing nothing from a father looking after his kid. Don't matter how much a piece of shit he is."

"He won't leave things there," said Ravy. "He'll want payback."

Vamps shrugged. "If he wants to come take a shot at us in our own manor, he's welcome to try. Right now, though, we got bigger things to worry about."

They took a moment to pause on the stairwell and look out of the windows.

The streets of Brixton had erupted.

Richard Honeywell

THE CHAOS ERUPTED with a lone gunshot, like the start of a marathon. Only, people did not break in the same direction towards a common goal. The rampage spread in every direction—people behaving more like startled deer than rational citizens.

As a police officer, Richard Honeywell's biggest concern was where that gunshot had come from—and who had fired it—but any chance of finding answers quickly eroded as the crowd broke into panic.

The reason so many of them gathered in Slough's Queensmere Shopping Centre was because of the giant television screen hanging from the rafters. Its purpose was to advertise products and televise sports, but for the last three hours, it had displayed nothing but news.

The news was not good.

The Thames Valley Police were on high alert, ready to assist the Metropolitan Police the moment anything happened on Oxford Street. Nobody could say what the stones were, or where they had come from, so they prepared for the worst. The problem was, the Thames Valley Police had their hands full on their own doorstep, without having to be on call for London. People in Richard's patch of Slough, for instance, had been on the cusp of panic since dawn, and by noon, they were all but ready to blow. That was why the gunshot had set them off like runners on the blocks.

It happened fifteen minutes ago—the attack on Oxford Street. The news was running a studio report where an authority on 'Terrorism Countermeasures' had been considering the possibility of a worldwide conspiracy regarding the stones. He dismissed it as impossible. Then the studio report cut abruptly to a view of Oxford Street. The stone in the middle of the road began pulsing and glowing, projecting a large net of colourful light into the air. Richard sensed it was a gate immediately. To him, it resembled the plastic loops children blew bubbles with, and those swirling, multicoloured suds were exactly the same as the net of light above the stone now. Yes, he had known it was some kind of gate.

But he never expected what came through.

The first creature to emerge was horribly burned—so disfigured that a fellow police officer on the scene rushed over to assist. The injured man had grabbed the officer by the throat and snapped his neck with a single hand. His skull hitting the pavement echoed from large speakers hanging from the shopping centre's rafters.

On screen, the City of London ignited.

In Oxford Street, what had been a rowdy, defiant mob now became a stampede of frantic animals. Reason and humanity deserted as men and women trampled the elderly and young to get away from the horrors at their back. In contrast, the people assembled in the Slough shopping centre had stood like statues, their necks craned upwards towards the television as if it were God speaking to them.

Then the gunshot had spurred them into action.

Richard's ears told him it had come from the western corridor of the shopping centre, over by the Nandos restaurant, but the assembled crowd fanned out so quickly that the shooter was swallowed up by the mass of egressing people.

Richard was one of seven police officers designated to the shopping centre, and as soon as he had arrived, he knew it would not be enough if a riot started. Seven men could not control five hundred. That was patently clear now as Richard fell to the ground, barged aside by a large man not watching where he went, and then swiftly trodden on by a business woman in sharp heels. He cried out as the skin along his left shin shredded. No one stopped to help him.

Taking kicks in every part of his body, Richard dragged himself over to one of the vendor carts that dotted the main plaza. This one stocked cheap sunglasses made to look like designer shades. A hollow underneath where the stall holder might sit on a stool, provided Richard shelter and allowed him to wait for the worst to be over.

His radio chattered on his belt, and he unclasped it. Hunched over, he pressed the button and responded. "Honeywell, over."

"Richard, you okay? It's Saunders. I'm over at Waterstones, and a herd of people just came running by."

Richard sighed. "Yep, that sounds about right. Some idiot fired a gun. I don't know what we're expected to do here."

"Should we arrest people?" asked Saunders.

"For what? Being scared? I don't blame them. I'm scared too. What the hell is happening in London?" A loud bang on the line followed by screaming. "Saunders, are you there?"

Silence for a moment, but then Saunders came back. "Sorry, a kid's been hurt. I need to go. Let me know when you have orders."

Richard was the most senior officer at the shopping centre—a sergeant—but that didn't mean he was responsible for giving orders. Usually, he would be back at the precinct organising task forces or training new recruits. Now and then he led operations when Reading FC played against someone the fans detested. Truthfully, he didn't know what to do. All he could think about was getting home. What he'd witnessed on television compressed his bones under the sheer weight of terror. The only reason he hadn't panicked was because he coiled inwards instead of out, choosing to accept nothing rather than panic at the reality. He had a job to do.

He got on the radio and told the other officers nearby to rendezvous at his position. The crowd thinned enough for him to emerge from beneath the vendor cart and stand up. Visions of a video showing him cowering being posted on YouTube went through his mind, but what could he have done? Let his spine get trampled and spend the rest of his life having his poor wife wipe his arse and empty his bladder? No way. Jen had enough to deal with looking after their son, Dillon.

Small groups of people remained in the area, almost all of them sobbing and hurt. One woman clutched her arm which pointed the wrong way from the elbow. Another guy sported a lump on his forehead the size of a golf ball—the glaze in his eyes made it seem like he was daydreaming.

Moans filled the air, but only one caused Richard concern. He followed the high-pitched keening to a motorised scooter overturned outside a chemist. His eyes next fell upon a handbag, its contents scattered, but he didn't see a body until he got close enough to peer over the scooter.

"Jesus!"

A frail old lady rested on her side, sobbing. The rubbery flesh around her wrist blackened from an obvious break, and a gash on her forehead dripped blood like a tap. Richard righted the scooter and shoved it away so he could lift the woman up and onto his lap. She whimpered, and it took several moments of gentle whispering to calm her. "You're all right, love. I've got you."

His colleague, Riaz, appeared then. When he saw the bloody old woman in Richard's arms, he got right on the line to Dispatch to call an ambulance. "What happened to her?" he asked once aid was on its way.

Richard shook his head. "People turned into frightened animals. Nobody's fault."

"Like hell it isn't. We should check CCTV."

Richard disagreed. "People were running for their lives. Nobody meant to hurt anybody else. The only person who needs locking up is the idiot who fired a gun and started the stampede."

"It wasn't a gun," said Riaz. "I spoke to the centre manager. Someone dropped a helium cylinder in the card shop, and a valve broke. No one got hurt, but it made a pretty hefty bang."

Richard gave the old dear on his lap a gentle pat and tried not laugh at the absurdity of it all. "There's an ambulance on its way, love. You have anyone we should call for you?"

The old dear gave no reply, only whimpered. Shock. At her age it didn't take much. From the look of her tissue-paper skin she was probably north of eighty. Poor girl must be terrified.

"It will all be okay," Richard reassured her again. He looked up at Riaz. "Regroup with the others and then check outside. The crowd all ran for it, but God knows where they'll end up."

"All right, Sarge. I'll be on the radio."

Richard watched Riaz hurry away, then went back to soothing the old woman on his lap. The other injured people in the shopping centre gradually snapped back into reality, which led them to moan about their pain. From what Richard saw, they were fine. Only the old dear on his lap was in a truly bad way—and perhaps the woman with the broken arm who now fell unconscious.

Richard tried to wipe the blood off the old woman's face, but it was so thin that it crusted. The smell was like copper pennies. She whimpered still, but now closed her eyes.

"Where's that sodding ambulance?" he hissed.

Richard grabbed his radio and called Dispatch, surprised when no one answered. Never in his twelve years on the job had Dispatch failed to answer a call. He persevered for five minutes straight, and was just about to give up, when somebody finally replied.

"Dispatch."

"Yes, it's Sergeant Honeywell at Queensmeade Shopping centre, what the hell is going on there?"

"It's all gone to hell," said a welsh accent he didn't recognise. "I'm not even supposed to be answering calls, but everyone is busy."

"Who are you, then?"

"I'm Nancy. I'm just an office temp. Heard your call going on for five minutes and couldn't take the noise anymore."

"Where are all the dispatchers?"

"Here," she said, "but they have call after call after call coming in. London's under attack. So is everywhere else."

"Everywhere else?" said Richard, but then decided he couldn't deal with any more information right now. "I need an ambulance sent to my location. An old lady is hurt."

"I'll see what I can do for you, but I'm not gunna lie, there isn't going to be much chance of getting you one anytime soon. The entire region is calling in for help. They're assembling the Army to go into the city."

"The Army?" It made sense, but Richard struggled to imagine the Army stomping down Oxford Street. "What does Command want us to do?"

"I have no idea, love. Just look after yourself. I have to go."

"No, wait. I need—"

The line went dead.

Richard looked at the old woman on his lap and felt himself shake. The moans in the shopping centre beat at his skull. The stench of blood made him want to gag. He needed to get out of there. Needed to do something.

A crash, and Richard looked around to see a group of young men kicking in the door to the video game store. The staff had all left, and the security guards, to Richard's astonishment, looked the other way. So much blood and panic must have turned their stomachs and sapped their will.

The gang of youths spilled into the store and started their rampage, kicking over display stands and grabbing anything they desired. One lad, in a white baseball cap, stood up front while his pals loaded him up with games, consoles, and other expensive hardware.

Then one of the looters spotted Richard kneeling outside with the old lady—realised he was a police officer.

"Fuck, there's a plod!"

They stopped what they were doing mid-rampage. The lad with the armful of game consoles peered over the top of the pile with wide eyes. They all made for the door at once.

Richard tried to get up, but couldn't get the old lady off of him quickly enough without hurting her. She moaned. "P-Please..."

The looters edged out of the doorway and hurried towards the exit, where they would hit the streets and disappear with their haul. It was now or never if he was going to stop them. Richard might be a forty-year old man, but he was good in a sprint. He only needed to catch one of them—and the lad with the armful of consoles would be sluggish.

The gang bolted.

Richard jolted, but didn't move from his knees. Ruefully, he watched them race out through the exit.

There had been no choice but to let them go.

The old lady needed Richard more.

"I got you," he said. "Someone will be here soon."

"T-Thank you."

Richard stroked her brittle, grey hair while trying not to think too hard about what was happening. He had a feeling things would get very busy in the hours ahead.

What the hell was happening in London?

And how long before it reached here?

2

The ambulance took over an hour, and only one paramedic arrived instead of the normal two. Richard helped the medic load the old dear onto the gurney and secure her in the back of the vehicle. The woman with the broken arm was ushered inside also. She had woken up enough to take a seat up front. Before the paramedic got going, Richard pulled him aside.

"Will she be okay?"

The paramedic was a tall gent with shaved red hair. He looked dog-tired, and when he spoke, it was obvious his vocal chords had strained.

"Honestly, I'm not sure if anyone will be okay today. She has a concussion, which is bad for someone her age, but she's lucky compared to some." He took a moment to rub at his eyes as if he was holding back tears. "It's been the worst day of my life; I can tell you. This is my fourth call-out in the last two hours. I didn't know people could act this way. I had to take a six year old to the hospital because someone pushed him in front of a bus while they were trying to steal a bike. I don't think the boy has a chance of pulling through."

Richard grunted. "People are afraid. It magnifies the bad behaviour. It's men like you who have to look after the innocent at times like this. People like this old lady were doing nothing except going about their day."

"Men like me and you," the paramedic corrected.

Richard frowned. "Sorry?"

"It's men like me and you who need to look after the innocent. It was good of you to care for this old lady. I haven't seen a police officer all day. What are you all doing? Things are completely out of control. No offence."

"I think we're stretched pretty thin. Most of us are on high alert to go into London, but that might already have happened. I've been here all morning, and I haven't been able to get in touch with my order-givers. Apparently, the whole country is under attack."

"S'what I've heard. Those gates are everywhere." The paramedic closed the ambulance doors and shook Richard's hand. He also gave him a card with a phone number. "Name's Oliver. You keep 'em safe, and I'll come get 'em if I can. The switchboard's a mess, so I figure it would be useful if us guys on the ground kept in touch."

Richard put the card in his pocket. "My name is Richard; I'll keep in touch."

They shook hands one last time. Then Oliver got in behind the wheel and reversed out of the shopping centre. Richard turned a quick circle, taking in the remains of the precinct. It felt like one of those snapshots in history—a scene to be played out on the news ten years from now. A haunting reel of shocked stares and broken windows. Only, Richard dreaded that what had just happened in Slough was a byline at most. Oxford Street was the headline.

Monsters.

He got on his radio and called in again, but not to Dispatch. He hailed the other officers in the area. Riaz came back. "We're assembled in front of the church."

"Okay, I'll meet you there."

Richard did not want to go to the church. He wanted to go home and check on his family. Jen and Dillon must be terrified. But it was to the church he went.

St Paul's C of E was right outside the shopping centre, and true to his word, Riaz was standing right there with two other officers beside him—Saunders and Jameson. Jameson was sitting on the ground.

"Where's the rest of the team?" asked Richard.

"Your guess is as good as mine. I'm just hoping they're not hurt. Jameson has a twisted ankle."

Jameson shrugged, embarrassed.

Richard looked around and saw that the church was acting as sanctuary for the injured and afraid. A vicar milled about, offering tea and biscuits to the various refugees—many of them children. Some people had been trampled so badly that they sported dusty footprints on their clothing.

"We're getting everyone out of harm's way," said Riaz, but the worst seems to be over. "It was the initial panic that did most the damage. It's calmed down now. In fact, the town is deserted."

"Calm before the storm," said Richard. "Soon as the sun goes down, kids will be out for a good time. Unless we get our act together first that is. Have you heard anything from Dispatch or Command?"

"Not for the last half hour."

"You spoke to Dispatch half an hour ago?"

Riaz shook his head. "No, I got through to Command."

"I haven't been able to get a hold of them. What did they say?"

Riaz didn't answer. In fact he looked away and scanned the crowd of shellshocked people.

"Riaz, what did they say?"

"It's bad, Sarge. They say this is happening everywhere."

"Rioting?"

"No. Not rioting. The attacks. They're happening all over the country. Everywhere there was a stone. They've all turned into gates."

Richard had to steady himself on a nearby wall.

Riaz nodded. "I know, it's hard to imagine."

"What did Command want us to do?"

Riaz waved an arm towards the church and the people gathered around it. "This. They want us to keep a police presence in the town centre. Everyone else has been called in to man a task force headed for London."

"So we're on our own," said Richard. He ran a hand through his hair and realised he was sweating.

"Hopefully, the other guys will turn up to help, but I'm guessing they might have panicked along with everyone else. Michaels has only been on the job a few months. I'll have his nutsack if he's done a runner."

"Let's not count them out yet. We need to wait for the dust to settle."

Riaz rolled his eyes and turned away.

Richard went over to the vicar. "Any tea left for a shaken police officer?"

The holy man smiled. A subtle smear of blood stained his chin. "Of course. Let me grab you a cup. Here you go. Thank you for all your help today, officer. It's times like these when strong men have duty."

Richard took a sip of piping-hot tea and chuckled.

The vicar seemed bemused. "Did I say something funny?"

"No, it's just that I was saying something very similar not so long ago."

"Then you agree? Those of of us who can must do what is needed. We all saw the scenes from London. We understand what is coming."

"And what is that, Vicar?"

"The end. Perhaps not of everything, but certainly of what we know. Hell itself came through that gate today—it could have been nothing else."

Richard said nothing.

"You're sceptical, Officer? Many are these days, I'm afraid. I don't begrudge you for it, but whatever you believe—something evil has arrived, and this is just beginning."

Richard put his teacup on the wall. "Well, we're in agreement there, Vicar. I hear the Army is going into the city. People won't know what to do. They won't cope with fighting in the streets."

"They will cope, Officer. You may trust in that."

Richard sighed. "These people are lucky to receive your help, Vicar."

"Please, call me Miles. And my help is but a drop in the ocean. As I said, we all must do what we can."

Richard nodded. "Yes. If you'd excuse me."

The vicar nodded and went back to making tea.

Hell, as a metaphor, was something Richard could grasp well enough, but as a real place...? Believing that demons, or something else malevolent, had come to earth...? It was a struggle for him to accept such ideas, but then what did he make of what he had seen? Camera tricks? A conspiracy? Maybe the media had been hijacked, and what everyone saw was mere trickery? That was more plausible than Hell falling upon them.

But the stones were real. Richard knew because he had colleagues who had encountered them first hand. And old lady had died beside one in the village of Crapstone, and Michael Bray, the local coroner, used to play squash with Richard before moving south. Michael Bray had described the stone that had killed the woman.

Unmovable, and unknown.

One stone of several thousand.

If not an invasion from Hell, then what? Aliens?

Richard wobbled and again had to steady himself against the nearest wall. It was too much to process.

"You okay?" asked Riaz.

"No, Riaz, I am not okay, but that's not my main concern."

"What is then?"

"My family. I need to go check on them, but I can't leave you—"

"No, you can't."

Richard looked at the man. "What?"

"Everybody here is afraid, and they are relying on our presence to keep them safe. You can't leave."

"Riaz, you do not give me orders..."

"No, but I know that your orders will be to remain here."

That he was being told what to do by a subordinate made him even more determined to do as he pleased. "Riaz, I will be gone thirty minutes at most."

"Thirty minutes when anything could happen."

"I need to check on my family."

"And so do others."

Richard clenched his fists. "I'm going. You hold the fort while I'm gone."

Riaz rolled his eyes. "Fine. Just get back as quickly as you can."

Richard took one last look at the mess he was leaving his colleagues in—maybe fifty people sat on the floor outside the church, or on whatever perch they could find. Children crying. Mom's sobbing. Fathers sombrely staring into space. He would need to come back. The vicar was right about him having a duty, but his biggest and most important duty was to Jen and Dillon. How could he protect others before he protected them? He needed to know they were safe.

Richard found his squad car and climbed in. He took off at speed—the street ahead eerily abandoned.

The calm before the storm.

3

Richard leapt out of his squad car and raced up his drive. His house was a semi-detached dormer, but the long hedges on either side of the driveway made it appear to stand alone. Jen stared out of the front window, almost as if she expected him.

"Oh, Rich, I've been so worried," she said when he passed through the door.

"I should have called. I just wanted to get here."

"You're here now." She held him tightly—a strong woman with the extra pounds she'd put on over the last few years. He was so exhausted that her grasp knocked the wind out of him. "Are you okay?"

"No. It's been a tough morning. Did you see the news?"

She eased away from him and looked him in the eye. "How could I not have? Every channel got interrupted. They cut into Dillon's cartoons."

"What? Did he see?"

She pushed a strand of blonde hair behind her ear and sighed. "He's in the kitchen. I put a DVD on for him."

Richard pressed his forehead against hers, too tired to do anything else, and then headed into the kitchen. Sure enough, Dillon sat at the table watching a Disney film. From his fidgeting alone, Richard could tell he was agitated.

"Hey, Dillon. Daddy's home. What you doing?"

"Watching Lion King."

Richard smiled and gave his son a hug. Dillon was always affectionate, but could be withdrawn if worried. That was why he returned the hug, but did not look at his father.

"Is everything okay?"

Dillon nodded, but still didn't look away from the television. Despite being twenty-three, he was no less innocent than a eight year old.

"Dillon? If you saw something frightening on the TV, that's okay. Sometimes programmes can be upsetting, but you're safe. Nothing is going to hurt you."

"Monsters," Dillon muttered. "Monsters can hurt me."

"There are no monsters here, Dillon. Just me and your mum."

Dillon finally made eye contact. The Brushfield spots in his irises—a characteristic of his Down's Syndrome—glistened beneath a film of tears. "Will you stay here, daddy?"

"I... I can't Dillon. I have to go to work."

"Are you going to fight the monsters?"

Richard leaned in and hugged his son, patting his back at the same time. "No, sweetheart. I just have to make sure everybody behaves. You know my job is important."

Dillon nodded. He normally idolised Richard for being a policeman, but today it seemed to bring him trepidation. Richard wondered if his son understood the danger his job now involved.

"I don't want you to go, dad. I saw the monsters on the TV. They were hurting people. Don't go out." His bottom lip quivered.

"Sweetheart, everything is fine. I'm not leaving for ten minutes, so watch your film while I go talk to mummy."

"I don't want to watch the Lion King," he said. "I want you to stay here."

"Dillon..."

"Maybe he's right," said Jen, entering the room and looking like she needed a stiff drink. Pity they didn't keep alcohol in the house.

"I'm still on the job, Jen. I only snuck away to make sure you were both okay. I'll be lucky to get away with this as it is."

"You never signed up for what I saw on the television just now, Rich. Will you have to go to London?"

"I don't know."

Jen blinked and tried to keep her tears at bay. She had to turn away as she spoke. "I'm not having you risk your life. Your job is to arrest abusive husbands and confiscate wacky backy. It's just a stupid job."

Richard was taken aback. Never had he thought of his occupation as a 'job'. A vocation perhaps, but really, he considered it his calling. He'd been doing it so long now that it was part of who he was. "It's not a stupid job, Jen. I have a responsibility to protect the people. If I abandon my duties, what does that make me?"

"A husband. A father."

He sighed. Some arguments could not be won. "Look, before I do anything, I need to see what's happening. Things are all over the place right now. Is the news still running?"

"It hasn't stopped all morning."

Richard went into the living room and picked up the television remote.

"Keep the volume down," said Jen, following him. "I don't want Dillon upset again."

"Neither do I." He switched on the television but did not need to change the channel. He could have been watching a disaster movie if not for the BBC News ticker running along the bottom of the screen.

It was all over. That was the way it felt. The amount of death on screen, the amount of destruction...

"Oh, God," said Jen. "It's even worse."

A helicopter recorded the video—obvious from the high elevation—but this time it was not a view of London. It was New York. Richard spotted the Empire State Building towering in the background. The Big Apple burned. Central Park teemed with fleeing bodies so small they might have been ants. It was hard to see from such height, but the denizens of Manhattan were under obvious attack. Richard could see the ants colliding and dancing—predators and prey coming together in mortal harmony.

It soon became clear why the helicopter kept such altitude. Amongst the chaos, the flames, and debris, stood something massive and indescribable. A giant.

The huge, naked man strode through the streets of Manhattan, a colossus leaving in its wake a trail of devastation. With ease, it plucked up a city bus and threw it into the air as if no more than a loaf of bread. A military helicopter zipped around behind it, peppering it with machine gun fire, but it did more damage to the surrounding skyscrapers than the giant. Glass windows exploded in a Mexican Wave along the side of a modern high rise. A studio reporter narrated the scenes they were seeing, but the man struggled to string together sentences, speaking in broken, garbled utterances.

How did you report the unreportable?

A loud bang from outside the house, distant yet not miles away. Richard went to the window and looked out. The street was quiet. A nice area, yet it backed up against a more urban district that would be a prime centre of unrest when the inevitable unruliness began.

Would the trouble spill over here? Was their home safe?

"What's happening, Rich?" Jen asked him.

It pained him not to be able to answer. What was happening? A terrible dream? What had happened to the ordinary, mundane world of yesterday?

"We need to prepare for the worst," he said, wanting to hug Jen but feeling it was important that they stay emotionally detached right now. "If the rest of the world is watching this on TV, then there will be a panic the likes of which we've never seen."

Jen swallowed, but took a steadying breath and nodded. "So what do we do? Do we lock up tight and ride it out?"

Richard thought about it. Considered boarding up the windows and arming themselves, but his gut told him it was a poor move. If the unrest spilled over into this street, they'd have no chance of escape. And could Richard, as a police officer, hole up and ignore what was happening?

"I think we should all leave, Jen. It's better if we stick together with other people than stay here by ourselves. Plus, if the government starts evacuating people, it will be better if we are somewhere visible."

Jen folded her arms and held herself. "Where should we go?"

"The church in the town centre. Some of my colleagues are already there, along with a big group of people. It'll be safer. If trouble starts, we'll be less vulnerable in a group. It's also my duty to look after everyone. At the church, I can do that while also having you and Dillon where I can see you."

Jen nodded. "Okay, then we'll all go there."

Dillon came into the room. He looked pale, making his freckles stand out like bugs on his cheeks. "Go where?"

Jen smiled at him. "We're going to church, honey."

"Church is boring."

"It won't be today," said Richard.

Lt Hernandez

THE USS AUGUSTA buzzed with excitement, and it was with great trepidation that Lieutenant Jose Hernandez disembarked alongside his commanding officer, Captain Adrian Johnson, who was the spitting image of Harrison Ford and twice as grumpy. With the strange stones all over the world suddenly coming to life and emitting ethereal nets of multi-coloured light, the entire east coast Navy had been recalled to Norfolk Naval Station for immediate briefing. Nobody knew what would happen, but no one could see how the stones represented anything good. They were alien.

Hernandez had it in his head that the world was about to have its first alien contact. His mind conjured images of the strange lights turning into giant projectors for intergalactic communication. Maybe the aliens would be peaceful, reaching out in friendship—or maybe they planned to offer an opportunity for subjugation before they began their impending invasion. Every time he thought about it, his stomach flipped like a pancake.

"Keep up, Hernandez, you're dawdling."

"Sorry, sir." He doubled his steps and moved back alongside Commander Johnson.

Norfolk Naval Station resembled a car park more than anything else from afar. Its paved shoreline housed a thousand cars on an ordinary day, but now it was crammed with twice that. As the world's largest naval station, Norfolk could comfortably house over seventy ships alongside its fourteen piers and over a hundred aircraft in its eleven hangars. Today it seemed small.

Navy personnel rushed everywhere, some in dress uniform, others in their patchy blue work fatigues. Hernandez himself wore his fatigues, but he now wished that—like Johnson—he had thought to change into his dress uniform. He would be lost in this crowd, indistinguishable from the lowliest sailor. A wasted opportunity. Times like these—times of crisis—reputations got forged.

"Look at that beauty, Hernandez," said Johnson as they hurried towards Hangar 4 where several dozen officers had assembled. He point ed to Pier 6, home to a floating monument, the USS New Hampshire.

The USS New Hampshire was the flagship of the US Navy. The latest Gerald R. Ford-class supercarrier, it was due to officially enter service next month, but here it was now, ready for action. Nuclear powered and highly automated, it was the most advanced naval craft in the world. Hernandez licked his lips at the thought of one day serving aboard her.

Not that Hernandez's own ship, the USS Augusta, lacked prestige. A modern Burke-class destroyer, it was no duck in the water, and could dominate most ships of equal size. Coincidentally, it had launched from this very naval station in 1993.

As they neared the wide-open Hangar 4, where a massive group of officers assembled in rank and file, something happened. Hernandez sensed it more than realised it at first, but he caught movement in the corner of his eye—saw people rushing more frantically than moments before. A panic had taken hold and was spreading.

"Something's happened," Hernandez muttered, slowing down and then stopping.

Johnson stopped too, but looked irritated. His intense green eyes were beds of concrete. "Keep your head in the game, Hernandez. I will not be late."

Hernandez looked around and became more certain that some kind of news had just broken. A young ensign sprinted towards the docks and Hernandez grabbed her. "What is it? What's happened?"

"New York is under attack. Orders are to offer support right now."

Hernandez glanced at Johnson, who had changed from being irritated to looking confused. The look he gave the young ensign could have boiled water. "What do you mean 'under attack'?"

The woman shrugged her arm free of his grasp. "I mean, those stones are exactly what we were all afraid of. They brought something here."

"What—"

"I need to go." The ensign sprinted away.

"We need to get to that briefing," said Johnson.

With no counter-argument, Hernandez followed his commander towards Hangar 4. When they joined the other assembled officers, the panic had spread over the entire station—men and women cursed and cried. Some of them were from New York or had family there. Many fled, heading back to their ships or cars. Most remembered their duty and stayed, even as salty tears stained their cheeks.

When Admiral Kirsch appeared at the front of the hangar dressed in full regalia, the vast space fell silent. The sixty-year old man looked forty, with a wide chest full of medals and thick brown arms hanging confidently by his sides. A lifetime at sea had hardened the man, and even a sedentary command role failed to soften him. When he scanned over the assembled audience, he seemed to look at each person individually. Hernandez felt a chill.

Kirsch spoke slowly, making sure each word stood alone. "We. Are. At. War."

The air vibrated. No one dared let out the slightest whisper.

Kirsch continued. "Ten minutes ago, New York City was attacked. Some of you may have seen the images already, but that shows nothing of the scale of what we face. Over six thousand black stones have been identified around the world in the last forty-eight hours, and as far as we can tell, every single one of them just opened up and spat out something alien. Our enemy: unknown. Their intentions: unknown. One thing we do know is that they are here to kill us. Man, woman, and child. The slaughter is going on right now, in New York, in nearly every other city you can name."

Someone in the audience let out a strangled sob, but no one dared turn to see who.

Kirsch let the slight interruption go. He went on, "Assembled in front of me are some of the proudest, toughest, and most intelligent men and women the United States of America has at its disposal. Each one of you dreads the possibility of war; I know it, but each one of you is ready for it—has trained for it. You pledged your service to your country, but your country does not need you. The world needs you. Our foe is vicious and unknown. We will be gaining Intel on the ground as we fight, starting blind and finding our way as we go. We will win though, make no mistake about that. The enemy has ambushed us, caught us by surprise, but that is their first and only advantage. We have guns. They do not. We have hardware. They do not. We have the United States Navy, the meanest SOBs on this whole goddamn planet. Do you hear me?"

A cheer erupted, but it lacked bluster. The officers were still in shock.

"Most of us will go from here to offer aid to New York," said Kirsch, "but there will be others of us with other destinations. The east coast alone is home to over a hundred of those God-forsaken stones. From now on, we shall refer to them as gates, because that, my friends, is what they are. Our enemy has come from someplace else—where, I don't give two shits—but we sure as hell are going to send them right back with their tails between their legs."

Another cheer. This one a little more enthusiastic.

Kirsch had grown red in the face now. "For the first time in our history as a species, we will go to war, not because of greed, religion, or politics, but for survival. We will, for the first time, be a united mankind, against an enemy that wishes to snuff us out. Are we, men and women of the United States Navy, going to let them?"

A cheer. "No!"

"I said, are we fucking going to let them?"

A resounding cheer. "No, sir!"

"Then get back to your posts. Man those engines, and get to war. Let our enemy gaze upon their reflections in puddles of their own blood. Let them—"

The ground shook beneath them. The air whipped up a breeze.

An explosion, deep and loud.

Pugnacity disappeared as panic came flooding back. The assembled officers stumbled. None of them knew what was happening. No one took charge. Even Kirsch looked confused.

Gunfire broke out.

"To battle stations," Kirsch bellowed. Even though no one had designated stations, it served well enough to get them all moving.

Johnson moved, but Hernandez couldn't get his feet going. The sound of continuing gunfire outside filled his veins with syrup and weighed him down. He'd never been in a firefight before. He was no marine.

"Get moving, Hernandez!" Johnson shoved him hard enough that it hurt. The pain snapped him into action, and he got moving again. Together, the two of them made a break for it. Outside, a pair of jeeps whizzed by, parting the confused crowd. Marines manned the rear-mounted machine guns.

Among the gunfire screams broke out.

At the rear of the station, away from the piers and towards the main roads, smoke billowed and muzzles flashed. Marines filed together, rifles raised.

They fell quickly.

"What the hell is going on?" said Johnson.

Hernandez stumbled as someone collided with his back. That was his only reaction though, for his gaze fixed on that ever-diminishing line of marines. One by one they fell, their heads dipping out of view beyond the crowd. The crowd itself snarled up as hundreds of navy personnel fled towards the piers—away from the road. Hernandez and Johnson would get caught in the crush.

"We need to get out of here, sir."

Thankfully, Johnson did not argue. "Back to the Augusta."

They turned and tried to run, but the way forward was too thick with bodies. They were forced to shove and elbow their way along, inch by inch. Hernandez felt the unseen threat at his back like an approaching forest fire. He could even imagine his flesh burning, peeling from his back in bloody strips.

Was the enemy here?

Had they been ambushed? Or was it like this everywhere?

They needed to get back to the Augusta. That was their home, and they could defend it. Here, at the station, they didn't even have weapons to defend themselves.

Screams of pain multiplied and intensified, spreading out in an arc around the centre of the station as if the crowd was folding in on itself. The sound of gunfire increased too, but not from the direction of the marines. It was coming from the piers. Crewmen lined the various ship rails and fired from onboard. Hernandez instinctively ducked as he worried about a stray bullet parting his skull. As if to prove his concerns correct, he saw a young Lieutenant flop to the ground as a spray of blood erupted from his neck.

"Where the hell is the enemy?" Johnson shouted. "I can't see a thing."

Hernandez didn't either, so he wasted no time replying. The question answered itself.

A creature appeared in the crowd, a burnt husk of a man. It looked right at Hernandez, but then swiped to its left, catching an oil-stained mechanic around the throat and tearing out his windpipe. The dead worker folded to the ground like a roll of old carpet.

Then the creature charged right at Hernandez.

Time slowed down. Hernandez felt his feet lock up again, and could only flail his arms and open his mouth to cry out. Johnson was behind him, unaware of the hellish monstrosity racing towards them.

The thing was so badly burnt that it left strips of flesh on the concrete with every bounding step. With each split second, it closed the distance between it and Hernandez, and its broken teeth ground together hungrily. Its gnarled fists groped at the air.

A young woman backed into Hernandez, and when she saw the burnt creature coming towards her, she screamed. The noise prodded Hernandez's senses and caused him to react. He grabbed the young woman by the shoulder and shoved her hard at the incoming monster. It collided hard with her, and the two of them went down, the burnt creature on top. It tore chunks out of the woman as she screamed and fought.

Johnson grabbed Hernandez by the elbow and yanked him. "Keep moving."

More of the burnt creatures threaded through the crowd, overrunning the entire base and attacking from all sides. Johnson and Hernandez would be ripped apart long before they reached the Augusta. The ship was berthed two hundred metres away on Pier 6, but it might as well have been two hundred miles away.

Where had the enemy come from?

"Rip 'em to shreds," a gruff voice shouted.

Hernandez turned to see Admiral Kirsch. The admiral held a large pistol in his hand and fired it like a cannon. A nearby creature's head disappeared like a red jelly someone had kicked. With Kirsch stood four marines, each of them unleashing from MP5 sub-machine guns. Hernandez realised then how many of the burnt men were within arm's reach of him. They began to fall everywhere, riddled with bullets from the dead-eyed marines.

Kirsch caught Hernandez standing still and shot him a withering glance. "What are you doing, man? Get back to your crew and join this fight. Now!"

Hernandez feared the old admiral more than any creature from the beyond, so he stumbled backwards into Johnson when shouted at. Before long, he was sprinting down the pier at a speed he hadn't known he was capable of. Even Johnson, an impressively fit man, struggled to keep up.

But it still wasn't enough.

The enemy was everywhere, and the way ahead was congested.

Hernandez looked back over his shoulder. An army of abominations flooded down the pier behind him. Fleeing sailors were flung to the ground and trampled, or tossed into the water like trash. Blood stained the concrete.

"We're not going to make it," said Johnson. "No way."

"The water," said Hernandez. "We swim for it."

Johnson went to the edge of the pier and looked down. "I don't fancy our chances, but it might be our only choice."

The creatures would be on them any second. Only a few men and women now between Hernandez and the ensuing tide of death. The cold, dark water churning beneath the pier looked little more inviting. If the sudden whip of its cold caress didn't blow their already overworked hearts, then the pull of the various ship props might drag them under.

What choice did they have?

Hernandez prepared himself to jump.

Out of nowhere, an enemy appeared and grabbed him. Not a burnt creature like the others, it was more like a monkey torn wretched by disease. Each of its arms ended in nine-inch talons, and its face was a twisted grimace of teeth. Hernandez was not proud, but he let out a yelp.

Johnson came to his rescue, kicking out at the creature and sending it sprawling. The creature clambered back to its feet and launched itself into the air.

Johnson stood his ground.

A blast of noise.

A mid-air impact altered the creature's trajectory and sent it tumbling off the pier and into the ocean. More gunfire erupted nearby and Hernandez ducked down. Johnson spun around and pumped his fist in the air. "Yes! Let them have it!"

The crew of the Augusta filled the pier and brought their M164As to bear. Four dozen sailors pulled their triggers at once, sending forth a blanket of fire. Johnson grabbed Hernandez and dragged him behind the other men, out of harm's way. He glanced back and witnessed legions of monsters flopping to the ground as their organs exploded and heads split open. The crew of the Augusta slammed in magazine after magazine. The gunfire was endless.

But the enemy kept coming.

"Fall back," shouted Johnson, taking command of his men. "Back to the ship."

The wall of rifles inched backwards, still firing, still reloading, but retreating. The enemy was not wary, even as they continued to fall. They came in continuous waves, a hellish banzai charge.

The sound of rifle's stuttering dry brought despair—the scratching of death's fingers on an empty chalkboard.

The first crewman fell, pounced on by one of the ape-like creatures. The attacker tore open his chest cavity and ripped free one of his ribs. More men fell behind him. Hernandez was aware that he was screaming.

"Back to the goddamn boat!" Johnson shouted.

The men turned and ran, most of their weapons empty and useless. Turning their backs led to a rout, but some of them might still have a chance. Hernandez raced to the front of the group, desperately reaching for the Augusta's distant gangway.

He had to get there. He had to make it.

When his boot came down on the metal ramp, Hernandez gurned with relief. Snot ran down his face, and his knees buckled, but he was gathered aboard by his crew. Johnson was right behind him.

"Pull up the ramp," Johnson shouted.

The ramp clunked and recalled itself.

The disfigured apes leapt onto it before it disappeared and began to clamber aboard.

Rat-a-tat-tat.

Port-side machine guns opened up and tore apart the enemy, re-moving them before they had a chance to make it onto the deck. Rein-forcements manned the rails with fully loaded rifles. The enemies on the pier were sitting ducks.

Johnson grabbed his nearest ensign, Cuervo, and barked into the woman's face. "Tell the bridge to get moving. We're too vulnerable sitting here."

"Aye, Captain."

Hernandez wiped the snot from his face and looked out at Norfolk Station. Smoke billowed from every structure. The sky was black. The enemy was everywhere.

Dead sailors lay scattered, and many of the smaller vessels in dock were being overrun, their crews besieged. Yet, it was something else that chilled Hernandez to his bones.

A thirty-foot giant strode along the main road towards the base, a thing of rippling muscle and sinew. Its face was a marble sculpture— a beauty to behold. But it was no man, and such beauty only hid its bloodlust as it reached down and crushed a fleeing jeep full of men. With every man it tore apart, it bellowed in triumph. It was a monster, greater and more vile than all before it.

Hernandez flopped against the railing, unable to talk.

It wasn't aliens. It was something worse.

2

"What is that?" someone asked.

Hernandez eased himself away from the railing. "I don't know, and I don't want to stick around to find out."

The Augusta had moved away from the pier, but that didn't mean it was free from danger. War still raged at Norfolk Naval Station, and the giant had only added to the slaughter. The crew gasped as the tow-ering creature picked up a fuel tanker as if it were a toy and hurled it through the air. It collided with the main runaway of the USS New Hampshire and exploded. Sailors screamed and threw themselves overboard as the searing flames engulfed them. A parked F15 fighter plane listed onto its side and came apart in another mighty explosion. More sailors screamed in agony.

Meanwhile, the bulk of the enemy force—the burnt men and disfigured apes—continued tearing apart those unlucky enough to be in their way. Droves of men and women had made it back aboard their ships, but just as many still lay stranded in the centre of the base, standing back to back and fighting valiantly, yet losing decisively.

"All munitions to the deck," Johnson commanded. "I want a continuous line of fire supporting those men and women still trapped on land. Let's turn this around."

Glad to receive orders, the Augusta's crew got to work. Hernandez retrieved his combat rifle and struggled to load it with a magazine. His hands were shaking. Back at the rail, he lined up his scope and started picking shots. The first four trigger-pulls missed, chucking up chunks of concrete, but the next one winged a disfigured ape. The creature had been about to leap on top of a bleeding woman, but hit the ground instead—its right leg disintegrated.

Hernandez gritted his teeth and picked his next target.

Another direct hit. The burnt man cartwheeled into the water.

The next thing his scope spotted surprised him: Admiral Kirsch was still alive.

His marines also. The old man had lost his cap, revealing a thick crop of white hair, and his dress uniform was now stained entirely crimson—but he was alive. He still held his weighty pistol, and the thing still fired like a bucking mule. The four marines with him placed their shots with lethal accuracy, but were clearly exhausted. They moved sluggishly, brought their aims around a little slower every time. Eventually, the creatures would close in on them.

"Help the admiral," Hernandez shouted, hoping he would be heard. "Hangar 2."

Peering back through his scope, Hernandez watched the added fire support take immediate effect. Burnt men fell one after the other. The four marines moved with renewed enthusiasm. Kirsch looked around for who to thank and soon spotted the Augusta. He raised a hand and saluted them, then went back to popping off shots with his massive pistol.

Hernandez's rifle clicked dry. He ejected the mag and jammed in another. Picking shots was easy because the enemy were everywhere. Had they all come out of a single gate?

Was there one nearby?

Contemplating the odds only made his heart beat faster, so Hernandez concentrated only on what he could see through his scope, and on pulling the trigger. Tat-tat-tat. His skull rang with the constant onslaught of noise. Nausea overwhelmed him.

"Fire on the big bastard," Johnson yelled.

Hernandez pulled away from his scope and realised the giant had made it over to the hangars and was decimating the remaining Naval forces. Kirsch and his marines scattered around their huge foe and opened up with their rifles.

The giant roared, its long blond hair whipping around its shoulders—a statue come to life. A god of destruction. It reached down and snatched up one of the marines, holding the screaming man for a moment and grinning. Then he lofted the tiny body forty feet into the air and watched it thud against the concrete with a sickening splat.

Kirsch circled around in front of the giant and stood his ground defiantly. He waved a hand at his remaining three marines and ordered them to run. They refused. The four men stood together and unloaded the last of their ammunition into the massive enemy standing over them.

The giant flinched, took a step back, and let out a devastating roar. It swatted away the small-arms fire like mosquitos on its skin, then swung a massive arm and clobbered a nearby communications tower. The metal scaffolding folded in on itself, and the mass of electronic equipment held atop it came loose and fell to the ground. Kirsch had been standing right underneath.

Hernandez looked away and cursed as the old man and his three marines disappeared beneath a huge pile of twisted metal. Those still alive and fighting nearby faltered. Their admiral had been killed. Their leader was dead.

Ensign Tyke stood beside Hernandez and shook his head in despair. "What the hell is happening, Lieutenant? I don't understand."

Hernandez took a breath and pulled a face when he smelt blood. "It will be okay, Tyke. We'll get ahead of this thing and—"

Tyke's head disappeared from his shoulders. One minute he'd been anxiously staring at Hernandez, then he was a pair of empty shoulders with a stump of gristle and bone for a neck. His body slumped over the railing and into the water.

Gunfire peppered the deck. More of the Augusta's crew fell.

Hernandez squinted through his scope, urgently scanning the battlefield. What he saw drained the blood from his veins.

The burnt men were picking up the rifles of dead sailors and using them to return fire at the various ships. The safety of being on board evaporated.

An almighty blast came from a ship's main gun somewhere. The noise of the battlefield was like living inside a swarm of bees. Disorientation. No way to tell what was happening anymore. Chaos.

"Sail out!" ordered Johnson. "Norfolk is lost. We need to get to sea. Engines full power. Go! Go! Go!"

The decks rumbled. The Augusta leaned starboard. Crewmen ducked behind the rails, taking cover while bullets whizzed over their heads like hornets. A junior Lieutenant fell onto his back when he was too slow to get down, and he lay there screaming like a child. No one went to help him. Not yet.

Hernandez crawled over to Johnson who had taken a knee behind one of the ship's two MH-60R Seahawk helicopters. One of them leaked from a pierced fuel line.

"Captain, should I call Command?"

"Already tried," said Johnson. "Nothing but noise right now. We have to relocate."

"Relocate where?"

"I don't know, Hernandez! Right now, I just want to get my ship and crew out of harms way. You're standing here doing nothing."

Hernandez was taken aback by the sudden venom in his commander's voice, but when he considered the stress of the situation, he understood. "What would you have me do, sir?"

"Check on the wounded." Johnson turned away and got on the radio. Clearly any conversation with Hernandez was over.

So Hernandez went to carry out his orders. The Augusta moved half-a-kilometre out from Norfolk's piers, almost out of danger, but the horror still flared back on land. Even now, rifles clacked and larger guns boomed. The giant had disappeared, but the burnt men still swarmed, mopping up whatever remained.

Hernandez just witnessed Pearl Harbour.

And survived it.

The Augusta's crew stood mostly intact. Hernandez estimated the death toll at no more than twenty. Not bad considering the fates of ships such as the New Hampshire.

Seaman Patrick briefed Hernandez about the ship's damage, and that too was within the realms of 'lucky'. Nothing powerful enough to pierce the hull had come their way, and the only severe damage was to the backup comms dish. It wasn't a problem, so long as the main dish remained operational. The Seahawk's burst fuel line could be easily repaired. They had gotten out of there with their butts intact, but what came next, no one knew.

Hernandez headed to his quarters and grabbed his cell phone—wasn't surprised when the call didn't connect. If the world was at war, the networks would be overloaded with panicked callers. He would keep trying though.

"What are you doing, Hernandez?"

Hernandez looked up to see Lieutenant Danza. "Trying to call home. My ma lives in Austin, and there was one of those stones there, I think."

"And my sister lives in Columbus where there's one too. Think I don't want to take a minute and make some personal calls? I'm sure everyone does, but we have to focus on our duties right now."

"It's just one call."

"And what if one of the crew sees you make it? You'll have three hundred sailors all demanding to drop tools and call their mothers. Once they get a hold of someone they love there'll be no getting them back, especially if they get bad news."

Hernandez saw Danza's point, but he wasn't about to take a dressing down by a fellow lieutenant—especially one beneath him by time served. Hernandez's rank and seniority placed him below only Captain Johnson. "What an officer does and what a crewman does are not the same thing. I don't need you to tell me how to conduct myself."

Danza studied him for a moment, a slight smirk on his face. "If you think that screaming like a little girl is how an officer should conduct himself, then you have it all wrapped up."

"I'm sorry? Care to explain what you mean by that?"

Danza shook his head and chuckled. "I mean that the entire crew saw you scream when that thing had you."

"I thought I was going to die!"

"We're US Navy. We're trained to die. And when we do, we don't scream like children."

"Fuck you, Danza. Go back to driving a taxi for Danny DeVito."

"Ouch, a Taxi joke. They never get old. Just watch yourself, Hernandez. You might be second in command, but everyone knows you don't have any balls."

Danza walked away, leaving Hernandez to clench his fists and fume alone in his cabin.

Who did that piece of shit think he was? Fellow officers were supposed to respect one another. He was probably just another racist prick who begrudged a 'spik' being in a position to give orders. Hernandez had dealt with dicks like Danza during his entire nine-year career. Snarling bullies who cried 'affirmative action' every time Hernandez got a promotion over them. They failed to see that he had an unblemished record and perfect aptitude test scores.

He tried to call his ma again but still got no connection.

Growing up in Austin, the ocean had always fascinated Hernandez. He never got to see it until his thirteenth birthday when his school took a trip to the Kennedy Space Centre followed by a day at Daytona Beach. The vastness of the Atlantic had mesmerised him for hours and almost frightened him too much to go in—but once he had...

Everyone in Austin loved water. In the heat of Texas, swimming pools were an everyday part of life, but the ocean was different. The sea was alive. And when Hernandez was around it, he felt alive too. That day at Daytona beach, he knew he wanted to spend his life sailing the oceans and seeing the world. He would not be another Latino who never left the city in which they grew up. His ma supported him, and his pops had died when he was young. He had no other family. He decided he would enter a new one: the United States Navy. While it had never been easy, it had also never been hard. While individuals within the Navy had their opinions, the institution itself was blind to everything except talent. Work hard enough, devote your entire life, and you could be admiral.

Like Kirsch.

Naively, Hernandez had only ever seen the benefits of the Navy. It wasn't until now he realised he might actually have to die in service of his country. The Navy was not his family. It was his master.

He headed back onto deck where things were now more or less back in order. The crew went about their duties. The injured were moved to the infirmary. Only bloodstains suggested they had ever been in a conflict.

Commander Johnson approached Hernandez on the aft deck, motioned for him to follow. He didn't say a word until they were out of earshot of everyone else. "I've had word from Jacksonville," he said. "We had two-thirds of our east coast fleet at Norfolk. No word on survivors yet, but the USS New Hampshire was destroyed, along with several more of our larger ships. It hurt us bad."

"Jesus Christ," muttered Hernandez.

"That's not even the worst part," continued Johnson. "We had over four-hundred officers assembled during the attack, including three admirals. The Navy is rudderless. Fleet Admiral Simpson has taken over east coast operations from Jacksonville, but he's just one man—and his best years are behind him."

"I heard he was retiring this year."

"You heard right. He's pushing on eighty."

Hernandez sighed. "So what are our orders?"

"To do what we can."

"What does that mean?"

Johnson shrugged. "Hell if I know. Guess it means we try to help out wherever we can until we receive something more concrete. My current plan is to head north to New York, or south to Jacksonville. I'm waiting on Intel to see which area is most in need."

Hernandez nodded. "Okay. I'll head up to the bridge and keep an eye on things."

"No, I want you to check our munitions. We expended a massive amount of ammo at Norfolk, and I need to make sure we can still defend ourselves if we head back ashore."

"Yes, sir. I'll have one of the—"

"I want you to do it."

"Any officer can supervise a simple munitions check, sir."

Johnson glared at Hernandez. "Yes, but there is only one officer to whom I am giving the order."

Hernandez stood silent for a moment, trying to figure out why he was being treated like a green-eared recruit. He thought better than to argue further. Something about the expression on Johnson's face seemed to challenge him to try.

Hernandez saluted. "Right away, sir."

Johnson dismissed him curtly.

Hernandez started away, and wasn't sure why he stopped when the ship's radio buzzed nearby. Perhaps habit made him pick it up. He cringed when Danza's voice came from the other end. The other lieutenant requested to speak to the captain.

"It's for you," Hernandez told Johnson, offering the handset.

Johnson snatched it. "As I was expecting a call, that makes sense. I thought I gave you an order, Hernandez?" He sighed. "Stand there a moment."

Hernandez stood at attention.

Johnson spoke with Danza across the radio for several minutes, saying little and listening lots. Eventually, he dismissed the other and replaced the handset. He glanced at Hernandez and rubbed at his chin. "There's a cruise liner docked at Charleston in need of rescue."

"I agree we should help."

"You agree? I never even stated my opinion."

"Oh, I just assumed."

"Well don't. Don't you dare assume my orders. We will head south, yes, but the cruise liner is not our concern. Civilians are not an asset. We need to focus our energy towards launching a counter offensive on our enemy. If Command is moving to Jacksonville, that's where we should be. A new fleet will be assembling. Our priority should be to join it. I'm sure my fellow commanders will arrive at the same conclusion."

"So, we're going to leave the civilians to fend for themselves?"

"I don't like it," Johnson snapped, "but I need to think about the big picture. If I need a morality lesson, you'd be the last person I'd ask."

Hernandez spluttered. "What does that mean? Sir, if you have a prob—"

"What it means is that I saw you throw that young woman to her death back at Norfolk to save your own skin."

"I..." Hernandez closed his eyes as he recalled his own cowardly actions. "It just happened. I didn't think about it."

"I knew her, Hernandez. She served with me on the USS Wickham before I took command of the Augusta. She was a good officer. Better than you. Her name was Gina Landis, in case you were wondering."

Hernandez couldn't think of what to say. It was true, he had tossed the woman into the monster, but she would have been dead anyway. Nearly everyone at Norfolk was dead. He hadn't changed anything except saving his own life. It was simple pragmatism.

"Sir, I'm not sure what you want me to say. We were fighting for our lives back there. That girl—"

"Gina!"

Hernandez sighed and began again. "Gina isn't dead because of me. She's dead because monsters attacked us. The same ones now attacking a cruise liner in Charleston, which you have elected to ignore."

Johnson sighed and pinched the bridge of his nose as if trying to calm himself. "Perhaps you're right, Lieutenant. Perhaps you're not guilty of anything."

"Thank you for seeing that."

"We'll leave it for a court martial to decide."

Hernandez blinked. "What?"

"Soon as we get a handle on this thing, I'll be discharging you and having you stand trial. You're a coward, Hernandez, and you'll answer for it. Now get out of my sight. You have munitions to count, and if I find you've missed a single bullet you'll spend the night in the brig."

Hernandez walked away, shell-shocked.

A court martial?

So much for his unblemished record.

3

Danza came to see him two hours in. By that time, Hernandez thought he would feint if he had to count another bullet. As much as ammunition as they had spent back at Norfolk, they still had more than enough for another conflict—an amount painful to count.

"Least the captain doesn't have you cleaning the latrines," said Danza, beaming.

Too miserable to give a comeback, Hernandez carried on with his count, sorting the 5.56mm NATO rounds into boxes, ten by ten.

"What did you do?"

Hernandez considered the answer. Oh, you know, just killed a girl the captain probably used to screw. No biggie. "I have no idea," was his eventual reply. "Just leave me to it. I can't count with you bothering me."

Danza picked up a clipboard and studied it. "You counted the .62 cal shells yet?"

"No."

"All right." Danza picked up a pen and started counting the heavy boxes of large shells for the MK 45 gun.

Hernandez sighed. "What are you doing?"

"Helping you out. Actually, I came to tell you that we picked something up on the radars, something moving along the seabed. We think a ship went down recently. Now that I'm here, I'll help you."

"I don't need your help."

Danza carried on counting. "I know, I know. You don't need anybody's help, Hernandez. You have that big, giant chip on your shoulder to carry you through."

"I can accept help. Just not from assholes like you."

Danza whistled. "Ouch. And I thought I was a nice guy. You still sore about what I said to you earlier? Maybe if you'd seen my point and admitted I was right, you wouldn't be down here playing number monkey."

"What point?"

"That you should think about what you're doing, and how it will look to the crew. Did you get a hold of your ma?"

"No."

"Then it was all for nothing. You acted in your own interests, and as an officer, that's not acceptable. I told you what would have happened if you'd started open season on cell phones."

Hernandez clenched his fists and tried not to explode. Danza had been right—even at the time he had seen that—but why did the smug son-of-a-bitch have to make such a big issue out of it? "Yes, okay, Danza, you were right. It was a bad decision trying to call home. I'm worried about my ma, and I didn't think."

Danza smiled, still smug. "See, that wasn't so hard. I know you didn't think about it, but right now you have a boatload of frightened men and women who need you to keep a calm head. The crew will be looking to us and Johnson to make the right calls."

Hernandez huffed. "Yeah, right. Tell that to Johnson. He just ignored a plea for help from a cruise liner full of civilians. You would know because you gave him the report."

Danza nodded. "Not our place to question the captain. He needs to consider the big picture."

"You sound just like him."

"Good, because he's led a distinguished career, and getting on the wrong side of him hasn't done you any favours."

Hernandez curled his lip in disgust and let his current handful of bullets fall back into the crate. "You agree with his decision? You think we should just leave civilians to die, to get murdered by those things?"

"And what if I did disagree? Would Johnson change his mind?"

"Command told us to do what we can. Johnson isn't following that order. If he's violating an order from above, then we have a duty to—"

Danza waved a hand. "Oh, give it up, Hernandez. A minute ago, you couldn't stand me, and now you're talking about the two of us relieving the captain of his command. I was there when Command gave the order. The subtext was that they were barely in possession of their sanity. Fleet Admiral Simpson is in charge, but he's yet to give any firm orders, so whoever is manning the phones told us to just do whatever we can. The truth is that there are no orders to disobey, so the captain can do whatever he wants."

"No he can't! He has a duty to his country. We all do."

Danza sighed. "I don't disagree, Hernandez. The thought of all those innocent people... But let's just hold off on the mutiny talk for now, okay? We are one of the few ships lucky enough to get away from Norfolk in one piece. Let's consider ourselves lucky and not push things until we know more."

Hernandez rubbed a palm over his face. What was wrong with him? He was overreacting. He was so angry at Johnson's treatment of him that petty revenge clouded his thoughts. Or was it fear? Johnson wanted to see him dishonoured and disgraced because of some stupid girl. Humanity was at war, but the man was acting upon personal agendas? Hernandez now worried about America getting its act together and dealing with this crisis. Would there be time for a Court Martial? Would Hernandez end up in prison after surviving death back at Norfolk? It seemed likelier that they would all perish at the hands of monsters, but what if...?

Johnson was a fool. Hernandez stood guilty of nothing.

"Just forget I said anything, Danza," he said.

"Already forgotten. Unless I need to use it against you later." He clicked his fingers, firing them like pretend pistol, and laughed. Then he started up the ramp that led back out to the aft deck.

The ship listed.

Danza fell to the ground, struck his head against a pipe. "What the f...?"

Hernandez dropped a handful of 5.6mm NATO rounds onto the floor and cursed. He hurried over to Danza and helped the man back to his feet. "A wave?"

Danza rubbed at his head. "From where? The sea is calm."

They hurried up the ramp and went out onto the deck where the two Seahawks stood idle. A couple of the ship's mechanics huddled there, having been working on the broken fuel line. "What was that?" Danza demanded of them.

The two mechanics shook their heads. One of them, Seaman Lyle Crane, sported a greasy smudge across his forehead. "Dunno, sir."

The sound of gunfire made all of their faces fall at once. It came from the bow, the opposite end of the ship.

Hernandez waved an arm at the two mechanics. "Battle stations."

At once, they ran off to arm themselves. Hernandez and Danza did the same, grabbing rifles from the armoury and heading for the front of the ship. The gunfire grew continuous.

"How are we under attack?" asked Hernandez. "We're twenty miles off the coast."

Danza said nothing. He had grown pale, but he kept heading towards the bow. Hernandez fought the urge to jump overboard and followed his colleague. When they reached the front, they found Hell had come on board.

The crew battled something on the decks—bloated creatures resembling men, their flesh hanging loose and waterlogged on their bones. The entire ship was under attack. Enemies clambered over the railings and spilled onto the decks. Those with rifles let rip, tearing the enemy to pieces as quickly as they climbed the railings, but others stood unarmed, forced to defend themselves barehanded. The enemy leapt upon them like hungry lions, tearing at their windpipes with sharp, slippery claws.

Danza raised his rifle and joined the fight.

Hernandez stood there.

Seaman Lyle Crane stood nearby and came running. "Sir, we were already under attack when I got here. Do you know what's happening?"

Hernandez shook his head. "I don't understand where they are coming from. We should have been safe."

Lyle's face appeared grey under the setting sun, and impending nightfall felt like a curtain ready to be pulled over mankind's corpse. Was this the end? Hernandez watched the abominations kill his crew. Yes. "Get on a radio. Call for help."

Lyle saluted and sprinted off.

Hernandez stood there. He watched his crew fall in a torrent of gore, their slimy attackers ripping them into lumps.

Danza circled back around, popping one of the bloated monsters in the head. It launched backwards over the rail and back into the ocean. "Hernandez, I'm on my last mag. You got ammo? Hernandez? Lieutenant?"

Hernandez looked at the man, but couldn't summon a reaction. Slowly, like a rusted robot, he reached into his trousers and pulled out a spare magazine. Danza snatched it.

"Thanks! Those things are coming right up out of the water. I see light down there, deep beneath the surface. I think... I think one of those goddamn gates opened in the middle of the Atlantic."

Hernandez stood there.

Danza gave him a shove on the shoulder. "Hey, Hernandez, get with it! I need your help. Johnson wants a team up on the conning tower to gain elevation. Can you handle that?"

Hernandez stood there.

"Hernandez, go!"

Blinking, Hernandez got his legs moving. His heart thudded in his chest and bile burned his throat like he'd drunk a cupful of bleach. He raced into the ship's interior, gathering whoever he could along the way. By the time he reached the top of the conning tower, he had seven crewmen and four rifles. He sent one of the men as a runner to gather more weapons.

Hernandez found his voice. "Okay, we need to keep the ship from getting overrun. Concentrate on the enemy trying to board."

As commanded, the men with rifles concentrated their fire at the railings. The problem was that bloated monsters had now started to come on board via the aft deck too. From the conning tower, Hernandez only had a decent view of the ship's bow. Someone needed to contain the enemy at the rear.

"Okay, Petty Officer Rossi, hold this position and keep those railings clear. Matthews will be back soon with more ammo."

"Yes, sir."

"I'm heading to secure the aft." Hernandez flew down the ladder so quickly he almost free-fell, lucky to make it to the deck without injuring himself. The first person he bumped into was Commander Johnson. He was alone and injured. Blood flowed from his right arm hanging limply by his side. He held a Colt 9mm in his left hand.

"Hernandez. You got a team up top, good work."

"Thank you, sir."

"Danza is pinned down. We need to offer support."

Hernandez shook his head. "Sir, we need to secure the rear. The enemy is flooding aboard there. If we can stop the tide, we can regain control of the decks."

Johnson looked back at the carnage behind him. Despite being surrounded, Danza led a large group of sailors currently holding their own. "Okay, let's go quickly."

Hernandez raised an eyebrow. "Just the two of us?"

"You see anyone else we have at hand? We'll gather men if we can find them, but we need to hold the aft now. The men you put up top will help Danza hold the bow."

Although it had been his idea, Hernandez felt a cold, wet fish in his guts as he considered what a suicide mission heading to the aft with only his injured commander as support would be. Yet, if he did nothing, the ship would be overrun. Even now, dead men slithered along the rails from the rear of the ship.

"Come on!" said Johnson, already heading off. He pulled the trigger on his pistol and hit a bloated creature standing in his way. "Let's show these fuckers what we do to stowaways."

Hernandez shouldered his rifle and took off after his commander. Johnson seemed to have snapped—it was the only way Hernandez could explain the man's lack of fear. Even with one arm, Johnson sauntered along with confidence, raising his pistol and popping off rounds at whatever creature got close.

Almost at the aft, they found a couple of crewmen taking cover inside one of the rigid hull dinghies that hung over the railings. Both men were unarmed.

"Captain, thank God."

"Winstead, Gallagher! Get out of there. Your shipmates are dying."

Both men leapt out. "We were caught unarmed, sir."

Johnson reached into his belt and pulled a Smith and Wesson revolver into view. He shoved it at Winstead then turned around to grab a fire axe from the wall which he gave to Gallagher. "Both of you, come with me."

Together, the four men reached the rear of the ship. The sun had fallen below the horizon, but the area was well lit by spotlights. The two Seahawk helicopters blocked full view of the deck, but it was clearly an enemy ingress point. They teemed over the rails.

Johnson took out two bloated creatures mid-step. Hernandez opened up on three more sludging towards their flank. The creatures were slow to move—bogged down by water—yet they could pounce several metres once they picked their target. That's what happened to Gallagher within moments. The man raised the pistol in time to let off a shot, but it was too late. The bloated monster fell on top of him and disembowelled him with a single swipe of its bony claws. Thinking fast, Winstead dropped his axe and scooped up the revolver; pulling the trigger, he blew the creature away.

"Good work, Winstead," said Johnson, slapping another mag into the butt of his gun and firing off more shots.

Hernandez took out another bloater trying to sneak up behind them. Its leg came away at the knee, but it continued in a crawl. Winstead picked up the axe again and brought it down on the back of the creature's skull. The blood spatter was jet-black in the moonlight.

"These things are smart," said Winstead. "This one was trying to flank us. They're not animals, not monsters... I think... I think they used to be men."

Hernandez raised his rifle and zeroed in on another creature coming over the railing. Winstead might be right. Although the enemy's blue, swollen flesh was monstrous, their nipples, genitalia, and most of all, their eyes seemed human. Had they really once been men?

Were they zombies?

Demons?

Hernandez swallowed and pulled the trigger.

The bloated creature fell down dead.

The three of them continued putting up the best fight they could. Winstead swung his axe whenever he could save a bullet, and Hernandez was on his last magazine—he made each shot count. Johnson, however, was a madman, emptying a seemingly endless supply of extended clips he'd brought with him.

The enemy kept on coming. There could be a thousand of them down there beneath the surface of the water. How much longer could the Augusta hold out?

Hernandez pulled the trigger on his last round. Winstead was too slow spotting a bloater coming up on his blind spot. It leapt onto his back and bit into his neck like a ghoul. Winstead fired his revolver over his shoulder and took care of his attacker, but he was hurt bad. He fell to one knee and tried to stem the torrent of blood leaking from his throat with the palm of his hand. He used the axe handle as a crutch to stop him collapsing completely. "I'm down," he gargled.

The enemy smelt blood. They focused their attacks upon Winstead and swarmed him. Hernandez ran out of ammo, so Johnson was Winstead's only chance, but his pistol was too slow to fight off the onslaught. By the time he'd taken down three of the enemy, another four made it over to Winstead. He cursed and swore as they descended upon him, but soon cried out in pain. He tried to swing the axe from on his back, but it was swatted away and skittered along the deck. It came to rest at Hernandez's feet.

Johnson bellowed at him. "Hernandez, help him!"

"I'm out of ammo, sir."

"I don't care. Do something!"

Hernandez snatched up the axe at his feet and gripped it tightly, but remained where he was standing.

"God damn it, Hernandez!" Johnson slammed in another clip and fired. He hit two of the bloaters on Winstead, clearing a space in the swarm and revealing the man beneath. Winstead was dead, torn apart like a basket of bread. Johnson let out an animalistic snarl and kept on firing. Hernandez picked up the axe and ran over to his side.

"We have to get out of here, sir. We can't hold them off with one gun. They're going to surround us."

Even now, it happened. The creatures sensed their advantage and spread out around the railings, waiting to close in like a net. They were smart.

"Sir, we have to go, now!"

"We're not going anywhere, Lieutenant. Do your duty and secure this area."

Hernandez looked at his superior officer—saw the madness in his eyes. The man had lost it. The blood on his face made him look like a snarling madman.

"Sir, this is suicide."

"This is duty. The enemy is aboard our ship. We will die before we let them take it." He fired off several more rounds, each one hitting its mark. More bloaters came over the rails. The smell of brine-soaked flesh overpowered them.

"I'm heading back to the bow," said Hernandez.

Johnson glared at him. "Forever a coward. I order you to remain here and do your duty, Lieutenant. If we die, then we die as officers of the United States Navy. We die proud."

Hernandez wobbled, his knees made of wet sand. He looked around at the railings and saw dozens of the waterlogged abominations all around him. They were surrounded by monsters. No way to survive.

"I won't die for you, sir." Hernandez lifted the axe and buried it in his commander's collarbone, splitting his neck away from his shoulders. Utter shock covered Johnson's face. He tried to speak, but couldn't.

Hernandez put his foot on Johnson's pelvis and yanked the axe free. He swung it again, burying it deeper into the ruined neck tissue like a lumberjack felling a tree. Johnson gurgled. Blood came out of his ruined throat in rhythmic gushes.

Hernandez snarled and pulled the axe free again. This time, Johnson slumped onto his back. "There's your honourable discharge, sir."

The creatures fell upon Johnson and tore him apart as he bled out on the deck. Several more stalked Hernandez, but he kept them at bay with mad swings of his bloody axe. He edged backwards, desperately hoping he would make it back to Danza and the others, and that the other lieutenant had things under control. Gunfire still blazed—both a good and bad sign.

With Johnson dead, the ship now lay in Hernandez's command. The thought excited him as much as it terrified him, and the fact that he considered such things now, in this moment, surprised him. The other thought in his head, bizarrely, was that if he died, the ship would go to Danza. He wanted that even less than dying.

But that seemed to be the way things were destined to go. As Hernandez backed up towards the ship's launch bay, hoping to slip in through the hangar and race towards the bow, he found himself cut off. If he tried to take the enemy at his back, the enemy at his front would fall upon him—and vice versa. He had no way of defending himself without leaving himself exposed.

This was it. The end.

Killing Johnson had been unnecessary because they had both been screwed.

The first creature attacked and Hernandez was ready. He swung the axe like Mickey Mantle clutching wood. The blade had so much elbow grease behind it that it took the bloated bastard's head clean off. It also left Hernandez unbalanced and out of breath. The next creature barreled right into his side and knock him down. He hit the deck; the enemy was on top of him. More surrounded him and closed in, ready to take their piece of flesh.

Hernandez whimpered. Time to close his eyes.

Rat-a-tata-tata-ta.

The sudden wetness on Hernandez's face startled him. He flinched and opened his eyes, pushed the weight off of his chest. The creature was dead, its body weeping black blood and sea water from a dozen different holes. The other bloaters had scattered, many of them dancing the death tango as bullets riddled their bodies.

Rat-a-tata-ta.

Hernandez kept low and dragged himself into cover inside the hangar's entrance. He dared peek out for only a single second to see who had come to his rescue. Had Danza secured the ship? The bastard would be a hero.

But it had been heavy machine-gun fire that had turned the tide. Something bolted down and chain-fed.

Hernandez saw the spotlights circle around and realised who had saved him.

It was another ship.

Vamps

THE STREETS WERE a chaotic mixture of fear and anger. As many people fled as stayed to throw bricks at shop windows and kicked in car windscreens. Fight or Flight. The concrete jungle of Brixton had become a plain old jungle, and only animals lived in it.

"We need to get out of here, man." Ginge leant against a lamppost and took great heaving breaths. "I mean, this shit is like Iraq or something."

"I don't see no soldiers," said Mass. "We could use a couple of AKs right now. Wonder if the newsagents across the road sells 'em."

"No one will be coming to help us," said Vamps. "You think they'll be sending police, or the Army, to help out Brixton when Oxford Street and Soho are in the shit? We don't matter."

Ravy ducked as a brick flew over his head. It hit the side of a bus stop and rained glass on top of the old man taking cover there. "Shit man. We're gunna get our heads caved in."

Vamps looked at the madness erupting all around him and felt disgusted. Their city was under attack, and the first thing people did was turn on one another. Why? To grab a fistful of fags from the newsagent? What made people act this way?

Fear.

"We have to do something," he said. "You think these monsters from Oxford Street are going to stay where they are? Those gates are everywhere. Where the hell would we even go?"

"Anywhere but here," said Ravy.

Vamps shook his head. "If I'm going to have to fight for my life, then I want it to be here, where I know the streets and the people. This is home, yo. Where else you wanna be?"

Mass was already on board. "Mr Tarq runs the newsagents. He let me off for shoplifting when I was a kid. Used to let my mum off when she was short too. He don't deserve to get his place trashed."

"Then let's get started," said Vamps. "Let's clean shit up."

"What the fuck?" said Ginge. "We ain't crime fighters. This morning we tried to sell drugs and then straight up robbed a guy."

Mass smirked, his wide chin jutting out. "Which shows what bad motherfuckers we is. Don't mean we have to stand around and watch our hood get jacked up though, does it?"

"Okay," said Ravy. "As long as you and Vamps do the fighting, I'm down."

Ginge sighed. "Fuck sake. Yeah, fine. I'm down too."

Vamps nodded, proud of what they were doing—proud of his friends. "Let's go save our corner shop."

They legged it over to Mr Tarq's newsagent and flew through the open doors like something from The Avengers. Vamps felt good as he said, "Shop's closed, bitches."

They grabbed a teenager helping himself to snack food and drinks and tossed him right out onto the street. The kid had been in the middle of piling half the shop's inventory into his carrier bags when Vamps walloped him around the head.

"Get the hell out of here, you little rat," Vamps snarled in the kid's face, flashing his fangs.

"Aw shit, man. You're Vamps. All right, I'm leaving." The teenager legged it, empty handed.

Vamps nodded to his boys. "See, home has its advantages, like a killer rep."

There was another two teenagers in the throes of anarchy, but they too headed away on their toes when they saw Vamps and his crew. Once the looters left, the shop was quiet, the chaos outside muted by the steel shutters over the front windows.

Magazines lined the floor like a glossy carpet and broken bottles of red wine gave the cramped space the look of a crime scene.

They heard moaning.

Vamps looked around but saw no one. He tilted his head and honed in on the sound until he realised it was coming from behind the counter at the back of the shop.

"There's someone back there," said Mass.

Vamps followed the moaning, took a moment, then leant over the desk.

A man shoved his hands up at his face. "Please, don't hurt me anymore. Just take it."

Vamps studied the old man, his grey hair befuddled and stained with blood, and felt his stomach turn. Fucking animals.

"It's okay, Mr Tarq." Vamps reached out his hand but kept his palm out and harmless. "I'm not going to hurt you. We came here to help."

Mr Tarq cowered. "Please!"

Mass came over and stood beside Vamps. When he saw the battered old man, he shook his head and cursed. It took him a moment to let go of his anger. "Hey, Mr Tarq, it's me, Alfie. You know me. You know my mum, Heather Masters."

Mr Tarq looked up at Mass and frowned. "Little Alfie Masters? Is that you?"

"Yeah, Mr Tarq, but not so small anymore. We came to help you. It's okay."

The old man nodded and slowly pulled himself up against the counter. He clutched his ribs and winced a few times, but he didn't seem too hurt.

Vamps made sure the old man was steady. "You okay, gramps?"

Mr Tarq bent forwards, in obvious pain, but reached out and patted Vamps on the shoulder. "Yes, my son. I am okay. Bless you for being good boys. I thought there were none left."

"Not many," said Vamps. "But it only takes a few."

"Yes, yes, my son, you are right. Please, I must close my shop. The world is a dark place today, and I wish to be alone to think on it. Take anything you want before you go."

"We don't need anything, gramps, but thanks."

"I'll take a snickers," said Ginge.

Vamps rolled his eyes. "Okay, we'll take one snickers bar, but that's all. You take care, Mr Tarq."

Mr Tarq patted Vamps shoulder again and went to inspect the damage to his livelihood. He locked the door behind them as soon as they left.

Mass looked at Vamps and nodded. "It feels good to do good, you know?"

Vamps looked back at the newsagent, now shuttered up safely. "Yeah, it does. No reason to stop now."

So they continued their mission of cleaning up the streets of Brixton, veering north and forgetting that the real danger was not so far away. It wasn't until they moved just south of Battersea Park that they realised how foolish their bravado was.

Across the Thames, London blazed. Like the nursery rhyme, it was burning down.

Military helicopters flew overhead, unloading from their side mounted machine guns. More gunfire came from the ground. Even a fighter jet arced across the sky. There was a war across the river and Vamps had led his boys right to it.

Ravy wrung his hands together. "Okay, think we might have gone far enough."

Ginge went pale, which made his ginger beard seem like a thatch of shining copper strands. "Thank God, because I was starting to think you were crazy. Can we go back home? We're not even in Brixton anymore. This here is Battersea."

Vamps nodded. "Yeah, time to call it a day. We did good work. How many heads we busted, you think, Mass?"

"Seventeen. I was counting. Plus we kicked that mugger in the arse."

Vamps chuckled. "Nice work on that one, Ravy. You really showed him."

Ravy grinned proudly.

"Let's not get carried away though," said Vamps. "Shit's pretty quiet now on this side of the river, so I say we don't chance our luck and go any further. Agreed?"

Everyone agreed.

So they took a breather and got going. In the last hour, Brixton had quieted down. Part of it was that the people wanting to get out had got out, but Vamps thought another part of it was that the reality had sunk in for most people—that there were monsters in the city—and had scared them off the streets. Once people's adrenaline settled, fear found its grip easier. Even Vamps was coming down off his high, and the sight of smoke billowing from the thriving centre of London made his lips dry.

Maybe he had been hasty leading the boys this far north, but they were okay, and they really had done a lot of good today. If they could just get back to their block and hunker down, they could plan what they would do tonight—and tomorrow. Vamps understood that his recent stint of vigilantism had come about because he hadn't known what else to do. Being pro-active seemed better than running around scared like everybody else. One thing the streets had taught him was that when you acted you weren't thinking, and when you weren't thinking you weren't afraid. If a Brixton boy spent too much time sitting around imaging being knifed, he'd end up a nervous wreck. And a nervous wreck was a lot more likely to get stabbed. London was a city where only doers thrived. If you hesitated, the streets would beat you down. That was as true in the financial districts as it was in Brixton.

They were halfway through the Patmore Estate now, heading back towards home. They heard a woman's screams.

"Where's it coming from?" said Ravy, rubbing his goatee anxiously.

"From that block over there." Mass pointed.

Vamps started marching. He thought the others might argue, but they didn't. None of them could stand by while a woman screamed for help.

They found out what was going on in the next street. A tattooed skinhead sat atop an Asian woman and shouted in her face to 'shut up' then called her a 'paki'. He punched her face and wrestled with her clothing. An older guy lay unconscious in the gutter nearby.

"He's trying to rape her," said Ginge, looking sick.

"Well, he ain't gunna succeed." Vamps narrowed his eyes. The sight of this animal taking advantage of the current chaos by preying on the innocent made his blood simmer. All the selfish, violent acts Vamps had seen today, but this was the worst. To rape someone...

It wasn't human.

The thug struggled to get the woman's trousers off. He reared back to punch her again.

Before Vamps knew what he was doing, he gritted his teeth and yanked out his grandfather's old Browning pistol. He'd never fired it before, but he pulled the trigger without hesitation. The bang was ferocious, but nobody flinched. Gunfire was normal today.

The thug slumped forwards on top of the woman, a penny sized hole in the back of his neck. Vamps had been aiming for his shoulder. "Racist motherfucker," he muttered as he lowered the gun to his side to disguise his trembling hand.

The woman slid out from beneath her attacker and clambered to her feet. She took a breath and said, "Y-you... you shot him. How...? Where did you get a gun?"

Vamps took a breath and fought to keep his heart from beating out of his chest. He kept his eyes off the man he had just killed and instead frowned. "Ask me no questions, I tell me no lies. You all right, darlin'?"

"I... Yes. Thank you. You're not going to hurt me, are you?"

Vamps glanced back at his boys, who bristled at her comment. After all the good they had done today, they still got treated like common criminals. "I just saved your arse, luv, and you accuse me of bein' a mugger and shit. I ain't gunna hurt you. We ain't even like that."

"Oh," said the woman. "It's just that you all look so... scary."

Vamps looked down at his baggy black jeans and chuckled. "Just how we do on the streets, innit? You dress how you want, and we dress how we wants. Just clothes, innit?"

"Thank you," said the woman, seeming to mean it greatly. Her attacker lay dead at her feet, but she didn't seem to care one bit. There were lots of people dead today, and this racist piece of shit was probably among the most deserving.

It was okay to kill him. Wasn't it?

"What's your name?" the woman asked.

"Vamps."

"Vamps?"

He gave her a wide grin, revealing his gold-plated fangs. "Yeah, Vamps. These are my homies: Mass, Ravy, and Gingerbread."

The boys nodded silently.

The woman shook each of their hands. "It's a pleasure to meet you all."

"You need to be careful out here," Vamps warned her. "There's some heavy shit going down."

"I know. I'm a journalist. David and I are trying to get out of the city. You should come with us."

Vamps looked at 'David', who was finally stirring. Then he looked back at her. "Nah, I'm sound, darlin'. These are my streets, d'you get me? Me and the boys are staying put, and any of them fucked-up, Freddy Krueger bitches wants to come take us on, they're welcome. This is our manor and ain't nothing gonna bowl up and make a mess of it. You take care, darlin'. Next time, just hand over your phone, innit? And 'ere, take this." He pulled a thin black stick out of his belt and tossed it her way. It was a metal police baton he had found abandoned in the street earlier. He'd always wanted one, but this woman needed it more.

The woman caught it, seemed to weigh it up in her hand, then did something that surprised him. She hugged him. "You're a hero," she said.

Vamps eased her away, looking awkward. "Easy now. I ain't no hero. Don't you go writin' 'bout me in your paper. I ain't news friendly."

The woman nodded. "I promise. Take care."

"You too."

Then Vamps took his boys and carried on heading back to Brixton. He'd just saved a woman from being raped. To do it he had killed a man. He wasn't sure how he should feel about that, but the boys were looking at him in a way he didn't like.

Looking at him like he just killed a man.

2

They got back to Brixton a short while later and had barely spoken a word to one another. They checked on Mass's mum at her flat, but the old dear was tired and confused about things. Mass decided it best to leave her alone. She always had the warden down the hall if she needed help. Ravy called his dad who worked in Slough. He was fine. So was his sister who studied at East Anglia. Gingerbread lived alone and didn't keep in touch with his family. Vamps lived alone too. That was the bond that made them all so close—they had each other and little else. Vamps had a half-brother some place, but his three true brothers stood right here beside him. The Brixton boys.

They decided to spend the night at Vamps' flat, first choosing to take beers up to the roof to watch the craziness. You could see right across the Thames.

Night hadn't yet taken its grasp on the city and the distant high rises still gave off their usual light pollution. In fact, if not for the stench of smoke in the air and the unceasing noise, it might've been a normal evening in the capitol.

"Shit, man," said Mass, pointing at the horizon. "The Shard is on fire. Can you believe that? Next year's Apprentice is gunna have to get a new opening."

They chuckled.

"You watch that shit?" asked Ginge.

"Yeah, man. Next year I'm gunna take part and show L.A. Shugs my business idea."

Ravy frowned. "L.A. Shugs?"

"Yeah, Lord Alan Sugar."

"What's your business idea?" asked Vamps.

Mass folded his arms and lay back in his deckchair with a smug expression. "Gunna sell digital light switches."

Vamps frowned. "Digital what-nows?"

Mass rolled his eyes like they were idiots. "Digital light switches. I mean, what's the deal with how up-to-date everything is, but our lights are the same as fifty years ago. I want to replace light switches with these little LED touch screens that let you adjust the brightness, set a schedule, and even have them adjust automatically based on the sunlight in the room. It's so simple man, and it wouldn't even be an expensive gadget to manufacture. People would lap it up. The world loves tech. I would do the same with plug sockets. Make 'em digital. Let you switch stuff on and off from your iPad."

Vamps was impressed. "You know, that's actually not a bad idea. I suppose it's bound to happen. Someone needs to get in and get it started."

"And when I'm L.A. Shugs' main man, I'll be a millionaire. Get us all out of this shit-hole."

"You'd share the money?" said Ginge.

"Hell, yes. We family. One of us makes it, we all make it."

"Word to that," said Vamps, putting up his beer for a toast.

They clinked bottles, but then Ravy said, "Too bad the world has ended."

Vamps groaned. "Way to bring down the mood."

"Sorry. I'm just saying... Look at this place. There's fighting in the streets, looting, monsters tearing people apart... That's some heavy shit."

Vamps looked out at the city. Gunfire lit up the dusk like fireworks. Most of it came from the direction of Hyde Park, which had been illuminated by high powered floodlights. Several helicopters buzzed in and out of the area. Was that where the Army had assembled?

Were they taking care of business?

Like Vamps had with that rapist?

He pulled out his grandfather's Browning and lay it across his knees, studying it. The brushed metal was scuffed and tarnished.

IAIN ROB WRIGHT

"How you get that thing, anyway?" asked Mass. "I don't think you ever told me."

"It was my grandpa's."

"Really? He was in the war?"

"Nah, man. He was a gangster, same as us. He robbed it off some dude back in his cat burgling days. Was too hot to sell."

Mass chuckled. "Wish I'd met the old guy."

Vamps smiled at the vague memory he had of his grandfather. "Yeah, he was a good crack. Died when I was eight, couple years before I met you lot."

"Good he stuck by you," said Ginge. "You know, after your dad did one."

The mention of Vamp's father brought silence. Vamps clutched his fists instinctively but gave no thoughts to his feelings. The lads didn't need to hear about some deadbeat knocking his ma around. Way Vamps considered things, he had no father. End of conversation.

He put his grandfather's Browning away.

For a while, Ginge had kept them updated from his phone's internet, which was patchy at best. They watched juddering videos of monsters from Hell—too many to deny their existences. Those gates led to some terrible place and the damned and dead were spilling out. Some of the monsters were so badly burned that you could see bone.

"Think this will all go away?" asked Ginge when an hour had passed. He had barely touched his beer, more an eater than a drinker. Mass, on the other hand, drank two bottles ahead.

"Like hell it will," said Ravy. "We're all fucked."

Vamps exhaled, took a swig of his own beer.

An explosion.

All four of them leapt up out of their deck chairs and went over to the edge of the roof. A fireball filled the night sky, blooming from the ground and heading towards the stars. Vamps gripped his beer bottle tightly as it swung next to his leg. "It's one of the helicopters. The fighting's moved to Hyde Park."

"How the hell did they take out a helicopter?" asked Ravy. "They have anti-air missiles now?"

"Maybe it was pilot error," said Ginge. "Zipping around all those tall buildings…"

Somehow none of them believed it. The distant fighting had intensified in the last hour. Things weren't going well. The Army was going all in.

Then they saw something none of them could quite fathom.

Ginge dropped his beer bottle to the ground where it shattered. "Is that… Is that a giant?"

The word sounded stupid, but Vamps knew no better way to describe what he saw emerging from the floodlights of Hyde Park. A giant man wearing nothing but a loin cloth. Like some massive caveman meant to fight Godzilla in one of those awful Japanese movies. But this was no movie.

A giant laid waste to Central London.

"We need to get gone," said Ginge.

Mass folded his huge arms. "Hate to be a pussy, but I agree."

"And go where?" asked Vamps. The beer in his throat tasted like acid.

Ginge held up his phone. "The web said parts of the south coast are still okay, Portsmouth, I think. Maybe we should head there?"

"Let's just boost a car and go," said Ravy. "I could cope with the thought of zombies or demons in the park, but I ain't sticking around for no giants. That thing could step across the Thames and be here in ten minutes."

Vamps took another look across the city. He placed the thing as at least thirty feet. If it wasn't standing in the park, it would be hidden behind the buildings, and if it slipped out of sight there would be no way of knowing how close it was. By the sound of it, the Army was letting loose with everything it had.

But the giant didn't fall. It was a titan—invulnerable.

"Let's bounce," said Vamps, deciding that living in a refugee camp in Portsmouth was better than surviving home any longer.

Ginge exhaled as if relieved. "Thank fudge for that. Actually, can we swing by mine to grab some food first?"

Mass punched Ginge's flabby arm. "We're about to run for our lives, man. We ain't stopping for no Cadbury's Cream Egg, buster!"

Ginge frowned. "Fine."

They headed into the stairwell and started down. Televisions blared in some of the flats, so people were still at home, which made Vamps wonder if sticking around was a good idea. His gut instinct told him to stay put, but after seeing the scenes in Hyde Park he had a bad feeling. Eventually, the battle would spill over into Brixton and beyond. Staying alive on the streets would be even harder than normal.

Halfway down the stairs, three floors up, voices came up to meet them. Someone had entered the entrance hallway on the bottom floor. Vamps knew because he heard the broken front door scrape across the concrete.

"You sure he lives here?" came a voice they all recognised.

"That's the fucking dealer who screwed us over," said Mass.

"You mean the one we robbed at gunpoint?" Ravy added.

Vamps peered over the bannister to the stairwell below. It was definitely him. Pusher.

Other people too. Three more guys and a kid Vamps instantly recognised.

Vamps reached to the bright green cap on his head. "It's that car-jacking piece of shit."

Mass looked at him. "Who?"

"I caught a kid breaking into cars this morning and put him on his arse."

"So you were fighting crime before you even met us today? You batman."

Vamps chuckled. "Batman would be good now."

"He lives in this building," said the car-jacker. "My mate Jasmine used to go out with him. Third floor, I think."

"Hey, I remember Jasmine," said Ginge. "She was hot."

Vamps shook his head. "Not now, Ginge."

Pusher started up the stairs with his entourage. "Gonna teach that piece of shit what happens when people mess with me. He's fuckin' dead. My kid was there."

Mass smashed his fists together. "Let's go choke this mother out."

"Wait up a sec." Vamps held back his bulldog and peered over the railing again. He watched Pusher ascend the bottom staircase—saw the stubby length of brushed steel in the dealer's hands.

A sawn-off shotgun.

"He's coming in heavy," said Vamps.

"You gunna get your gun out," asked Ravy nervously. Still no one had mentioned that he had shot a man earlier. Vamps didn't know how they felt about it.

He didn't feel good about it himself.

Vamps kept his voice low. "Back to the roof. We need to lie low."

Mass looked at him slack-jawed. "We gunna run?"

Vamps nodded. "Don't matter how tough you are in a gunfight. Anybody can catch a bullet. I ain't gunna risk that, so let's bounce."

They hurried back up the stairwell towards the roof. Pusher was making enough of his own noise not to hear theirs, and by the time they made it up, they were all pretty sure of a clean escape.

Vamps shoved an old roof tile under the door to wedge it shut. There was no reason Pusher should think to come up here, but just in case. "We'll stay up here till the coast is clear. Then we'll think about getting out of the city."

"Good thing it's a warm night," said Ginge, clutching himself.

"Good thing you're carrying ten-stone of fat," said Mass, punching his friend on the arm.

"Screw you, man."

"Shut up," said Vamps, or I'll go get Pusher to shoot you myself.

"He don't wanna shoot us," said Ravy. "He just bluffing."

Mass huffed. "You turn up at someone's manor with a sawn-off, you ain't bluffin', man."

When they heard the shotgun go off, the point was made. They fell silent, eyes wide.

Who the hell had just caught a bullet?

Vamps went over to the roof edge and looked again to Hyde Park.

The giant was gone, but things had never been more dangerous.

Richard Honeywell

RICHARD FELT BETTER with his family close by, but still felt a weight on his shoulders as he kept a watchful eye on the people in the church. There were a hundred of them now, mostly the vulnerable and lonely. Some had brought along cans of beer, which wasn't against the law, but bode ill for the evening. Drunk people were not the easiest to control in a panic, and panic could swoop upon them at any moment.

The church had an old television set that the vicar set up in front of the wooden lectern. The news played constantly but showed nothing to make people feel any better. It showed horror not hope, but people could not look away. In the centre of London, Big Ben's ornate clock face was blackened and charred while a battle raged on in nearby Hyde Park. The Army fought monsters in the street, monsters from Hell, if you believed what the more paranoid talking heads claimed. Gates to Hell had opened and demons sought to purge the earth of humanity. The insane thing was that Richard believed it. He could think of no better explanation for what he was seeing on the news.

Demons were here.

And they were everywhere.

In the last hour, the television had flashed multiple scenes of devastation from Tokyo to Bogota where barefooted Colombians fired guns in the street. There had been few scenes of triumph, except for a brief ten seconds of footage from Damascus which showed the entire city armed and ready. The peaceful nations of the world were the ones doing badly. Geneva had been laid to waste with barely the slightest resistance. Swiss pacifism had been a death warrant to its people.

Dillon was bored, but an old lady named Shirley was doing her best to keep him occupied by playing eye spy. The kindness of a stranger was a powerful thing in times like this, and Richard felt a swell of emotion every time he looked at the old woman caring for his son.

"Romantic, in a way," said Jen, holding a cup of coffee between her hands whilst leaning against a weathered pew. "Like the way people huddled together during The Blitz."

"People died during The Blitz," Richard told her. "And people have been dying today."

Jen nodded, but didn't seem to regret her comment. She placed a hand on her husband's arm and looked him in the eye. "I'm just saying, it's times like these when people pull together. We all make each other stronger by sharing courage and compassion. I'm proud of you for looking after all these people, Rich."

Richard didn't feel like he was doing much good, and he told her so. "I'm just babysitting. The real work is in London. I feel terrible for admitting it, but I'm glad I'm not there."

"I'm glad too, but that doesn't mean you won't be needed here. These people," she looked around at all the stragglers and oddballs that sat on the church's stone floor or slouched on its pews, "they see a police officer present and automatically feel safer. Don't underestimate how important you are."

"I don't underestimate it, Jen, but I worry that if things get worse, all these people will look at me for direction. I don't have a bloody clue."

"Cross that bridge when it comes."

Riaz came in from outside and strolled down the centre aisle between the pews. He went right up to Richard. "It's dark outside now, and Glen just radioed in from Cider Hill. We got some kids playing up."

"Can Glen handle it?"

"No," said Riaz. "He's one man, and he said there's half a dozen of them."

Richard nodded. "Are you going to assist him?"

"No, we will assist him."

"I'm not leaving here," said Richard, glancing sideways at Dillon, who was growing bored with eye spy.

"Look," said Riaz. "You've already abandoned your duty once to go get your family, and I can understand that to a degree, but they are here now and safe. I won't allow you to stay here and do nothing while the streets turn into a jungle."

Richard straightened up and scowled at his colleague. "You're not in a position to allow me to do anything."

"Maybe so, but as a fellow police officer, I am requesting your assistance, and unless you have a bloody good reason not to give it, I'll be reporting you to the SI."

Richard opened his mouth to speak, but Jen squeezed his arm. "It's fine, Rich. You need to go do your job. Don't worry about me and Dillon. We're fine."

Richard swallowed a lump in his throat as he tried to decide. He watched Dillon stand up and inspect the various church paraphernalia. Before long he would start messing with things he shouldn't. Then he would break something.

But the damage outside the church would be far worse if looters were allowed to scurry around unchecked.

"Okay, Riaz, fine. Let me say goodbye to my son."

Riaz nodded, but looked annoyed even at having to wait one minute more. Richard ignored his colleague's attitude and went over to Dillon.

"Hey, Dil-Dil," he said. "I'm just popping out, but I'll be back soon."

"No, dad, don't go outside. The monsters will get you."

Richard gave his son a squeeze to calm him. "No, they won't. The monsters are far away. I'm just going out to see a friend at the other side of town. I won't be long. While I'm gone, I need you to be good. Don't mess with anything you shouldn't, and do what mummy tells you, okay?"

Dillon, nodded whilst pouting at the same time. "It's boring here, dad. They won't let me change the channel on the telly."

"I know, but we all have to stay here for a while before we can go home."

"Because of the monsters?"

Richard didn't want to alarm his son, but he also wanted him to understand. "Sort of, Dil, yeah. We just need to make sure the monsters stay where they are."

"Can you get my books, dad?"

Richard sighed. His son loved to read—something Richard and Jen had tried to instil in him at an early age as a way to support his Downs. It had worked, and Dillon often read the Harry Potter books cover to cover. Child's encyclopaedias were also a hit—especially if they contained facts about animals. "I don't think I'll have time to go back, sweetheart, but if I see any shops open, I'll see if I can grab you a magazine."

"Okay, Dad," he nodded forlornly. "Love you."

Richard kissed his son's forehead. "Love you too, son."

Jen was still standing nearby, so he gave her a quick hug before he left. He was about to say something to her when Riaz cleared his throat irritably.

"I'm coming," Richard snapped. He followed the other officer out of the church doors, but was stopped by the Vicar.

"Ah, officers," said Miles. "I just want to say again how very grateful I am to have you here. People are afraid. Part of me wishes I never turned on that television, but I suppose there's no hiding from the horrors we face."

"No, thank you, Reverend. It's been a massive help giving all these people somewhere they can come together for morale support."

"I suppose you two are on your way to deal with those less interested in such things?"

Richard nodded. "Unfortunately, times like these bring out the worst in people."

"I don't honestly think there has ever been 'times like these', but I take your point. Please remind anyone you meet that there is still room at the church and a mug of hot tea if they want it."

"We shall," said Riaz. "Thank you again, sir."

"Please, call me Miles. 'Sir' should be reserved for men in ties, don't you think?"

Riaz was eager to get away, and his reply was short. "Yes, Miles, I do. Goodbye now."

As they walked away, Richard pulled his colleague up. "You don't have to be so rude, you know. That man has done more to help than anyone."

"Serving tea isn't a help. We need to clamp down on nuisance behaviour before it takes hold. He's just getting good publicity for the church."

"That's a little cynical."

He shrugged. "Perhaps."

Richard wondered if Riaz was Muslim, and if that was why he took exception to the reverend and his church. He decided he was too ignorant of such things to ask. Nor did he know Riaz particularly well.

Cider Hill lay at the edge of the town centre where the shops changed into offices. A booze shop traded there next to the bus station, so it was often a problem area where anti-social behaviour was concerned. The walk took them ten minutes.

Glen, a round-faced man with a persistent smile, had parked outside a recruitment firm. He waved out the car window at them as they approached. "Didn't want to make a move until I had backup."

"What do we have?" asked Richard.

"Six or seven kids boozed up at the bus station. They raided the office by the looks of it."

Richard put his thumbs inside his belt and sighed. "Don't know what we're supposed to do with them."

"Lock 'em up," said Riaz. "Same as any other night."

"But this isn't any other night, Riaz. The whole world went to Hell in a hand basket today, if you didn't notice. Bunch of kids pissed up at the bus station is not the concern it would usually be."

"Crime is still crime. If an innocent person wanders into the bus station and gets attacked, that's our failure."

Richard nodded. "I agree. My only point is that it seems stupid to ride them all to lock up. Is anyone even manning the jail tonight?"

Glen nodded. "I've been back and forth on the radio with Suzie at the desk. There're a couple uniforms in—Sutton is there."

Sutton was another sergeant, like Richard—a decent copper. Richard nodded. "Okay, we'll call it in once we've dealt with the situation."

"Let's get a move on then," said Riaz.

Glen took the car down the road outside the bus station while Richard and Riaz hurried along on foot. The rowdy teenagers inside were kicking over bins and climbing the timetable boards like monkeys. The amount of beer cans on the floor was enough to fill a wheelie bin with.

Riaz was first in, racing at one of the lads before they saw him coming.

"Fuckin' pigs," one of them shouted, breaking into a run.

Richard dodged sideways and met the escape of one of the lads. The two of them smashed together and went down to the ground. Richard got the better of the scuffle and ended up on top. The lad's baseball cap rolled across the floor and left his face exposed.

"You were at the shopping centre earlier today," said Richard. "You trashed the games store."

"I dunno what the fuck you're on about, pig."

Richard yanked the lad to his feet, trying not to let the stench of alcohol overpower him. "We'll soon jog your memory, son. There'll be plenty of CCTV footage to remind you." He saw the flash of worry spark through the lad's eyes and was satisfied. He turned around and saw that Riaz had apprehended two other lads, holding them at bay with his CS gas canister. Outside, Glen had gathered a fourth hoodlum and had him up against the car. Three of the youths got away.

"You okay, Riaz?" asked Richard, shoving his prisoner around and slapping on handcuffs.

Riaz nodded, a satisfied expression on his face as he manhandled the lads in his possession.

They got the prisoners handcuffed and took them outside, sitting them on the ground in a line outside the off license. "You've really made quite the time of it today, haven't you?" said Richard.

The group of lads stared sullenly at the ground.

Riaz nodded at Glen. "Call it in."

Glen used the radio in his car and got through to Suzie. They chatted back and forth for a minute while Riaz and Richard dealt with the prisoners.

"You know what a scumbag you have to be to be out causing trouble at a time like this?" said Riaz. "People are scared. People are dying just a few miles away in London. What the hell do you think you're doing?"

No one spoke.

Riaz kicked one of the lads. "Answer me, you little shits."

Richard reached out and nudged his colleague back a step. "Okay, Riaz. We have them."

Riaz shrugged away. "I'm just disgusted. Disgusted at this country. Disgusted at degenerates like this who think they can do what the fuck they like."

Richard saw the hysteria on his colleagues face. The way his eyes darted about, and his lips twitched. "Just calm down, Riaz. You know that this is what happens. Most people are behaving, trying to help."

Riaz shook his head and took a moment. "I know. Damn it, I just wish we were better, that's all."

Glen climbed out of the cruiser and approached. "We can't take 'em in."

Richard frowned. "What? Are the cells full?"

"No, the cells are empty, and so is the station. Suzie said that Sutton has told everyone to go home to their families."

"Sutton did that?" Richard couldn't believe it. Sutton was too dedicated to abandon his post. Where things really that bad?

Yes, of course they were.

Glen sighed. "I know it's crazy, but Suzie was just about to leave herself. She said the officers who joined the task force in London haven't reported back in hours and that Command isn't answering.

We've been forgotten for the time being, so it's up to us what we do. There's an all-out war in the city by all accounts."

"So what do we do with these scumbags?" asked Riaz, his anger rising again. "We can't just let them go."

Richard grasped his arm. "We'll figure something out."

One of the lads bolted up and tried to make a run for it. It was an absurd act, seeing as his hands were cuffed in front of him. He made it three steps, waddling like a penguin, before Riaz swept his legs out from under him and sent him crashing down onto the curb.

"Fuck man! That's Police brutality."

"Tell it to someone who cares," Riaz hissed. "Stand up once more and you won't be able to try again."

Richard had to move Riaz back again. The man was clenching his fists. "Riaz, just calm down. They're just a bunch of kids covering their fear with reckless behaviour."

"Yeah," said Glen. "Just relax, Riaz. You're frightening them."

"I ain't scared of nuffin', blud," one lad mumbled.

Riaz looked like he was about to go off again, but an approaching vehicle made the three officers turn. It was an Army jeep, and it stopped when the driver saw them and pulled up beside the curb. A soldier stared out at them from the back of the uncovered vehicle. An Asian woman sat in the driver's seat.

"Bout time we got a little help," said Richard, putting his hands on his hips and sighing with relief.

"I'm not here on behalf of the Army," said the soldier. "I'm just getting these two reporters to their offices."

Richard peered into the back of the jeep and saw the soldier was sitting next to another man, and there was a little girl sitting between them and staring glumly at the back of the seat. He grunted, not wanting to sound afraid as he asked the question. "Oh, how are things in the city? Still bad?"

The soldier shook his head. "No, not bad. Finished. There's nothing left in London. The Army got destroyed. I might be the only soldier left from Hyde Park."

Richard felt a wave of nausea wash over him. "Shit. What the hell are we dealing with, here? Is it really monsters?"

The Asian woman nodded from the driver's seat. "We're at war, and we need to be prepared. Everybody, not just the Police and Army. We all need to be ready to fight."

Richard tried to comprehend what the woman was getting at. He ended up huffing. "Fight monsters? You must be joking. People won't fight. I've just spent half the night trying to stop people robbing each other."

"If we don't work together, we don't have a chance," she said to him. The young woman's hard expression made him shift uncomfortably.

"Just do what you can, Officer," said the soldier. "Those kids you have under arrest, what did they do?"

"What didn't they do? Breaking into shops, kicking in car windscreens, joyriding..." Richard didn't know why he was exaggerating. He wondered if he was panicking.

"You need to talk to those boys," said the reporter. "Tell them what's coming. Give them something to do, and they'll be glad to be of use, I promise you."

Richard sneered. "What? You want me to deputise a bunch of thugs?"

The soldier nodded adamantly. "Yes! We just lost an army in Hyde Park. This country needs fighters. You have a bunch of them sitting in the road. This isn't just a news of the week event. This is it—the big summer blockbuster, end of the world, fight for survival type of gig. You have a chance to make a difference, Officer. Get your men and those boys ready, because war is coming to us all."

Richard looked at everyone inside the jeep, then back at the soldier. "You're not joking? This is really the apocalypse or something?"

"Everywhere is under attack, you probably already know that. It's going to fall on men like you to fight back. There won't be a British Army to sort this all out. It's going to be fighting in the streets and dying in pain. It will be youngsters, like the ones you have under arrest, that will fight for our survival. So go tell them what they're up against before it's too late."

Richard nodded, feeling stunned. He felt like he was discovering that he had been sleeping during some great event. He had known things were bad, but these people, driving around in a battered Army jeep, made him realise that the situation had progressed far beyond his current understanding. They had seen things he had not, things that had made them understand. "Okay," he said. "I'll round 'em up and get 'em to work. Every able-bodied person I can find will be ready, you have my word."

The soldier saluted him. "What's your name?"

"Richard Honeywell."

"I wish you well, Richard. Stay alive."

"I... Yes, you too."

The woman shifted into gear and got going. Richard stood in the middle of the road, stunned.

Glen wandered over to him a moment later. "Do you think he was telling the truth? You think the Army is gone?"

Richard shrugged, watching the jeep's taillights disappear at the end of the road. "Why would he lie?"

"I don't know."

"If the city really has fallen," said Riaz, "then we need to fall back and find support. The Army in London wasn't the country's only defence."

Richard felt his shoulders drop. "Perhaps not, but the Army in London would have been our best defence. If it fell, I don't hold up much hope for anything else." He began to pant. "And what about the other stones? We're being attacked from all sides. There's nowhere to fall back to."

What was he going to do? How did he keep Jen and Dillon safe? By gathering up a bunch of vandals and trying to build a fort? Insane!

"But we're safe," said Glen. "Slough isn't under attack."

"Oh, wake up, Glen," said Riaz. "If London is defenceless, the enemy will have free rein to spread out and attack the surrounding areas. We're as close as you can get to London without being part of it. We're next."

"Then what do we do?"

Richard felt dizzy. He felt far away from his own body. He gazed at the line of youths sitting on the curb. Although they were likely afraid, their bravado was deeply ingrained. They would not dare show their worries. Richard needed to do the same. "We do what the soldier told us to do," he said, desperately wanting to follow orders, even if they came from a stranger. "We prepare ourselves to fight. No one is coming to protect us or our families, so we need to do it ourselves."

Riaz tutted. "You're an idiot if you think that's a good idea."

"I don't think it's a good idea. I think it's the only option we have."

"My wife and daughter are here," said Glen. "If there's nowhere I can get them to, then I'll fight any amount of monsters to keep them safe. If we have to stay here and fight, then I'd accept it head on."

Richard nodded, trying not to fall down where he stood. "Me too, Glen."

Riaz sighed. "Let's just head back to the church. Maybe we can put our heads together and figure something out."

Richard motioned towards the youths seated on the curb. "We have some recruiting to do first."

One of the lads on the curb lurched forward and vomited.

"That's up to you," said Riaz. "I want no part of it."

Richard sighed when Riaz departed in a huff, but was pleased that Glen stayed with him. The two of them faced the expectant youths together. Richard placed his hands on his hips as he spoke. "If you lads are still in a mood to wreck stuff, you might get another chance. Only, this time you'll be wrecking what I tell you to."

The lad who was still missing his white baseball cap, looked confused at first, but then he looked up and grinned.

2

Richard couldn't believe the time when he glanced at his watch. 6AM. They had worked right through the night. Now that he realised the time, he let out an almost endless yawn. Most people in the chilly church interior had bedded down well before midnight, sleeping fitfully on blankets supplied by the vicar.

Richard had last checked on Dillon and Jen a little after 1AM. They had been snoozing, and he'd dared only to pull a blanket up over Dillon's shoulder before going back outside to work. Lots of work to be done.

As it turned out, the four youths apprehended at the bus station were surprisingly eager to help, almost like they'd been waiting longingly for direction. It further convinced Richard that their drunken antics had been fear of not knowing what to do.

Aaron approached Richard now, white baseball cap reunited with his head. He was the gang's obvious leader, and the other three rallied behind him when he had agreed to help Richard. For the last few hours they had been working on a barricade across the main road. It was looking good

"I'm knackered, boss. The sun's coming up. Can me and the lads get our heads down?"

Richard nodded. "Go find somewhere quiet at the church and I'll give you a shout if anything happens. You and your friends did good job today, Aaron. We're lucky to have you."

The praise seemed to surprise the lad. "Thanks. Suppose we all need to stick together."

"Unless we all wake up from a terrible dream, things have changed, and we only have each other."

Aaron headed off while Richard inspected the lad's handy work. The church was surrounded by roads on two sides and a large pedestrian zone on the others. Aaron and his friends, along with several others from the church, had broken into several cars and removed the handbrakes. They rolled the cars into the road to block anything from approaching. In addition, they pinched a bundle of scaffolding from a parked builder's truck and constructed a small platform from which to keep watch. The remaining poles were shoved through the car windows to face the road like porcupine quills. It would make scaling the barricade that much harder. It wasn't Hadrian's Wall, but it might slow the enemy down, and it would make the people in the church feel safer.

Richard felt like a general, penned in and awaiting a last stand.

Yet, despite his fear, Richard could not suppress another yawn. He headed to the church. Birds waking on the roof began their chorus, remarkably calm and ordinary. Usually, the sound of birds singing at dawn depressed Richard—it meant a restless night of sleep was ending, and a tired day at work was beginning—but today it might be a sign that the world was not yet lost. The birds still sang.

Riaz sat on a wall outside the church. He looked ghostly, with the whites of his eyes the most visible part of him. "Your worker bees done for the night?"

"They did good," said Richard. "Better to have them on our side than a thorn in our side."

"I suppose you're right. I lost it at the bus station."

"That was hours ago, Riaz. Don't worry about it. We're all under strain. None of us know what's coming."

"Glen spoke to someone at HQ a little while ago. London has been abandoned, but there's a new task force assembling in Portsmouth. Our armed forces are being recalled from abroad, but the Middle East is under attack too, so it will be hit and miss how much of it comes back."

Richard closed his eyes and inhaled. "I can't believe the whole world is under attack by demons."

"Judgement is upon us."

"You believe in God, Riaz?"

He shrugged. "You know many Muslims who don't? I believe in Allah the Supreme and Almighty, but to tell you the truth, I've been wondering for a while if he still believes in us."

"What do you mean?"

"I mean I've been doing this job too many years. I've seen too many husbands beat their wives, too many stabbings and rapes. Too much of everything. We are not godly. We do not deserve Allah's love. This is what we deserve. What's happening now."

"A massacre?"

"A cleansing. We have failed our creator. When an artist makes an irreparable mistake on his canvas, what does he do?"

Richard shrugged.

"He throws the canvas away and starts a new painting. We will not win this war, Richard. Mankind is not supposed to." With that he walked away, not towards the church but towards the barricade.

Richard went inside the church and headed to the altar where he had left Dillon and Jen sleeping. He found them sleeping still. As quiet as a mouse, he slid down beside them.

Snores filled the cavernous space, travelling high into the rafters. Richard wondered how long it would be until it was the sound of screams.

"Dad?"

Richard rolled to see that Dillon had opened his eyes. "Hey there, sweetheart."

"I was worried."

"I'm fine. I've been working."

"Are the monsters here?"

"No, Dillon. No monsters. You're safe."

Dillon closed his eyes again, and for a moment, looked like he would fall back to sleep. Then he opened them again and appeared even more awake. "Can we go home?"

Richard kissed his forehead. "Not yet, sweetheart. We need to stay together, all of us in the church, for a little while longer."

"Until it's safe to go back?"

"Yes."

"Will it ever be safe?"

Richard was about to answer, but saw that Jen had opened her eyes too. She looked at him, but did not speak. "I don't know, Dillon," he told his son. "The truth is that things might get very frightening, and daddy will have to fight very hard to keep you safe. Whatever happens though, you and your mum need to stick together, okay? Even if it means leaving me."

He had expected Dillon to protest, or even cry, but his son surprised him by nodding. "People in the church talk about the monsters. They said they will be coming to hurt us."

Tears brimmed in Richard's eyes. He wanted to lie—God how he wanted to lie—but he couldn't. Not now. "That's true, Dillon, and I need you to be big and brave. Everyone is frightened, and that's okay, but we all have to be one big family and look after each other, so today, Do whatever mummy tells you to."

"Are you going out again?"

"No, Dillon, not yet. I'm going to get some sleep."

"But then you will have to go out again, because you're a sergeant?"

Richard understood his son was trying to make sense of things, to put things in order. He wanted to know what to expect. "Yes, because I am a sergeant, and the other policemen need me to tell them what to do."

Dillon nodded. "Okay."

They all lay there for a moment, the three of them, listening to the snores of fifty strangers. Eventually, the sun broke through the stained glass windows, and a bejewelled shaft of light came down from the ceiling.

"Never thought I'd see the day you dragged yourself into church," said Jen, reaching out a hand and stroking his hair the way he loved. Already it made his eyelids droop.

"Me either. Guess I've been wrong all these years. I hope God hurries up and helps us, because I'm not sure I can do much on my own."

"You're not alone, Rich. There might be a lot of bad things going on, but you'll never be alone. We'll face this together. You, me, and Dillon."

"Right now, that's the only thing I'm holding on to."

"Good, because I'm proud of you."

He glanced at her. "You are?"

"Remember before we got married, when you joined the police force? We stayed in that hotel in Torquay—The Silver Fish."

"Oh yeah."

"And we took a few beers onto the beach one night and spoke about our dreams for the future."

"I remember. You stepped on a shell and cut your foot."

She chuckled. "I did, didn't I? Before that, though, you told me you wanted to join the police force and make a difference. You wanted to help people."

"I remember."

"But all you've done these last few years is complain about how all you seem to do is chase, punish, and lock up. Nothing has done any good. Nothing has changed."

Richard sighed. His thoughts on the effectiveness of modern policing were often depressing. "Weed seizures and pub brawls. I've grown tired of it."

"I know you have, honey. That's why I'm proud of you, because you never let it jade you. Today you inspired a bunch of teenagers into helping out instead of punishing them for the sake of it because it wouldn't have done any good. You gave them a chance to do something useful. You empowered those boys, and they broke their backs working for you tonight."

"How do you know that?"

"Because I got up in the middle of the night and watched you. Miles made me a cup of tea, and we shared a cigarette. He told me all about what happened at the police station."

Richard had spoken at length to Reverend Miles about what was coming. The poor man had been awake the entire night, bringing Aaron and the others tea and coffee to keep them going. "The boys surprised me," he admitted. "It was a reporter from the city who told me to enlist their help. Not sure I would have considered it myself."

"You would have. You see the best in people, Rich. That's why I love you."

"I love you too, Jen. So much. If anything happens..."

She shushed him. "We'll face it together. Get some sleep."

His wife continued stroking his hair, and sleep was exactly what he did.

3

The refugees at the church had swelled throughout the day, but the group grew unbalanced with children and elderly. Richard understood that most families were probably hiding out in their homes, but it was those young parents and teenagers that they needed. If this was to be Slough's defensive force, they needed strong men and women. That was why Glen and the other officers had gone out in the squad car to spread word that there was sanctuary at the church. The only one to remain was Riaz.

Richard, meanwhile, had slept until a little before noon and then got right back to building defences. Aaron and his friends were back at the growing barricade and had been adding to it with chairs and tables taken from the storage room of the church. It now stretched from the sidewall of J.Roberts Accountancy right across the road to the Fisherman's Feast chip shop. It was next to the chip shop where Richard spoke to Aaron.

"We're going to need to get some munchies, boss. I'm starving, and I bet everyone else is too. If we're all going to hang around the church, we can't live on the vicar's tea and biscuits."

Richard felt his own tummy rumbling. It was almost three o'clock, and he hadn't eaten since yesterday at breakfast time. "I know. We need to sort that out or people will begin to grumble."

Aaron motioned to the chippie's large glass window. "Could get the grills on in there. Mikey used to work at a takeaway and could probably get everything cooking. Would mean breaking in though unless we can find the owner."

"Break it," said Richard, surprised by how quickly he came to the decision.

Aaron smirked. "You sure, boss?"

"We need to feed everyone. This isn't going to get cleared up in a weekend. We will have to do whatever we need to."

"You're a copper I can get on board with, you know that?"

"You caught me on a bad day."

"Your mate was looking for you."

Richard frowned. "Who?"

"The other copper. The Asian one."

"Riaz?"

Aaron shrugged. "He was sat on the wall outside the church."

Richard turned and crossed the road, heading back towards the church. Sure enough, he found Riaz sitting on his usual perch. "You were looking for me?"

He pulled out his phone and waved it. "I've been getting network coverage this afternoon. Allowed me to do some research online."

"Great. Have you learned anything?"

"I started with the normal searches, reports from the BBC, etc. Things are as bad as I thought. It's the end of the world."

Richard sighed. There was nothing to be gained by making such grand statements, even if they were true. "Okay."

"Then I went narrower, tried to find out how long we have left. The enemy is on the move, but they seem to be forming up around the country into several larger armies. Each army is being led by a giant."

"Sorry," said Richard. "Giants?"

Riaz huffed. "People online are calling them angels because of scars they have on their back that look like wings. There's one in London. It was there during an attack on Hyde Park. The RAF hit it with missiles, but it didn't even bleed."

"And it's coming this way?"

Riaz shrugged. "Don't know."

"So where did you learn all this?"

"The Slough Echo."

"The newspaper down the road?"

"They've been gathering the facts and posting them online. That's the reason I was looking for you. Apparently, the enemy has some kind of aversion to iron."

Richard tilted his head and paid close attention. "Iron?"

Riaz nodded. "According to the Echo, the demons, or whatever they are, can't cross a line of iron. Thought that might be useful for your barricade."

"It's our barricade, Riaz. We're building it to keep us all safe."

"You really think it will make the slightest bit of difference? We can't fight what's coming."

Richard sighed. "Can we beat what's coming, I don't know, I admit it. But the least we can do is fight it."

"Why fight when it's pointless? Why not run and enjoy the time you have left with your family?"

"You think I don't want to do that? Of course I do, but where would we be then?"

There was the nearby sound of glass shattering.

Riaz leapt up off the wall. "Those little shits!"

Before Richard could stop him, Riaz was racing across the road towards the chip shop. Aaron and his three friends were currently putting through the large plate-glass window by throwing bricks.

Richard shouted after Riaz, but it did no good. The officer ran up behind Aaron and grabbed him around the collar, spinning the lad around. "What do you think you're doing?"

"Get your hands off me, pig!"

Riaz snarled. "I'll drag you into a cell and guard you myself."

"Riaz! Riaz, it's okay."

Riaz glanced sideways at Richard. "How is this okay? It was a bloody stupid idea leaving these trouble makers on the street."

"I told Aaron to put through the windows," said Richard.

"What? Why?"

"Because we all need feeding, and this chip shop is sitting here abandoned and full of food."

Riaz released Aaron and shoved him away. The lad smirked but looked a little shaken in the eyes. Riaz glared at Richard in a way he did not like. "This is somebody's business. What right do we have—"

"For Christ's sake, Riaz! What the hell is the matter with you?"

"What's the matter with me? I'm a police officer hearing that another police officer just condoned wanton destruction of property."

Richard shook his head and pointed a finger in Riaz's face. "No, it's more than that. You've been in a foul mood since last night, which is fair enough considering the circumstances, but what I don't get is how one minute you're telling me we're all doomed, then the next you're trying to enforce the law as if everything is normal. What is going on with you?"

He slapped Richard's finger out of his face. "I'm not having this conversation. You want to play at being Mad Max, fine, but it's a waste of time."

"Why is it?" said Richard. "Why are you so eager to give up?"

Riaz shoved past Richard and marched away. As he stormed off he shouted over his shoulder. "Don't forget about the iron. It might just let you live a few minutes longer."

"That guy is a dick, man," said Aaron.

Richard patted him on the back. "It's my fault. I should have involved Riaz in what we were doing."

"He don't want to be involved. All he does is sit around stink-eyeing us."

"I'll talk to him. For now, just get those fryers on. I'll go get you some volunteers from the church."

Aaron took off his baseball cap and ran a finger through his hair. With a smile he said, "I always wanted my own business. Guess I'm in the fast food game now."

"Well, be good at it or it'll end up being a free for all."

Richard headed back to the church, and when he announced that food was in the process of being delivered, an excited chorus of hungry moans broke out. Dillon sat on the steps up to the altar, so Richard went up to him and pulled out the item he'd tucked in the back of his trousers. It was a Beano comic he had taken from a basket outside of a charity shop. Dillon grinned at the sight of it.

"Dennis the Menace. Thanks, Dad."

Richard gave him a hug. "You're welcome."

Jen came over. "How's it going?"

"We have a decent wall up now. Riaz told me he's learned that the demons can't cross iron."

"Demons? Are we calling them that?"

"Yes, and there's giant angels too, apparently."

She broke out in laughter.

Richard grinned. "You don't believe me?"

She covered her mouth and stopped herself. "No, I do believe you. That's the problem. Demons, angels... It's just so absurd. Whenever I try to make sense of it, I start to go insane. I mean, we haven't even seen these things. It all feels like a big practical joke, you know?"

"Let's hope that it is. I would rather feel stupid than afraid."

"Well, we're okay for now at least. I'll take Dillon to go get food at the chip shop. Maybe we can find a way to help out."

The thought of his wife and son having a task to occupy them sounded good to Richard, so he told her, "Go ask for Aaron and say you're my wife. He'll be glad to have your help; I'm sure."

She nodded. Before she left, she rose on her tiptoes and kissed him on the cheek. "I'm still proud of you."

Richard sighed. "Just let me know as soon as you stop."

"Can't see that happening."

Richard stood in the church while most everyone filtered outside and across the road to the chip shop. Faced with a brief moment of peace, he sat down on a pew and stared up at Jesus who hung from a cross above the altar. Richard had never believed in him before, but he wondered now if the man had been real—in the sense he was God's son and looked down on humanity. Was it truly demons stalking the earth, or something else entirely? Was Riaz right: that they would all perish without the slightest assistance from heavenly forces? Despite

Richard's atheist views, there was something fateful about ending up at a church. He felt somehow protected.

"Do you feel his presence?" asked Miles.

Richard started, but then settled back down. "Not sure I do. I don't see any sense in this."

"And yet, there is sense to be made. It's happening for a reason, just not one we understand."

Richard laced his hands together in his lap and took his eyes off Jesus and turned them to Miles. The man was still donning his cassock and collar. If it had been Richard, he would have changed into something more comfortable. "What is your take on all this, Miles? Is there a religious perspective?"

"There is a religious perspective on all things, not that it's always helpful. In my opinion, for I cannot speak higher than myself, I believe this is a war that started somewhere else. I think forces above us are in dispute, and perhaps we are just a staging ground. Maybe we have been caught in the middle."

"You mean like Heaven and Hell? They are fighting over us?"

"Earth is heavenly by its very nature, for it is of God. I imagine God's enemies would like to see humanity fall. It would be the ultimate insult to him."

"So we're collateral damage?"

Miles nodded gently. "To believe we are anything more important would be vain."

"I suppose you're right. Does the bible say anything about this kind of thing?"

"Depends on which version you read. Some of the American sects would tell you this is a tribulation, that we are all being tested for worthiness of Heaven. They call it the Rapture. C of E is a little less dramatic. Perhaps the Antichrist has been among us, and we missed him. There is so much evil in the world it would be easy to dismiss him as just another tyrant or greed-monger. Maybe he brought war to us without us even noticing."

"I haven't seen the four horseman yet."

"Nor shall you, I am sure. Such things are simple allegory. What I believe, however, is that if there are forces of evil, then there is also good. If the devil has come to Earth, I believe wholeheartedly that the Messiah will follow. As bad as things seem, we may not have seen everything play out just yet."

Richard patted the man's knee. It seemed appropriate. "I can get on board with that."

"Then there is hope."

"It's about all we have."

Miles put his hand on top of Richard's. "Feed yourself, Officer. You are our totem, and we need you strong."

"Totem?"

"The focus of our collective spirits. People will follow you, gaining strength from your strength. Keep care of yourself. Go eat."

He nodded. "A question first."

Miles leant forward. "Yes?"

"Does this church have anything made of iron?"

Miles looked confused, yet he gave the matter some thought.

A short while later, Richard went outside. He was pleased to find a long, orderly queue outside the chip shop. People were calm. Yet, imagining how they would be during an attack made Richard shudder. Would they scream and run? Probably. Could he change it? Unlikely.

Perhaps though.

Richard bypassed the crowd and went to the barricade. He climbed up onto the scaffold and turned to face the queue. "Hi, hello." He cleared his throat. "I would just like to address you all briefly, if that's okay."

People nodded. Some muttered.

"Thank you. Many of you have already met me, but I would just like to introduce myself properly. I am Sergeant Richard Honeywell. Until the last few days, I worked at a desk and planned minor drug raids and arrests. I was never a soldier, and I can't say I've ever been in real danger. I suspect that is true for most of us. Recently, I met a man who was a solider, however. He was at Hyde Park during last night's attacks. Things went badly. London is abandoned—I don't know if you already know that. The rest of the country is under threat too. It appears the enemy is everywhere."

A few of the crowd whimpered. A mother cupped her son's ears.

Jen looked up at him from the rear of the crowd. Dillon was eating a packet of crisps. Richard couldn't help but look at them as he spoke. "Like many of you, I have a family to protect, and the urge to run away is strong. But there's nowhere to run, I assure you. We will be forced to defend ourselves soon. Perhaps today. Eventually, those monsters we all saw on television will be here. What we do then will determine our futures. If we turn and run, the enemy will hunt us down and pick us off one by one. If we stand and fight..."

"Why would we stand and fight when the British Army couldn't?" an older man shouted.

"Because you have no choice, sir. If you don't fight, you will die. Maybe you'll get to live a day longer by running, but you'll die."

More whimpers from the crowd. "Stand and fight, and we have a chance. If groups like us resist, our numbers will begin to add up. Maybe we won't survive—I hate to say it—but if we take some of the enemy with us, we make it that much easier for the next group of people forced to defend themselves. We will prepare, and do our best to be ready, but I urge you to conquer your fear and fight those sons of bitches. They are here to exterminate us. They are here to kill our children and step over our corpses. Are we going to let them?"

"No," said Shirley, giving Richard a supportive smile.

"Fuck no!" said Aaron, standing in the chip shop's doorway. He wore an apron and held a ladle in his hand which he thrust into the air triumphantly.

"I'm with you," shouted Jen.

"Me too," said someone Richard didn't recognise.

"What choice do we have?" cried someone else.

A couple more spoke out in support, but the rest of the crowd did nothing more than mumble. It was impossible to know what they would do, but Richard was confident he had done all he could. He'd explained the odds and what was required. It was down to them now.

"Good speech," said Riaz once Richard had climbed down off the barricade. "I'm sorry."

"For what?"

"For letting my hang-ups affect what you're doing."

Richard frowned at him. "Just tell me what the problem is Riaz."

"My son was in the city. I haven't heard from him since this began."

Richard felt the news like a gut punch. "I'm so sorry. I didn't even know you—"

"His mum and I are separated, but I visit him one weekend a month. Maybe we didn't have the best father-son relationship, but he was my boy."

"I understand. How old is he?"

"Six."

"You must have been young?"

Riaz nodded. "I was twenty-two. Part of the reason it never worked out with Tariq's mum. I was too involved in myself back then."

Tariq. Richard logged the name, wishing he knew more about his colleague. He patted him on the arm, but it was clear Riaz didn't appreciate the contact. "Look, I can't imagine what you must be feeling, but we are fighting here to stay alive. Tariq might still be out there. Give yourself a chance to find out."

"I think I already know well enough."

"Don't give up on your son, Riaz. If you want to be a good father, don't give up."

"HELP! Please, help."

Riaz and Richard looked around at the same time. The shouts came from beyond the barricade which was now too high to see above. Richard clambered back up onto the scaffold and looked towards the road. Two cars had pulled up on the curb, and people spilled out onto the pavement. The man shouting was covered in blood.

"Help us, please. We have an injured man with us."

"Of course," said Richard. "Let me make way for you." He hopped back down from the barricade and grabbed Riaz. "Let's move some of this out the way. We have people coming in."

Several volunteers helped, and together they pulled back the scaffolding poles and other junk piled up on top of an old Rover shunted up against the chip shop's wall. By the time Richard got another view of the road, seven people were standing there. Four women and two men. The two men carried a third between them—an injured man.

Glen.

Riaz spluttered with surprise. "Glen! What happened to him?"

The man who'd been shouting for help shook his head. "We don't know. I found him lying by the side of the road. I was heading out of town, trying to find help. He's in a bad way, but he told us to come find you all. Can we come in?"

"Yes!" cried Richard. "Come on in."

They slid Glen across the Rover's bonnet and allowed Riaz and Richard to grab a hold of him. While the newcomers climbed the barricade, Richard eased Glen onto the floor. He was muttering something.

Richard frowned. "What is it, Glen? Tell me what happened?"

"They... They're here. They're coming."

Glen lost consciousness just as Miles arrived with the things Richard had asked for.

Rick Bastion

RICK SAT AT his piano but didn't feel like playing. The time had come to say goodbye to his beloved baby grand and his vast Edwardian home. Time to say goodbye to his life. And maybe hello to his death.

Maybe then I'll fade away
and not have to face the facts.
It's not easy facing up when your whole world is black.

Of course, he wasn't alone. His companions—Maddy, Diane, and his brother Keith—all paddled the same sinking boat. The world ended the moment demons and angels invaded it. That Rick had fought and survived while millions of others died was enough to keep him fighting. It was his duty. His companions felt the same way. None of them intended to accept death.

That was why they were leaving tonight beneath the cover of darkness. Rick's home was surrounded by iron bars, but it had eventually been assaulted anyway. It was unsafe to remain, and their only chance of survival was to find help. Not that they were certain of finding any. Diane's internet searches had grown bleaker by the minute, and only the Echo provided any meaningful hope. In the last few hours, their website had been down more often than it was up, but it was via the newspaper they had learned about the power of iron. The demons could not easily assail it and were injured by its touch.

The other ace in their pocket was asleep on the living room couch. Daniel was a Fallen Angel. It was from him they had learned what was happening. The black stones around the world had summoned portals to Hell, and the damned were coming through them to claim the earth as their own. In doing so, their leader, The Red Lord, hoped to force a confrontation with God himself.

Daniel was injured—possibly dying—and it was because he had given part of himself to bring Rick back from the dead after an ancient demon with long black hair had crushed his skull. Rick owed his life to the Fallen Angel.

Maddy came up beside Rick, a blank expression on her face that suggested she was thinking.

"You okay?" he asked her. "You're thinking about your husband." Maddy had wanted to go home to get her wedding ring, the only part of her deceased husband she could hold onto since his body was lost somewhere in the ruins of Milton Combe.

She sighed. "One day, I will go home and grieve for him properly."

Rick smiled. "And I promise I will help you do just that."

"Thanks, Rick. You going to play something?"

Rick looked at the ivory keys in front of him and reached out, fingers hovering. Instead of playing, he placed down the lid. "My playing days are over. I've promised myself that one day, when all this is over, I'll come back here and spend whatever days I have left playing music. Who knows, maybe I'll even be a pop star again."

"I'll be first in line to buy your CD."

"I've got our bags piled in the hallway," said Keith, entering the living room. A large bruise stained his cheek from the last evening's battle with the long-haired demon—which now lay dead in the garden along with several of its minions. The stench was growing pervasive.

Rick climbed up from his stool and forced himself not to glance back at his piano. He'd said his goodbyes. It was time to go. "I'm ready if you are."

"We should get Diane to do one last check online," said Maddy. "Check it's still safe to head south."

It was a good idea, so they went into Rick's oak-timbered office where Diane was napping. When she noticed them, she started—everyone's nerves were on edge—and they asked her to do another check of the internet.

"Sure," she said, sleepily. "The connection is getting spotty, but I'll give it a go." She opened Rick's laptop and tapped at the keyboard. "The Slough Echo is still up," she said a moment later.

"Any news?" asked Keith.

"Hold on, let me see. Yeah, Portsmouth is still a safe zone. The Army is being recalled from abroad, and that's where they are coming in. Apparently, the Echo has a military liaison at their office who is keeping them in the loop about things. The information should be up to date, and... hey, listen to this, someone managed to close one of the gates in Syria."

Keith frowned. "Syria? How does that help us?"

"Because it shows there are ways to hit them back," said Rick. "It shows other people are still fighting."

"Great. Another few thousand gates and we should be all back to normal."

Rick rolled his eyes. "It's better than nothing."

Keith looked at his watch. "It's almost ten PM. If we want to make the most of night cover, we should move. We make it to the motorway if we can, but if not we stick to the countryside."

Keith thought he was in charge, as always, but Rick didn't argue. What his brother was saying was sound. The motorways were potentially troublesome, but if they were free of demons, they would be the fastest route—with farmland to escape to on either side if they encountered danger.

They gathered in the hallway before the large front doors. For a time, Rick had been a hermit behind those heavy slabs of wood, a failed pop star too embarrassed to be seen in public. Now, he was a blooded warrior about to step out into the deadly wilderness. Each of them held weapons: Keith and Rick iron pokers, Diane a baseball bat, and Maddy wielded both an old field hockey stick and a chef's knife.

"I still say we leave Daniel here," said Keith, glowering back toward the living room.

Rick shook his head. "No way. He saved me." The others didn't know Daniel's true nature—that he was inhuman—but Rick told them he had been rescued from certain death by the guy. Daniel was coming along, no matter what.

Keith huffed. "Fine, fine. He'll slow us down something terrible, but I understand he's one of us, I suppose."

Not exactly, thought Rick.

"I've put the wheelbarrow just outside," said Maddy, "along with a duvet and pillow. He'll be a bit cramped, but should be comfortable."

Maddy was a paramedic. Rick was glad to have her along because she had a nurse's compassion. "Thanks, Maddy. Keith, you want to give me a hand?"

Keith shrugged and followed after his brother. They approached Daniel on the sofa and picked him up between them like a length of old carpet. The Fallen Angel stirred momentarily, opening his eyes and staring at Rick, but then he went back to sleep.

"Guy's as light as a feather," said Keith. "That will make wheeling his arse around a little easier."

Rick knew Daniel had possessed an anaemic hospital patient on the brink of death, so the lack of body weight was understandable. He also knew that if Daniel died, he would be whisked straight back to his prison cell in the lowest pits of hell. God had punished his revolting angels harshly, but betraying the Red Lord would bring Daniel even harsher punishments. Even Lucifer bowed to the mysterious power pulling the strings of this war.

Maddy unlocked the front doors while Keith and Rick carried the Fallen Angel to the awaiting wheelbarrow. He fit inside easily. Rick positioned the pillow behind his head.

It was time to go.

Rick took one last moment to appreciate the home he had spent the last six years living in—the symbol of the success he had once achieved. Its high, gabled roof had twin chimneys like ears on the head of a looming monster, yet it had only ever felt safe to Rick. The iron gates surrounding the property had saved their lives.

Movement. A flicker of a shadow beyond the driveway floodlights. Rick squinted. What the hell?

"Whoa, whoa," Maddy cried.

Rick spun to see Daniel's wheelbarrow tipping over. He acted quickly, threw out his hands to keep it steady. Soon as he had, his eyes went back to the end of the driveway. Had someone been there? Rick was certain he had seen a person.

But the stranger was now gone.

"You okay?" asked Keith, seeing his confused expression.

"Yeah," said Rick. "I thought I saw someone."

Keith looked concerned, scanned the gates nervously. "Who?"

"An old man... An old man sweeping."

"You saw an old man?"

Rick felt stupid. "I thought I did. He had a broom, I think. I must... I must be seeing things."

Keith grabbed his shoulder and looked at him. "You still okay to do this?"

Rick wasn't sure. "Maybe I have a concussion or something. We can't stay here any longer, though. We need to find help."

Keith gave his shoulder a hearty pat. "Then let's go."

They moved down the driveway, trundling Daniel along in the wheelbarrow. Rick couldn't help but look around anxiously. Couldn't shake the feeling that someone had been watching them. Watching them and sweeping the ground.

As they passed out of the gates, Rick noticed a pile of dirt gathered on one side of the road along with a trail—like a broom had swept across it.

2

They stopped at a petrol station one hour after leaving the house. So far the going had been good. Although walking through the rural village streets resembled walking through the ruins of a sacked settlement, there had been no sign of demons—live ones at least. Their bodies lay all over the place. The problem was that for every demon corpse, there were five human ones. The sheer horror of it was what led Rick and his group to take a breather inside the petrol station.

Tears filled Maddy's eyes, but she would not allow herself to sob. "I'm not sure I can cope with any more. Did you see... did you see that little girl?"

Everyone nodded. It had been impossible to miss the little blonde girl with bloody pigtails and two torn-off arms. Her body lay propped against a road sign like some kind of warning. The harsh glow of the nearby lamppost made her sallow cheeks almost translucent. A blonde woman lay dead beside the girl—perhaps her mother. Before moving on, Maddy lay the girl's stiffened body in the grass. Even for a paramedic, it had proven too grizzly. She had barely said a word since.

Keith put down his iron poker and went to the petrol station's buzzing refrigerator. He snatched a bottle of water and uncapped it. After taking a swig, he looked around. "Looks like people left everything and ran for their lives."

"What else could they do?" said Diane, holding herself and stepping carefully. "People must have been so afraid. So many dead. No one was ready for any of this. I was training to be a childcare worker. I'm supposed to be spend my days in a nursery surrounded by laughing children, not walking through dead bodies."

Maddy gave the girl a hug. "We're alive, and so are other people, I'm sure. We will find them, I promise."

Diane wiped at the tip of her nose. "Where have all the demons gone now? I mean the ones that were here in the village. They couldn't all have been with the ones that attacked us. You think any are still here?"

"The demons are all assembling into armies," said Keith. "The ones that attacked us must have come from the gate in Crapstone, but they only swept through here on their way to someplace else. We head south. We'll be fine."

Diane seemed unsure, but she nodded. Rick approximated the girl to a nervous bird, yet she had survived a lot and still placed one foot in front of the other. Diane was stronger than she realised.

"Let's grab a few supplies," said Keith, moving over to the confectionary aisle and gathering chocolate bars. With his large gut, Keith would last longest if they were forced to starve.

Fortunately, that didn't seem like it would be the case. The petrol station was fully stocked, and it was reasonable to assume other places were too. If they died, it would be quick and painful and at the hands of a demon. Rick picked up a sausage roll and tore open the packet. When he bit into it, the lights winked out.

Diane moaned.

"There goes the power," said Keith. "Bound to happen sooner or later."

Rick swallowed the mouthful of pastry and wiped his mouth with the back of his jacket's leather sleeve. "Does that mean the power stations are offline? Have things got even worse?"

Keith shrugged, like he knew it all and was tired of explaining. "More likely the grid has been compromised. Not like they can send an engineer to go fix a fallen power line at the moment. Better to switch it all off and divert power where it's needed. This is the government making smart decisions. Somewhere, someone is still in charge."

"I hope so," said Rick, but wasn't sure he believed it. More likely, the power stations were unstaffed, their engineers deserted or dead. Was the enemy smart enough to attack strategic targets? Had they knocked out the power on purpose?

The demon with the black hair had certainly been in possession of his wits. He had spoken to Rick, told him of the Red Lord's plans. All of humanity gone.

Maddy picked up a couple of bottles of sports drink and took them over to Daniel, still unconscious in the wheelbarrow. "Hey, Daniel, can you wake up and take a sip of this?"

Daniel murmured.

"Daniel," she said, shaking him gently. "We need to keep you hydrated. Can you just take a little bit of this, please?"

Daniel's left eye peeled open, and his lips parted. Maddy placed the sports drink against his dry mouth and slowly tipped it in. After a few moments, he spluttered and began gulping thirstily.

"That's it," said Maddy. "Drink as much as you can. It will give you a little boost."

Daniel took another glug, but then started choking.

"Easy," said Maddy, patting his back. It didn't help. Daniel continued choking so violently that he almost tumbled out of the wheelbarrow. Rick rushed over and grabbed his arm to keep him from thrashing.

"Hey, it's okay. Calm down."

Daniel opened both eyes and gasped for air.

"What was in that bottle?" asked Keith. "Poison?"

"No, it was a vitamin drink." She held it up in front of her.

Rick read the label and groaned. With added iron. "It is poison. At least it is to him."

Keith stared at him. "What do you mean?"

Rick found himself in a hole and decided the only way out was to tell the truth. "Daniel is one of them. He came through the gates."

Keith backed away from the wheelbarrow and raised his iron poker. "You mean he's a demon?"

"No, he's an angel. One of the Fallen. He was trapped in Hell and escaped with everything else, but he isn't one of the bad guys. He saved my life. He's been trying to help us."

"Like hell he has. He's a goddamn spy!"

Rick snarled. "Then how come we're still alive?"

"Beats me, but we need to deal with him right now."

All the while, Daniel continued to choke.

Maddy pointed at Diane. "Get me some water. Now!"

"What are you doing?" Keith spun to face her.

"Trying to stop him choking."

"Let the bastard choke."

Maddy pointed a finger in his face. "No! I trust Rick, and I haven't seen Daniel do anything to harm us. I would at least like to help him survive long enough for him to answer my questions."

Diane hurried back with the water. It was peach flavoured.

Maddy shoved the bottleneck into Daniel's mouth and upended it. Daniel gagged on the new liquid, but some of it went down okay. After a few moments, he drank voluntarily. The choking and hitching subsided.

Daniel was lucid.

Rick peered at him, eyes wide. "Daniel, you're awake?"

"S-so I am. What's that... that terrible taste in my mouth?"

"That might be the iron we just gave you."

"T-the what?"

Rick shrugged. "Sorry. We've been waiting for you to wake up."

Daniel blinked, his eyes droopy and like he could fall back to sleep any moment. Despite that, he glanced around. "Where?"

"We're at a petrol station. We decided to make a break for the south coast. There might be help there."

"Rick says you're a demon," said Keith, looming over Daniel.

Daniel didn't seem ashamed of the fact—maybe he was too out of it—and nodded slightly. "One word for me, I... suppose."

"You're one of them."

Daniel shook his head adamantly despite his weakness. "No."

Keith nodded, just as adamant. "Yes."

"I'm not one of them."

"Then help us," said Maddy.

"Too... weak."

"You see?" Keith pointed a finger. "He's working to bring us down."

Rick knocked his brother's pointed finger downwards. "Yeah, because Hell would really send a Fallen Angel to bring down an accountant and a fading pop star. I'm telling you, he's on our side. He..."

"He what?" Keith had grown red in the face, the collar of his dirty shirt seeming to grow tighter around his fleshy neck. "What were you going to say, Rick?"

"He... He brought me back to life. I was dead—my skull crushed—but he fixed me. Brought me back from the dead."

Keith burst out laughing. "You've lost it. You've bloody well lost it."

"No, I haven't. I'm telling you!"

Keith looked at Rick, and the smile slipped away. "Maybe you're right. Maybe you haven't lost it. Maybe Daniel has got to you. Maybe you're determined to screw us all over."

"Keith!" Maddy put her hand on her hips. "He's your brother!"

"Is he? Came back from the dead, apparently. Isn't that what demons do? Wouldn't that make him a zombie? Doesn't sound like my brother to me." He prodded Rick in the chest.

"Back off," Rick snarled.

Keith prodded him again. "I want to know what the hell is going on here. I won't die. Marcy and Maxwell are still out there somewhere, and I intend on getting to them."

Rick shoved his brother hard in the shoulders, rocking him back. "You mean the wife and son you cheated on? Screw you, Keith. You're not the boss of anything, and you don't decide what happens. Daniel is with us, and I am fine."

"Rick?" Maddy was staring at him. Keith backed away cautiously, his poker held up in front of him.

"Oh God," Diane put a hand to her mouth.

Rick shook his head. "What? What is it?"

"Just... look in the mirror," said Maddy.

Look in the mirror? What was she talking about? There was one of those curved mirrors at the end of the aisle which allowed the sales assistant to glance around the corner. Rick went over to it. It was dark, so when he looked up, he couldn't see himself clearly. He only saw his own eyes.

His eyes were glowing red.

Rick staggered backwards in shock, colliding with a shelfful of cleaning supplies behind him. "What's wrong with me?"

Maddy came up behind and grabbed him. "Just sit down. On the floor, now."

He allowed himself to be lowered and pulled his knees up while he sat there in stunned silence. Maddy rubbed at his back.

"What's wrong with me?" he asked again, realising he was shivering.

"Shh, take deep breaths. Everything is okay."

Rick realised his heart was thudding like a tambourine, but slowly, gradually, he calmed down. "Am I... Am I normal again?"

Maddy looked into his eyes. She nodded. "Yes."

"I told you; he came back wrong," said Keith.

Maddy glared at him. "Enough, Keith. Nothing's changed. We're all heading south to find safety."

"You're insane. He's one of them now."

"Can we stop fighting?" said Diane. "Let's get what we need and go. I don't like being stuck inside here. It's too cramped. When I was twelve, I got locked in a cleaning cupboard at school for a whole hour. Tight spaces have freaked me out ever since."

Keith ran a hand through his slicked-back hair and exhaled. "Fine, let's get what we can in our packs and get back on the road. Let's just forget about the facts Daniel is a demon and my brother is possessed. Nothing to worry about, I'm sure. Maybe that old man sweeping Rick saw was Jesus, come to whisk us all to safety. Everything is sodding hunky dory."

"What did you just say?" Daniel struggled to lift himself up out of the wheelbarrow. "What was that you said?"

Keith didn't even bother to look at him. "I'm not talking to you, demon. You're a spy."

"What did you say about a man sweeping?" The force in Daniel's voice shocked them.

Frowning, Keith broke his own assertion and turned to Daniel. "It was a joke. Rick was seeing things. Thought he saw an old man sweeping. Not surprised, seeing as you supposedly knitted his brain back together."

Daniel groaned. "The Caretaker. We need to leave here. Right now!"

"Wait, you mean he's real?" said Rick. "I really saw him?"

Daniel gritted his teeth as he struggled to climb out of the wheelbarrow. He gained an inch before falling back down. "The Caretaker is very real. If you saw him, we are all in very serious danger."

"Who is he?" Diane's hands bunched up against her mouth.

"Hell is a place full of monsters," said Daniel, "but even Hell has its bogeymen. They say the Caretaker was the slave who used to clean up the blood at the Roman Colosseum after Christians were put to death there. The Romans saw the blood as tainted and sent only the lowliest servants to deal with it. For decades, the slave watched while devout men were put to death, fed to lions, hanged, or stabbed. Over time, he became numb to their suffering—to all suffering. He became amoral. Near the end of the slave's life, the gladiatorial combats stopped, and killing in the Colosseum ceased. The slave found himself without purpose. After a lifetime of cleaning up the blood of Martyrs, he had developed a need for its scent, for the tackiness against his fingers. For its taste."

Diane groaned. "Oh God."

Daniel continued, his strength returned as he told the story. Maybe it was fear giving him a boost. "Eventually, the slave could rest no longer. He needed to spill blood himself, to continue his life's work. He started with his master, causing a minor slave revolt. First, he bathed in the blood, before cleansing it from his skin and from the floor. He left his former master on the dirt outside his home, mimicking the thousands of Christians who had perished on the sands of the arena. For another ten years, the slave continued his quest for blood, drinking from his victim's necks as they bled out. It was the cleanest way to remove the liquid. No blood on the ground. It was his job to keep the ground clean. It had always been his job."

"He sounds like a vampire," said Maddy.

Daniel nodded. "Perhaps where the myth was born. Rome was deathly afraid of the old man who stalked its shadows, cleansing citizens of their blood. Roman Emperor Honorius promised a captured Gaul his freedom if the man hunted down the monster and slew it. The

Gaul, once a druid of his clan, tracked the murderous slave down by butchering a dozen sows and draining their blood into a vat at the edge of the Rubicon River. The sickly scent drew the old man out of Rome, as desired, the very first night. The moon was full, and now, truly a monster, the murderous slave's teeth were stained permanently red from the blood. The Gaulish druid ambushed the slave and drowned him in the great vat of blood, bringing a poetic end to the creature who had stalked the streets of Rome. The emperor decreed that the vat be sealed and buried with the old man's corpse inside, forever to be soiled by the clotted blood of pigs."

"How do you know all this?" asked Diane, still covering her mouth.

"I know nothing for sure," Daniel admitted. "The Caretaker has become a myth throughout the hallways of Hell, his story whispered between the damned. The old slave has swept the burning halls for so long that I no longer remember when he first appeared. What I do know is that he wasn't amongst the Fallen."

"What does that mean?" asked Rick.

"I mean that the original inhabitants of Hell are the Fallen Angels. Lucifer created Hell to be his own kingdom and started claiming damned souls to serve him after that. In other words, aside from the original Fallen Angels, every single soul ever sent to Hell was once a man. The Caretaker walked this earth as a human being once. Then, one day, he ended up in the fiery abyss for his sins. For hundreds of years, he has swept the infernal hallways and kept them clean of blood. But blood is never ending in Hell. It flows like air. The Caretaker grew even more mad than he had been as a man. Eventually, just looking upon him as he went about his business would curse you to misery. To gaze upon the Caretaker is to invite him upon your soul. He will drain you of everything you are and leave madness in its place. He is feared, even by those in Hell. Even by Lucifer."

"And I looked upon him," said Rick.

Daniel nodded. "That is why we need to leave."

But it was too late. The petrol station's front window shattered, and something terrible came inside.

3

The windows burst in a hail-storm of glass. Rick grabbed Maddy and pulled her into the aisle. Diane and Keith scattered too, leaving Daniel stranded like an upturned terrapin in his wheelbarrow. The Fallen Angel was straining to get up.

Demons filled the petrol station—burnt monsters and ungodly primates. An infernal gang from the pits of hell. Who and what had they been in life?

Rick cursed himself as the demons came closer. He had left his poker next to the fridges when he'd grabbed a sausage roll. Now he was defenceless. At least Maddy still held her hockey stick. She had kept it the whole time inside the petrol station and also had hold of a knife. She handed the blade to Rick.

Rick took the knife silently, crouching low in the aisle and trying to see his attackers in the dark. They were spread out, moving to all corners of the room.

"There's no way out," he said, strangely numb to the fact they were probably all about to die.

"So we fight," said Maddy.

"Hey," Rick hissed after her as she broke into the aisle. "Get back."

The sound of sweeping.

The pitter-patter of blood.

"Get back," came a shaky voice. "Go back to Hell, you big shit!"

Rick frowned. Was that Daniel? What was he doing? Unable to leave his companion to face the enemy alone, he hurried after Maddy to face their possible deaths.

Out on the main floor, Daniel had stood, yet kept one hand on the wheelbarrow as though he might stumble back in. He had his other hand up in front of him, a fist clenched at the demons amassed before him. They were seemingly held in place, unable to close in on him.

They cowered.

Sweep!

Maddy moved up beside Daniel. Rick joined her.

Sweep!

Daniel glanced sideways at them. "Thanks for abandoning me, buddies."

"Sorry," said Rick. "It happened so fast."

"I forgive you. Any ideas on what to do now? I can hold these buggers in place for a few minutes, but I'm too weak to keep it up."

Rick watched as the demons edged forwards. One of the primates began to hiss and spit. "How are you controlling them?"

"Because an Angel has dominion over Hell, but that only means so much on earth. They'll resist me, eventually."

Rick could see the truth of it. "We have to run."

"Where?" asked Maddy. "They have the front door blocked.

"There's a back door," said Keith, shouting across the room. "Over here."

Rick turned to see his brother standing beside a door. EMPLOY-EES ONLY.

"Go," said Daniel. "Get out of here!"

Sweep!

"He's coming, isn't he?" said Maddy. "I can hear him sweeping."

Daniel looked at her. "He's already here, luv. You just can't see him yet."

Rick grabbed Maddy and shoved her towards the back door. She resisted for a moment, but then got moving. Rick stayed where he was.

"Rick, what are you doing?" shouted Keith. Diane and Maddy had arrived by his side.

"I told you," Rick shouted back. "I'm not leaving Daniel."

"You're a fool," Daniel sweated as he continued to cast a spell over the enemy—a weakening spell, as the burnt men and their fellow monsters edged closer. "A damned fool."

Keith shouted again. "Get away from there."

"I'll meet you down the road, Keith. Follow the road and you'll come to a car dealership. I'll meet you there."

Keith wobbled on the spot, back and forth, towards the door, towards his brother. "Rick!"

"Just go! Get out of here."

Maddy went to make a run back towards Rick, but Keith dragged her away.

Then they were out the door, all three of them. Gone.

"What do we do?" Rick asked Daniel.

"Use what I gave you."

Rick frowned. "What do you mean?"

"I mean the reason I'm so weak is that I transferred part of my essence into you when I brought you back. As long as you're alive, I can do little. But if you help me."

"Help you?"

One primate broke free of its thrall and leapt at Rick. Rick flinched and slashed with the knife Maddy had given him. The creature tumbled back, a thin line widening along its throat. Black blood sprayed out onto the floor.

The burnt men growled.

Sweep!

"Quickly," said Daniel. "Concentrate and help me."

"Concentrate on what?"

"On making this go away."

Rick didn't understand what Daniel was telling him to do, but he raised his hand and clenched his jaw with effort. He studied the demons in front of him, bore into them with his eyes. Imagined them being gone.

One of the creatures spoke. "You will rot where you stand. I will tear you limb from limb—"

Rick ground his teeth and squinted his eyes.

His head throbbed.

"I will track down the remaining children of this earth and... and..." The demon's words trailed off. Its lidless eyes flickered, went wide.

Its fire-ravaged body began to smoke.

Rick trembled. "W-what's happening?"

"Just go with it," said Daniel.

Like a Plasticine sculpture beside a fire, the burnt man drooped, flesh sagging from its cheeks and pools of blood forming beneath its feet. It struggled and vibrated, but could not move from where it stood.

Then the other demons began to sag too. They thrashed madly, but it was like they were glued to the floor—a floor that was unbearably hot. Rick knew that the heat was not coming from the floor though. It was coming from him and Daniel.

The first creature suddenly popped. The sagging flesh of its cheeks burst open—like two giant zits—and blood and pus spattered everywhere. Rick fought back his revulsion and continued to concentrate. One by one, the demons burst open, and within moments, only pools of viscous material remained where they had stood.

Rick gasped, his arm dropping as if the bones had been removed. His body cried out, aching all over, but Daniel caught him as he fell. "Such power isn't meant for a man," he said.

"I... What did I do?"

"You just purged your first demons. Well done. Now, let's get out of here. The Caretaker wants you."

Sweep. Sweep. Sweep.

Rick pushed himself up out of Daniel's arms and turned towards the staff door at the back. He took his first step towards it when something yanked him backwards.

He stared into the face of a monster.

Yet, it was a monster without a face. Beneath a thatch of clumped grey hair was a smooth, fleshy oval. Somehow, it still managed to stare into Rick's soul, and he felt himself tremble, not on the outside, but on the inside. Something sharp held a fierce grip on his soul and was pulling, tearing, yanking.

Rick tried to scream, but his lungs turned to cough syrup, and he gargled. Inside his aching skull he heard words. Clean, clean, clean. You shall be clean.

"Let go of him. As a Lord of Hell I command you."

Rick felt the grip on his soul loosen, but not completely. The abomination still had him. That empty, featureless face still looked down on him.

"I said let go!"

Rick felt himself being pulled savagely, but this time it was his body, not his mind. Daniel had him by the arm and was yanking him like a rag doll. They stumbled towards the back door.

The Caretaker produced a broom and swept up the messy puddles left by the demons. And he whistled.

Without a mouth, the abomination whistled.

It was a merry tune.

Daniel dragged Rick out the back door of the petrol station and into a small stockroom. The fire door at the back was hanging open, and they spilled through it into the awaiting night.

Daniel huffed and puffed, sweat pouring from his face. Despite being at death's door only an hour ago, the Fallen Angel had once again been called upon to rescue Rick. How much longer could Daniel keep going?

"We need to find your brother."

"D-down the road," Rick muttered as he tried to move on his own steam. He took one step after the other, but each movement threatened to floor him. "H-he let me go, The Caretaker. You made him."

"I did no such thing," said Daniel wearily. "I surprised him, caught his interest, but he didn't let you go. You're a mouse, Rick. The Caretaker wants you, but first he wants to play. You have Angel blood inside of you, and he's never cleansed an Angel before. He'll be coming after you, Rick. No matter where we go."

"Then what do we do?"

"For now, we find your brother."

But when they made it to the car dealership, Keith was not there.

4

Daniel helped ease Rick onto the bonnet of an expensive saloon. The bodywork dented, but the time for worrying about property damage was over. Corpses lay everywhere—salesmen and customers alike.

In the darkness, their silhouettes threatened to leap to life at any moment. It was only upon closer inspection that their caved in faces told the truth—that they were long dead.

Rick always thought dead bodies were supposed to reek enough to make a man gag, but so far his nose detected only a subtle meat smell—like old bacon.

"They didn't wait for us," Rick moaned. He could forgive his brother fleeing back at the petrol station, but to not even wait for him…

It didn't feel right. Keith might have put his own safety first, but Maddy wouldn't have. She'd been the first one of them to stand and fight back at the petrol station. In fact, she was the least afraid of them all. Rick supposed the death of her husband figured into that. Did she even care if she died? Maybe she did, and that was why she, Keith, and Diane had reached the car dealership and kept on running.

Rick was alone.

And the Caretaker was coming.

"What exactly happened back there?" Rick asked Daniel. "What did I do to those demons?"

"You expunged a demon back to hell. An exorcism of sorts, but as the demons were inhabiting their own bodies, their souls departed and left their bodies as empty vessels. They'll be stuck in Hell now, part of the essence of the place, unless…"

"Unless what?"

"Unless they possess a human being."

"I thought demons couldn't do that because of the iron in our blood?"

"The iron in a human being's blood only prevents a Heavenly creature from possessing a human. It was a way for God to ensure that Angels could never abuse his creation or escape to earth. The lowliest inhabitants of hell, however—the peasants if you will—they can inhabit a human being because they were once human themselves."

"What are you saying? That if the demons on earth don't kill us, the souls still trapped in Hell will possess us?"

Daniel shook his head. "No. Possessing a human isn't easy. To reach out from Hell... Let's just say, it's not something you're in danger of right now. We should try to find the others. They must be near. They left only ten minutes before we did."

"Yeah, but they were running, and we were limping."

Daniel pulled a face. "Good point. Maybe we can use one of these cars."

"You saw the roads. We wouldn't get past a block."

"Can you walk?"

Rick pressed his fingers against himself, probing for injury. It was conclusive—everywhere hurt. But he could move.

"I can manage. How about you, Daniel? You don't look good."

As if embarrassed, Daniel stood straighter. "This body won't last forever, not with the strain I keep putting it under. If I don't rest up and heal soon I won't be able to help you anymore."

"You said I took part of your... essence. Is there any way I can give it back?"

"Yes."

"How?"

"By dying."

"Right, so let's not go with Option A."

Daniel smiled, the first time in a while. "You really think your brother would abandon you?"

Rick snorted. "Keith is one of the most selfish people I know, but I don't think he would. He loves me, in his way."

"Then what happened to him?"

"That's the part that worries me. Maddy and Diane are with him."

Daniel hobbled over to the lot's office and peered inside. It was locked up tight, with only a single window cracked. "I suppose we pick a direction and hope for the best."

Rick hated the uncertainty of it, but he lacked a better solution. They had left The Caretaker less than half a mile away, and he could be upon them again very soon.

You're a mouse, Rick.

And the cat is coming.

Rick glanced at the road. It split off in two directions via a junction. The junction led to Crapstone, one of the first places to be hit by the demon invasion. The other route led towards the motorway. Their plan had been to head towards the motorway.

"We go this way." Rick pointed. "Crapstone is dangerous, but this way leads to the motorway. Keith would have stuck to the plan."

Daniel nodded. "Seems sensible to me. Let's just hope your brother didn't take to the fields."

Rick looked on at the farmland bordering the rear of the car dealership and thought it was a distinct possibility. If Keith had escaped across the fields, the route Rick was about to take would carry him in the opposite direction. He might never see the others again.

"Here goes nothing."

Rick and Daniel exited the car dealership and started down the road. With the lampposts dead, it was like walking through an abyss, the moon—a bare sliver—giving off little in the way of light.

"So, you really knew Lucifer?" Rick asked after five minutes or so.

Daniel glanced sideways and seemed uncomfortable. "Yes."

"What is he like?"

"Arrogant. But fair. He believed God had no right to rule the lives of Angels—that such beings of great beauty and intelligence should be free. Many of us agreed with him, and Lucifer posited that if Angels contemplated revolting to gain their freedom, then they were entitled to it. A lowly creature does not care if it is free or not, only that it is fed, warm, and safe. A creature such as an Angel or man yearns to make its own decisions. Lucifer dreamt of a Heaven where Angels were free to fashion their own destinies. He was the first democrat, with God a Monarch needing to be unseated."

"You believe that too, Daniel?"

He shrugged. "God is great, and his compassion endless, but he is also in a position of eternal dilemma. Every decision He makes helps some and hurts others. Whichever side is suffering most will inevitably blame him and desire freedom from His will. I believe God should bestow the same indifference upon Angels that he has done on mankind. For millennia, he has stood back and refused to interfere on earth, even while millions of you cry out for him. Yet, he keeps his angels on the tightest of leashes. It is something I do not understand, nor ever will."

"So you would still join Lucifer if you ever had to do it over again?"

Daniel frowned. "And spend eternity in Hell? No thank you. Despite what I think, I now understand that God made me, and that gives him the right to do whatever he wishes. Since being cut off from Heaven, it's made me realise how much I was a part of it, and it a part of me. I yearn to be back home, and despair that I never will be. Hell is a place of torment and pain, yet it is the lack of love that hurts most. The lack of a gentle touch or friendly word is enough to make a soul brittle, forever on the edge of shattering. It is a lonely place. You have no idea how lonely."

Rick shuddered. "I can't believe Hell is real. That people go there."

"People do not go there. Monsters do. You are not a monster, Rick. You will never see Hell."

"Even though I've been an atheist my entire life?"

Daniel shrugged. "A product of society. It is not your fault that your parents did not instil in you belief, or that your era is dominated by science. How could God blame a child for not believing in him when that child was never told of his existence? The metrics of old no longer exist. All that matters now is a person's virtue. Do good and you will be rewarded. Choose a path of strength, and it will lead you to paradise."

"Then should you not be allowed back into Heaven one day, Daniel? You are doing good now."

A shroud fell over the angel's face, even darker than the shadows either side of them. "No."

"But—"

"I said, no. There is no forgiveness for one who has looked upon the Abyss. My presence, my knowledge of the damned, it would taint Heaven. Only purity exists there. My soul is tarnished."

Rick said no more. They walked in silence for an hour after that, until they neared the motorway's entrance. Instead of heading down the slip road though, they carried on to the roundabout and peered over the railings at the wide road below. In the pitch-black darkness, the line of cars abandoned end to end seemed like a giant endless snake—a steel serpent without end. But while the great serpent remained still, there was movement.

People were alive down there.

Rick leant over the railing and pointed. "Other survivors."

Daniel pulled him back and shushed him. "Take a closer look."

Rick frowned. There were people. Rick saw them moving in the darkness—human movement, not the erratic, inhuman shuffling of the demons.

But then he realised that there were demons too.

Rick watched survivors walking with demons. The survivors moved in a line, demons at the front and back.

"What are they doing?" Rick turned to Daniel. "What the fuck are they doing?"

"Keep your voice down!"

Rick pursed his lips and glanced back down at the motorway. With no light to see by, it was impossible to make out individuals in the line. They were tied together—or chained—like a line of slaves in an old movie. The demons were hustling them along like cattle.

Being led to slaughter?

"Why are the demons not killing them?" Rick kept his voice low. "Why are they moving them along?"

Daniel sighed. "Remember what I was saying about possession? All those disembodied souls in hell? What you're looking at is a production line of brand new cars."

"I don't understand."

"These people will be used as vessels to house demon souls."

Rick felt sick. The sight of people below being led to their doom like lambs... "How?"

"Best not to go into that," said Daniel, "but they can only be possessed in proximity to a gate. They need to be near Hell for a disembodied soul to reach out and grab them."

Rick started towards the slip road.

"Rick, where are you going?"

"To help those people."

Daniel hurried after him. "Are you mad? There's probably thirty demons down there."

"And three times as many humans. If we free the survivors, we can overpower them."

"You're naive, Rick. Even if there were three hundred survivors down there, they're afraid and weak. They'll fall like flies."

"We have to do something. Maddy might be down there."

Daniel raised an eyebrow.

Rick grunted. "What? Why are you looking at me like that?"

"Just find it interesting that your biggest concern is Maddy and not your brother."

Now that he considered it, Rick wasn't sure about the reason either, but he tried not to over think it. "Because my brother is an asshole."

Daniel nodded. "Yeah, he is."

"What if this is the reason they weren't at the car dealership waiting for us? What if they were captured? I won't stand back and allow all those people to be possessed. We're at war, Daniel, you said it yourself, and right there is an enemy supply route. If we do nothing, all those people will end up being used by the enemy as tools. If we free them, they will add to our strength. So whose side are you on, Daniel? Are you truly here to help or not?"

Daniel shook his head slowly and glared at Rick as if he wanted to slap him. Quietly, he said, "I am here to help. I am on your side. If that is not clear by now—"

"Then prove it, Daniel! Time to commit. Not just to helping me, but helping the cause. This is war, and we need to hit back. That travesty down there is our chance. I don't have a choice—my friends and family might be down there. You don't have to help me, but I'm going either way."

Rick started walking, ducking his head and creeping towards the slip road that would take him onto the motorway. He wondered how well demons could see in the dark. Not well, he hoped.

Daniel appeared beside him, also ducking. "You're going to get killed, you know that?"

"It's a risk I'm willing to take. Like you said, only place I'll be going is Heaven. So what's to fear?"

Daniel didn't reply, but something about the anxious expression on his face made Rick worry. What wasn't Daniel telling him?

They reached the motorway ducking behind an abandoned lorry. The chain gang was a hundred metres ahead, the nearest demon far enough away that hiding was easy. The problem would be when the sun came up, or if the whole group of them stopped to make some sort of camp. Then Rick would have to think more seriously about what he planned on doing. Following them was his only plan for now, but eventually he'd have to act.

How would he take down thirty demons?

Was it even possible?

He was going to find out.

Vamps

"**Y**O, VAMPS, I can't do this, man."

They had just come to the aid of some Chinese tourists and things had got heavy. They'd ended up retreating across the Thames and were now even closer to the danger zone. It had left all of them shaken. Vamps looked at Ginge and shook his head. "You've seen what's happening to our streets, Ginge. We don't got no choice but to help out. Things are fucked. People need us."

Ginge had grown pale, as he always did when he was tired. It made his red hair stand out even more. His expression was the same as Vamps' five-year old nephew, Bradley, when he wanted sweets but got cabbage. "Vamps, man, we ain't heroes. We gangsters."

"Yeah, we gangsters, and another gang is moving onto our turf."

Ravy joined the conversation. "I never signed up to fight no monsters."

"Me either," said Mass, shrugging to express that he was up for it anyway. "Just the way it is."

Vamps looked at the bricks and broken glass covering the roads and pathways below. "We never signed on for nothing. We were born and raised, yo. This fight came to us. We go out and we help, just like we did yesterday. We stopped some bird from getting raped. Do you not get that? She's probably alive because of us."

"Vamps is right," said Mass. "I like how it feels. I mean, what's going down is shit, but I liked the feeling when we helped people yesterday."

Ravy sighed. "Fine, but eventually we gonna die. This ain't the boys from West Ham, this is some serious shit. Not to mention that psycho, Pusher, is on our case."

"Way I see it," said Vamps, "the chances of us dying are pretty high whatever we do. Least this way we get to go down swinging."

Ginge sighed. He looked over the roof ledge and went silent. A moment later, he said, "All right, I'm in. What's the plan?"

Vamps grinned. "We go out and head towards the first scream we hear. Arm up, boys, today ain't gonna be the day we die."

They grabbed their weapons and headed into the stairwell. On the third floor they were forced to stop when they stumbled upon a body.

"Ah, fuck, man," said Ginge.

The lad's face was a mess, half of it missing. Ravy covered his mouth and gagged.

"Guess that explains the gunshot we heard last night."

Vamps reached up and took the green beanie hat from his head. He knelt down and placed it over the car-jacker's ruined face. "Time I gave this back to you, blud. Sorry you got in the middle of this."

Mass didn't look as cocky as usual, and instead of slapping his fist he wrung his hands. "Pusher shot the poor bastard in the face. That's cold."

"He's lost it," said Ginge.

Vamps glanced at the dead car-jacker and nodded. "I think a lot of people have lost it at the moment. Let's get out of here."

The fighting in the city had continued through the night, but the city had grown quiet now. Cold too, with the dawn sunlight insufficient for bringing warmth. Dead bodies littered the street and started to smell, yet the scent of blood was not as pervasive as the pong of shit. Vamps had never seen a dead person—not until he'd killed the rapist yesterday—but it seemed like they all shit their kecks before moving on. It wouldn't be long before the streets teemed with disease. Perhaps tonight they would finally head out and make for the coast.

Right now though, they had to patrol the streets. When this war ended, and if they lived, they might just get some respect. No more being kept down by society because of being young and broke. They would be warriors. When the shit hit, the upper classes were nowhere to be seen. No middle-class heroes in a ground war.

A jet flew overhead—gone as quickly as it arrived.

"Hey," Ginge pointed. "Something's going on down there."

Vamps put a hand over his eyes to shield his sight from the rising sun. He thought he saw a bus in the distance "Piccadilly circus. If that's a working bus, why the hell isn't it trying to bounce? They should be fleeing as fast as the wheels will take them."

The brightly lit signs on the corner of Piccadilly Circus were scorched and blackened from fires in the shop below. The bus stopped. It was no city bus or open-topped tourist coach, but a plain white bus with darkened windows. The air brakes hissed, and the exit door folded open. A man in a grey suit exited and lit a cigarette. Vamps' street senses acted up. Something was wrong about the bus driver. He was too calm—the way he stood in the street smoking like nothing had happened. A pile of torn-up bodies lay not ten feet away from him.

"Hold back, yo." Vamps put an arm up. He crept to the side of the street, sliding in and out of the alcoves to keep his approach hidden. Somebody else got off the bus—another man in a suit. This one was younger than the other and as stocky as a wrestler. He had long blond hair like a young Hulk Hogan. In his hand, he held a length of chain and yanked on it. The first in a line of handcuffed men and woman spilled out of the bus, the chain attached to their throats.

"Is it a prison bus?" asked Ravy.

Vamps shook his head. "No way. Travelling prisoners wear matching uniforms to stop 'em runnin' and blendin' in. I know because they moved me from Belmarsh to Brixton after some fuckers from Angell Town tried to off me. I had to wear this shitty grey tracksuit. Those people over there are wearing their own clothes."

"Then who are they?" asked Ginge.

Mass put a hand on the pavement and ducked lower, almost prone. "Who are the dudes in suits?"

"I dunno," said Vamps. "Let's watch what happens."

They moved over to a delivery van and stooped behind it. Vamps stuck out his head to see what was happening. The two suited gentlemen brought the line of prisoners into the middle of the road and made them kneel. A sleek black Mercedes pulled out of a side street. It parked up, and a chauffeur stepped out and opened the rear door.

Vamps covered his mouth when he saw who exited next. "No freakin' way!"

Ginge frowned. "Who is it? You know that dude?"

"Yeah, man. That's the fucking Prime Minister."

Mass whistled. "That skinny fucker is the PM? We should go over. If we help him, we'll have it made, yo."

"Innit," said Ravy. "I voted for that guy. He said he would stop war in the Middle East."

Mass raised an eyebrow. "You voted, buster?"

"Yeah! My dad said our vote is what makes us all equal."

Vamps was certain the man was John Windsor, Prime Minister, his jet-black moustache a dead giveaway. In a black suit, he strolled before the line of prisoners and spoke with the jailors. The chained men and woman pleaded and begged when they saw their reigning PM, but the man acted as though they weren't even there. One woman sought to rise to her feet, but the chauffeur hurried over and kicked her kneecap. She screamed and grabbed herself. The chauffeur shut her up by kicking the teeth out of her mouth. He left her there choking on blood.

"What the fuck, yo," said Mass.

Vamps clutched his grandfather's Browning, making sure it was still there. "This shit smells wrong."

"Yeah," said Ginge, uncharacteristically brave. His outrage had overtaken his fear. "We should go pop that motherfucker right in the mouth. He cut my nan's benefits last year."

Vamps had been about to break cover, but he leapt back down when he spotted demons spilling into Piccadilly Circus.

"What the fuck?" said Mass, his face dropping. "There're hundreds of them. We need to bounce."

Vamps agreed, but he couldn't help but watch. The Prime Minister and his companions seemed unafraid of the demons, even as the line of prisoners screamed in terror. The demons surrounded the area until Vamps could no longer see what was happening.

"I'm fucking off," said Mass.

Vamps nodded. "I'll meet you at the Lyceum. I'll be right behind you."

"What are you talking about?" said Ginge. "We need to get out of here."

Vamps waved his hand. "Get the hell out of here, boys. The Lyceum. I'll be there. I promise."

They didn't seem to like it, but they got going, and once they fell out of sight, Vamps turned around and climbed up onto the van's roof to get a better view. The demons were not attacking the PM. In fact, Windsor seemed to address them as though they were his goddamn constituents. One creature—a burnt man at least a foot taller than its fellow demons and sporting singed dreadlocks—stood directly in front of the PM and nodded his head obediently.

Then the strangest thing happened: one of the human jailors in charge of the line of prisoners handed over their chains to one of the burnt men. The demon led the frightened people away. Windsor headed back towards his Mercedes, smiling. Vamps had been around dealers most his life, and he had just seen a deal go down for sure. Sure as shit.

But what the hell was the deal?

And what the fuck was the Prime Minister doing out here trading the lives of innocent men and women to these demons?

The anger the question summoned made Vamps grip his gun tightly, his finger tickling the trigger.

But it would be suicide to fire a shot. The demons had only just left. It was time to leave.

Vamps crept to the edge of the van, about to climb down when he heard a shout. "Hey, you over there!"

Vamps had been spotted.

Oh hell no.

With no time to waste, Vamps threw himself from the top of the van to the ground below. As he hit the pavement, his ankle folded sideways. Electricity ran up his right knee.

God dammit.

Vamps hoisted himself up and hobbled away, glancing back over his shoulder. The PM dove back inside his Mercedes like an attempt had been made on his life, but his cronies gave chase. They were much faster than Vamps, and the fact he had a gun would not help him, because they carried some of their own. Bigger ones.

The only question now was who would get to Vamps first—his boys or the bad guys. No way did he want to end up in chains like those people. Shit just got worse.

He ducked into a side street, heading towards the Lyceum. He thought about leading his pursuers away from Ginge, Mass, and Ravy, but he too afraid to play hero right now. He needed his friends. His family.

He needed help.

But the Lyceum lay a couple blocks away. He wasn't going to make it.

Blindly, Vamps threw back his arm and fired off a shot. The report was loud and made his temples thud, but he didn't miss a step and kept running. He got up to running speed, but a sprint was beyond him.

He fired another shot behind him.

Then another.

Then they were firing back at him.

Vamps dodged behind a vegetable cart on the pavement and threaded himself between two parked cars. His chest heaved in and out.

Another shot rang out. A car window shattered.

Fuck me, I'm gonna die out here in the street. Just like my ma always worried I would.

Another shot hit the ground in front of him, kicking up chips of whatever shit roads were made of. Vamps realised he was moaning out loud as the fear escaped from his throat.

Then his boys appeared, looking dazed and confused, but there to help him. They had his back.

Mass led them down the road. Vamps waved an arm for them to take cover. "They've got guns. They've—"

Another shot rang out and sailed so close to Vamp's head he felt the wind on his ear. Panic seized him, and his legs turned to jelly. He wobbled and fell. The road rose to meet his chin and suddenly he was laying on the ground as stiff as a board. The sound his body made sliding along the ground was like a watermelon hitting concrete. The Browning tumbled from his hand and clinked against the curb.

"All of you, down now!" One of the PM's men shouted.

Vamps drew his head back and watched Mass freeze. His hands went up, and he got down on his knees. His expression could have melted ice, but his rage wasn't enough to stop a bullet, so he did as he was told. Ravy and Ginge too.

The PM's men split off to opposite sides of the road, keeping Vamps and the others in the middle. The cronie on Vamps' left was dark-haired where his partner was blond. It was the blond who grabbed Vamps and shoved him roughly to his feet. Vamps eyed up the Browning in the gutter.

"Don't do anything stupid," said the blond. "I'll leave you to die right here in the gutter, you peace of shit."

Vamps gave up on the gun. Instead, he turned towards his captor. "The fuck you doing working with the demons?"

"This is London. It's all about the politics. If you aren't with the reigning party, you get stepped on."

Vamps glowered. "They'll string you up for this."

"When? Haven't you had your eyes open? This isn't a war, it's a coup. Humanity isn't top of the tree anymore, and never will be again."

Vamps felt dizzy, his chin throbbing, and he was too nauseous to fight. Mass, however, cursed and swung a punch. He knocked the other guy right on his arse and snatched the gun from his hand. He spun on the blond man holding Vamps and looked like he was about to pull the trigger. Then his arm fell slowly to his side. His jaw fell open, even as the PM's cronie leapt back his feet and struck him upside the head and knocked him out cold.

Vamps turned around to see what had stopped his friend in mid-fight. It wasn't hard to figure things out.

The seven-foot demon with long black dreadlocks grinned like a deranged monster—exactly what it was. Demons filled the entire road like a football mob.

"Ah, what do we have here?" said the dread-locked monster in a thick Jamaican accent. "More fuel for de fire. Take dem to de warehouse."

The demons in the road parted as Vamps and his boys were led away.

2

Vamps' arms were numb by the time he was led inside the warehouse at the back of the theatre district. His blond captor had shoved his hands so far up behind his back that he could scratch his own head.

They were now inside some kind of prop factory. Mannequins stood before massive wooden backdrops. Pretend cars parked beside plywood furniture and cabinets. One wall was almost entirely lined with masks, including one that looked an awful lot like Shrek.

"You better hope I don't get another shot at you," Mass told the brunette cronie, who now sported a rather severe black eye.

Ginge and Ravy were silent, afraid. Instinctively, they moved together.

The blond prodded Vamps in the back with his gun. "In here!"

Vamps staggered into a cage full of people, perhaps two dozen. It was meant to be a storage cage for the warehouse stock, but it had been turned into a prison. Those inside all wore blank expressions. A young woman in the corner had pissed herself, sitting with her bare feet in the puddle.

Mass went in behind Vamps. The door swung shut and locked them in. Their two jailors left.

"I'm going to kick the shit out of those fuckers," said Mass, smashing his fist against the cage and making the whole thing rattle.

"Chill out," said Ravy. "You're going to bring them back."

"Good! You think I want to rot in here? They best come back so I can snap their necks."

Ravy folded his arms. "Look, man. We alive. Let's just be grateful right now. I'm tired of this shit. I want to see my family again one day."

Vamps said nothing. His ankle was swollen and causing him pain, but it kept him lucid. He looked around at his new companions and saw they had been frightened beyond the point of usefulness. These weren't gangsters from Brixton or hooligans from West Ham. They were city workers and shoppers—ordinary people used to worrying about car tax and mortgage payments, not demon invasions or being locked up. Come to think of it, who on earth really was ready for this shit?

Ginge pressed his forehead up against the cage and started panting. His cheeks grew bright red, but his clammy forehead looked like it had been rubbed with chalk.

Vamps patted his friend on the back. "We'll be okay, man. I promise."

Ginge sighed, keeping his head pressed up against the cage. "We should have made a run for it like everybody else. What the hell were we doing?"

"We were doing what was right. Hold your head high because we didn't run."

Ravy joined in. "Yeah, Ginge. You a gangster. For real. The only reason I stuck around was because you did. I was like, if Ginge has got the balls to face this, then so do I."

Vamps patted him on the back again. "Be proud, man."

Ginge sighed. "How can I be proud when I wanted to run the whole time? It's only because you and Mass were so down with sticking around that I didn't have a choice."

"You had a choice, Ginge," said Vamps. "You stuck by me because you're brave. You didn't tuck tail and run like the rest of this city because that's not how you roll."

Ravy put a hand on Ginge's back and rubbed gently. "We family, man. We stick together no matter what. We stick together."

Vamps looked at Ravy and nodded. "We stick together."

Ginge lifted his head away from the cage, a criss-cross indentation pressed into his forehead. "And now we're going to die together."

"Got that right!"

Vamps looked up just in time to see a punch flying at his face. It clocked him on the point of his chin and sent him reeling backwards. He stumbled over his bad ankle and ended up on his arse.

Pusher glared down at him, a snarl on his face. "You crossed the wrong motherfucker. You think you can crash my pad and wave a gun in my face? Karma's a bitch." He kicked out at Vamp's head, but was knocked off balance by Mass who shoved him up against the cage. Mass, in turn, was set upon by two of Pusher's guys who emerged from the crowd and smacked him in the back of the head. A fight broke out. Those not involved scurried to the edges of the cage.

Vamps leapt up quickly. He grabbed Pusher's shoulders and planted a head-butt on the bridge of the bastard's nose. Enraged, he growled and retaliated with a kick to Vamp's stomach. Both of them staggered backwards, nursing their pain.

Vamps clenched his fists by his sides.

Pusher did the same.

Ginge fell on the floor and screamed as one of Pusher's boys punched him in the ribs. Mass came up behind the guy and lifted him off the ground, slamming him down on the concrete hard enough that he didn't get back up. "Welcome to cage-fighting, bitch! I'll be your guide."

Vamps dodged towards Pusher. "I will knock your fucking teeth out."

Pusher leered. "You can try."

The two of them crashed together, whirling dervishes as their limbs lashed out at one another as they spun in a brutal dance. Pusher clubbed Vamps in the ear. Vamps planted a kick to Pusher's left knee. Both of them snarled, their pain masked by adrenaline.

A gunshot stopped the fight as quickly as it had started. Everyone inside the cage froze. Vamps and Pusher faced each other, both of them panting, both of them bleeding, but they didn't make a further move.

The two cronies appeared, each of them brandishing guns. The blond's gun smoked from the recent gunshot. It was Vamps' grandfather's Browning. "What the hell is going on here?" he asked.

Vamps kept his eyes on Pusher. "What's it look like?"

"It looks like you're causing trouble. I don't like troublemakers."

"Then perhaps you shouldn't go around kidnapping them."

The blond man scowled. "Who started this?"

Vamps looked at Pusher accusingly, but he said nothing. He wasn't about to snitch on anybody—not even a piece of shit like Pusher.

"We're sorry," said Ravy, his voice cracking. "We'll be quiet."

The blond man approached the cage and stared at Ravy. "Do you promise?"

Ravy nodded. "Yes."

"Okay. Good. Just tell me who started it. You can tell me. I'm not a bad guy. Name's Barry."

Ravy stepped back from the cage. "I... Nobody started it. It just happened."

Barry kept his eyes on Ravy. He spoke slowly. "Who started it?"

"No one, like I—"

Bang.

In a fraction of a second, Barry brought up the Browning and yanked the trigger. The people inside the cage went wild, erupting like monkeys at the zoo. Vamps was knocked sideways and re-twisted his ankle.

Barry held up the smoking Browning and smiled. "Got quite the kick on her. Guess they don't make them like they used to."

Vamps tried to speak, but he was too much in shock. He crawled along on his stomach, fighting his way through the panicked crowd. "Get out of my fucking way. Move!"

He climbed up onto his knees and shoved his way passed a fat guy in a suit. Then he found himself face to face with Pusher. This time, though, Pusher didn't raise his fists. He looked at Vamps anxiously, then moved his eyes to the side.

"Look!"

Vamps spotted Ravy lying on the floor and clambered over to his friend. The bullet had struck his chest, and his breaths came out in whistles. "Ravy, fuck man. You're gonna be okay."

"He's fucked," said one of Pusher's guys, but Mass shut him up by punching him in the side of the head.

"Shut the fuck up, bitch."

Pusher didn't react to his boy getting beat down. He stood behind Vamps in silence, looking down at Ravy as he lay on the floor panting.

Ravy tried to speak, but all that came out was, "S-sorry."

Then he was gone. Vamps lifted him across his lap and held him in his arms. It was a long time before he could let go.

3

Vamps and Mass placed Ravy up beside the back wall and covered him with a blanket they snatched from a frightened young couple in the corner. The man and woman would have to deal with being chilly, because Vamps wasn't about to leave Ravy where everyone could gawp at him. He deserved better than that.

During this time, Pusher and his two boys kept their distance and nursed their wounds. Vamps, Mass, and Ginge had wounds of their own, but the worst pain was in their hearts.

Ravy was dead, and no matter how Vamps looked at it, he knew it was his fault. He'd been insistent that they stick around in the city. It had always been a crazy thing to do, but now it seemed downright absurd. What had he been thinking? Why was he so stupid?

"This is messed up," said Mass, his thick arms folded in a nervous gesture that was entirely unlike him. "I... I can't deal with this anymore. Ravy is gone. He's really gone, isn't he?"

Vamps had no words, so he embraced his friend briefly and let go. Mass would be okay, to a point. It was Ginge who needed looking after.

Since watching his best friend get shot, the big guy had sat up against the wall, rocking back and forth gently and staring at the blood on the floor.

Vamps shuffled down beside him. "You okay?"

Ginge didn't even acknowledge he'd been asked a question.

"Ginge, man. Let me hear you. Are you still with us?"

Ginge blinked. His eyes brimmed with tears.

"It's the shock." Pusher crouched in front of them both and examined Ginge with a quick glance. "I had a buddy who went the same way when he saw his sister jump off the roof of his tower block."

Vamps frowned at his enemy. "Back up. I don't need to be seeing you right now."

"Fair enough. Just letting you know I call a truce. No good to be fighting each other right now when we have a bigger enemy."

"I said back up."

Pusher sighed, but kept his palms up, and he moved away. "Sorry for your loss, G."

Vamps went back to his friend. "Ginge, man, we need to find a way out of this."

Ginge stared into space.

Vamps sighed and got back to his feet. If Ginge needed time, okay, but they still needed to find a way out of this cage. Vamps couldn't afford to sit around and do nothing. All the same, he was surprised when he saw the Prime Minister standing on the other side of the steel mesh.

The prisoners all gawped as the leader of the country stood before them proudly, his chin lifted towards the ceiling. His black moustache twitched as he spoke. "I'm extremely sorry for your ordeal. It is never my intention to watch any citizen of this great nation suffer. Unfortunately, certain sacrifices need to be made in times of exceptional circumstance."

"Why are you doing this?" one of the prisoners asked.

The PM seemed pained by the question. He reached up and ran his long fingers over his bony chin. "I am faced with difficult decisions, ma'am, but my number one priority is keeping people safe. All of you here are safe, I assure you. You need not worry. I implore you to cooperate and understand that everything that is happening is happening in the interests of this nation."

"Are you fucking deluded?" asked Pusher. "You're caging people like animals. I have a goddamn son I need to get back to."

Windsor scanned the crowd and located Pusher. "Would you rather be dead like everyone else? I have saved you by bringing you here. Don't you see that? I am working with our guests to ensure a peaceful handover of the city."

Vamps couldn't believe what he was hearing. He'd seen a handover all right—a handover of innocent people to demons. No wonder the Army didn't get the city under control. Their leader was in cahoots with the enemy. Had the demons likewise co-opted other world leaders? Was this less a war and more a hostile takeover?

But what if Windsor was being sincere? It was true they were alive rather than dead. What was the Prime Minister's angle? Why were they locked up in this cage?

Vamps stepped up to the cage and studied the PM. "Are you really trying to help us?"

Windsor gave a politician's grin which gave away nothing. "Of course. I was elected to serve the people of Great Britain. I assure you I am doing all I can."

"I know where there are more people in need of rescuing," said Vamps, deciding to test the PM's reasoning. "Let me out of here, and I'll take you to them."

Windsor tilted his head with interest and took another step towards the cage. "Tell me where they are, and I'll go get them. They'll be brought right here into safety."

Vamps shook his head. "No deal. You let me and my friends out, and I'll show you."

Windsor went silent. He studied Vamps with his dark eyes until a small laugh escaped his lips. "A good attempt, my friend, but I'm afraid you'll have to lie a lot better to fool me. Good try. I can see I must keep an eye on you." He pointed a finger and wagged it like a school-teacher telling off a pupil. "Bravo."

Vamps reached through the cage and grabbed the PM's finger. He twisted it and yanked Windsor up against the cage.

Everyone gasped.

The PM was silent, his jaw locked, his eyes narrowed. "Unhand me immediately."

Vamps held the PM in place for a few seconds, suddenly realising how rash he had just been. The sight of the smug prick made him lash out, but now he had crossed a line that would probably result in him getting a bullet like Ravy. "P-Please, sir," he said. "Just let me out of here. I can tell you anything you want. I know the city—the parts you don't. I know where you can find all sorts of things. I can be useful to a man like you. Please let me out."

Windsor yanked his hand back and moved away. He straightened out his suit and offered Vamps a look of contempt. "I will have no deal-ings with the likes of you. There's nothing you know that I do not, I assure you. You should be ashamed of yourself for trying to prostitute yourself. What kind of example are you setting to your fellow citizens? We are not mercenaries, and I will not abide the services of one. Good day to you all, and remember what I said: Cooperate and you will all remain safe."

The PM marched away, leaving Vamps slumped up against the oth-er side of the cage. From behind him, Pusher grunted. "Man, that was shameful. You were almost down on your knees ready to suck him off."

Even Mass was upset. "Yeah, man, that was pretty disgusting to watch."

Vamps made sure Windsor had gone before he spun to face the others. "Just doing what I had to do."

"For real?" asked Mass.

Vamps smirked. He shuffled his arm and allowed something to slide out of his cuff and into his hand. He examined the expensive fountain pen for the first time as he displayed it for Mass and Pusher. "I needed to distract the wanker while I half-inched this."

Pusher frowned. "You stole the Prime Minister's pen. Man, you really is small time."

Vamps sighed. "Don't you get it? They want to treat us like prisoners, we should act like prisoners. This pen is stainless steel and sharp as fuck. I just got me a prison shank, yo. Can't wait to use it."

Pusher stepped back, looking worried.

But Vamps had other targets in mind.

4

Vamps tried again to get a response from Ginge, but summoned only a solitary tear down his friend's left cheek. "Come on, Ginge. We're getting out of here, I promise, but I need you back in the game. Mass and me need your help."

Ginge blinked, and another tear spilled down his cheek. Vamps sighed and left him alone again. Pusher had been right—it was shock—but what were you supposed to do for someone in that situation? Was it right to leave them alone, or should Vamps be shaking Ginge roughly and slapping his face like they did in the movies.

Comedies mostly.

This was no comedy.

"He still being a whiny bitch?" Pusher folded his arms and pulled a face.

Vamps turned to him. "What did you just say?"

"He needs to man up. Thought he was a Brixton Boy?"

"He is."

"Then he should start acting like it."

"He was man enough to rob your ass yesterday."

Pusher shrugged. "Only after I robbed you pussies first."

Mass hulked up his shoulders, his massive trapezius muscles like the hood on a cobra. "You 'bout to get another beat down, blud. Then we'll learn who the pussy is, buster."

Pusher laughed. His boys moved up beside him, but he waved a hand to keep them back again. "Nah, lads, this is between me and the punk with pretty little gems in his pussy mouth."

That was the last straw. Vamps went at Pusher with both hands. He grabbed the back of his skull with his left and threw a punch with his right. Pusher took a fist right in the eye, but was quick to knee Vamps in the stomach and double him over. He followed it up with a hammer blow to the back of the head. Vamps hit the floor.

Pusher kicked him in the ribs.

Mass went to get involved, but Vamps waved him off, panting. "N-No! This is one-on-one."

"Yeah," said Pusher, grinning. "One man against one pussy." He smashed his fist against Vamps' cheek and almost knocked him out. It took everything he had to hold onto the last threads of consciousness.

Vamps moaned, tried to get up, but had his arm booted out from under him.

Another kick to the ribs.

"What is the meaning of this?" Barry marched into the warehouse, still clutching the Browning.

Pusher backed away, his hands out in front of him. "Hey, this guy is causing trouble again. It's all him."

"I... I need help," said Vamps from on the floor. "I need to tell the Prime Minister something. Just get me out of here and put me in another cage, and I'll tell you everything. This guy is going to kill me."

The suited man frowned, seeming to assess the situation before acting. "What do you know?"

"W-what don't I know?" said Vamps, spitting blood. "I know where there are people hiding out all over Brixton. I know where to get guns, drugs, money. You can have it all. Just get me somewhere safe, and I'll tell you."

"You're a fucking disgrace," said Mass. "I thought I knew you, Vamps."

Barry pointed the gun at Mass. "Quiet, you."

Then he unlocked the cage and stepped inside, keeping the Browning out in front of him the whole time. He knelt and patted Vamps with his free hand. "Okay, up! We're leaving, just you and me. You're going to snitch about everything you know."

Vamps scrambled to his feet. "Yeah, man. I swear. I'll tell you everything. One of the people in this cage has a weapon."

Barry backed up, raised the Browning in front of him. "Who?"

"Me!" Vamps shoved the fountain pen right into the bastard's jugular. The bleeding didn't start until he pulled it out again. Then, like a geyser, it exploded in great rhythmic bursts that covered everything. Barry grabbed his punctured neck and sprawled against the cage wall. Even as he was dying, he raised his arm to point the Browning at Vamps.

Pusher backhanded the man in the face and broke his nose. He dropped the gun, and he used the hand to cover his face as blood continued pouring out of him. Then his legs gave way, and he collapsed onto his knees.

Mass leapt forward and booted the piece of shit in the chest, knocking him onto his back where he went still. "It's just politics, bitch!"

Vamps examined the bloody fountain pen in his hand and grimaced with disgust. He had just killed his second man in as many days. He tossed the pen to the ground, yet somehow he knew the killing wasn't done. With that in mind, he knelt to pick up his grandfather's Browning. Pusher attempted to do the same, and they ended up face-to-face with both their hands hovering over the antique pistol.

The next two seconds seemed to last forever. The air went out of the room. Nobody spoke.

Pusher backed away, grinning. "Hey, man. I was just picking it up for you."

Vamps gathered the Browning and straightened up. "I believe you. Let's just get out of here."

Pusher nodded to his boys. "Come on."

They filtered out of the cage, but Vamps noticed that many of the prisoners remained—too scared to move? Vamps turned, unable to abandon them without thought. "You stay in there you'll die. Take five minutes, think things through, then decide how you want to spend what's left of your lives."

Mass helped Ginge up off the floor, and together with Vamps, they got moving. Ahead, Pusher and his boys looked for weapons amongst the warehouse props. As long as Vamps was the only one with a gun, things might just turn out okay.

Mass readjusted his grip on Ginge. "Ginge, man, move your bloody legs. I ain't carrying you across London."

Vamps shot Mass a worried looked. "Maybe some fresh air will wake him up."

"Epping Forest it is then. Hey, you remember that time we went there to smoke weed and ended up getting lost?"

Vamps chuckled. "Yeah, man. Ravy went full-castaway after ten minutes. He was trying to make a fire and contemplating the rest of his life in the wild."

"He was high as fuck."

"We all were."

"Vamps?"

"Yeah, man?"

"What do you think we'll find out there?"

Vamps could think of only one answer. "More reasons to fight."

CAPT. Hernandez

DAWN WAS FAST arriving, which made the other ship all the more a ghostly visage. It had appeared from nowhere—from the shadows themselves—but it had brought the light with it. Salvation.

After leaving Captain Johnson on the helicopter deck, Hernandez fought his way to the ship's bow. It would have been impossible if not for the covering fire of the other ship. Several times, demons had set upon him only to explode into pieces under machine gunfire.

The men he had positioned atop the conning tower were still alive, and so was the group led by Lieutenant Danza. The other officer gave Hernandez a hearty salute. Things hadn't looked like they would end well for a moment there.

Hernandez staggered into the bridge, where Ensign Connelly had already patched him through to the Coast Guard frigate sitting at port-side. The other vessel's captain introduced himself as Captain Guy Granger.

Hernandez picked up the receiver. "Thank the Lord for you, Captain Granger. Thank the Lord. You saved our bacon. Once those things were onboard we couldn't stop them coming. It was you cutting them to ribbons on the water that turned the tide. Your men are heroes. Over."

"That they are, Captain. Over."

Hernandez sighed. "Not the captain. Commander Johnson died in the attack, a stray bullet from one of your men, I believe. I'm Lieutenant Hernandez. Over."

"I'm sorry about your commander," said the other captain. "My crew did the best they could. Over."

"I understand. Our decks were swamped with monsters. We would've lost far more men if you hadn't been here to help. Over."

"Do you know where those creatures came from, Lieutenant Hernandez? Over."

"Affirmative. Our radar picked up an anomaly on the seabed in this area. The things must have swum right up out of the depths. They were so bloated and malformed that they must have been sunk right down low. Over."

After a moment of silence, Captain Granger: "Then it appears these hell gates are beneath the oceans and on land. We should all keep an eye on the radar and steer a clear course. Over."

"Copy that, Captain. We fled Norfolk hoping to regroup, but ran right into another battle. Over."

"You were at Norfolk? So were we. Did you see how things ended there? Over."

Hernandez rubbed the back of his hand holding the receiver against his sweaty forehead, then put it to his mouth. "There's nothing left. The USS New Hampshire went under and took a thousand men with her, but several vessels got away. We count our blessings. Over."

A sad reply came back, yet not one seemingly ready to quit. "At least some of us got out alive. We're not beaten yet. Over."

Hernandez nodded, despite the other man not being able to see him. "Copy that, Captain. Gives us a chance to regroup and head back to coast. Now that you saved us, we'll be able to fight another day. Naval Command is operating out of Florida now, and all ships are to make their way to Jacksonville. It'll be a pleasure to have the Hatchet along for the ride. Over."

"Negative. The Hatchet is crossing the Atlantic. Over."

Hernandez frowned. Was there something he didn't know? "Why? Over."

"I have a personal matter to attend to. Over."

A personal matter, at a time like this, when the whole of the United States was under attack? Was the man off his meds? "We have orders to assemble at Jacksonville," Hernandez said plainly. "Disobey and you'll be considered a deserter. Over."

"Call it what you want," came Captain Granger. "I'm going to the UK to get my kids. Over."

"I can't allow you to do that, Captain Granger. The Hatchet is United States property, and your men have a duty to protect their country. You need to return to coast, or relinquish command to someone who will. Over."

Hernandez took a moment to inspect his crew—for they were now his—and saw they were bloody, panting, and badly shell-shocked. They needed a show of strength to rally behind. Danza stood nearby and was staring at Hernandez. Hard to read what the man was thinking.

"With all due respect, Lieutenant Hernandez, I don't take orders from you. Over."

Hernandez squeezed the handset and placed it right up against his mouth. This was a battle of authority, and if he had any chance of maintaining his integrity, he needed to show he was not a commander to be trifled with. Captain Granger had gone rogue, and that would not do. "The US Coast Guard has been ordered to relinquish command to the Navy. I am the senior naval officer in this region, and I am taking authority of your vessel. I will have one of my junior officers take command of your crew. Prepare to be boarded. Over and out."

"You sure about this?" asked Danza, quietly enough that no one else heard it.

Hernandez realised he had a lump in his throat and struggled to remove it before speaking. "We have a duty. The United States needs every one of its assets to help in its time of need. We cannot allow a rogue Coast Guard captain to steal a ship and crew right in front of us."

Danza nodded and seemed to agree. "You're right, but that Coast Guard captain just saved our lives."

"What's your point?"

"That if we fire on them and kill them, our own men will be con-flicted. If a fight breaks out, you'll be asking them to kill the people to whom they owe their lives. Americans."

"My crew owe their loyalty to the US Navy, nothing and no one else."

Danza nodded. "I don't think Captain Granger will lie down and let us board. He'll fight, which means we'll lose more men. Men we need right now."

"What exactly are you getting at, Danza?" Hernandez snapped.

"I feel it's my duty to play devil's advocate. Just tread carefully is all I'm saying. Sometimes you have to lose a few battles to win a war."

Hernandez disliked having to argue his case, but he hesitated a moment to consider Danza's words. Was the officer right? Had he committed to a winless action?

It was too late to change course. To back down would ruin any chance of gaining the crew's respect.

Hernandez gave his orders. The Augusta drifted in close enough that the hulls of the two ships almost touched. The remaining crew lined up along the railings, but they did not point their rifles—yet. Hernandez preferred the situation be concluded without gunfire, but would use whatever force necessary. Even after their losses, his crew still possessed two rifles for every one of the Hatchet's, and the Augusta itself had three times the armaments. They could sink the Hatchet if it came to it, but to do so would defeat the purpose of this whole action. Hernandez wanted command of the other ship—the beginning of his very own fleet that would sail back to the mainland and begin a quest of heroism and bravery.

Hernandez approached the railing, wondering if it put him at risk of a bullet, but knowing that he needed to show confidence. "Tell your men to stand aside, Captain Granger. I hereby seize this vessel in the name of the United States Navy."

Captain Granger stood at the opposite railing, also without a weapon—two generals meeting across the battlefield. "Your access is denied, Lieutenant Hernandez. I am the captain of this ship, and my word is law. Be grateful for your rescue, and take your men wherever you choose, but they will not come aboard this ship."

Hernandez narrowed his eyes, and spotted then that there were several civilians on board the Hatchet, besides the servicemen. "You have American citizens on board. Do you plan on kidnapping them?"

"No man or woman is here against their will. In fact, any who wish to join you now may do so." Granger turned around to look at his civilians, but not one of them stepped forward to leave.

"You have them scared," Hernandez remarked.

Granger smiled so widely that it was easy to see even at distance. "Considering you were all but dead in the water when we arrived, I think maybe it's you they are afraid of. The men on this ship survived the attack on New York, the attack on Norfolk, and now the attack on the USS Augustus. They are safer with me than anywhere else. They are survivors and—as my own Lieutenant called them earlier—warriors. We came to aid you in your time of need when running away would've been easier. My crew is fearless and ferocious. Come aboard if you dare, Lieutenant."

Hernandez laughed like a hyena. "You really think you will win a fight against my ship, Captain? You don't stand a chance."

"Perhaps, but are you willing to lose the men it will take to put us down? I promise that for every one of us you take, we'll take three of yours. We have two machineguns and my ship's main gun aimed at you, not to mention about a hundred rifles. I'm over-manned, you see. That's what happens when you win fights—you get stronger. I look at your crew, Lieutenant, and all I see is fear and exhaustion. They have lost their commander and inherited you. How long do you think they will tolerate your command if you force them to kill fellow Americans? Fellow Americans who just saved their lives. Or perhaps they won't have to tolerate you much longer. Maybe the very first shot fired will be right at your forehead. You're a pretty good shot, aren't you, Lieutenant Tosco?"

Another officer on board the Hatched raised his riflescope to his eye and grinned. "Aye, aye, Captain. I can shoot the nut-sack off a navy officer from a hundred metres. In fact, I'm ready to pull the trigger right now."

The situation was slipping from Hernandez's grasp, and he knew it. Bile burned at the back of his throat. He tried to respond but tripped over his own words and ended up offering nothing but bluster. He shifted uncomfortably and retreated a step. The small act of moving away sent a shiver of unease among the crew and Hernandez saw them waver, uncertainty in their eyes. Captain Granger had used the same thinking that Danza had warned of, and now that the man had voiced it, it was in the men's heads. Could they commit to a firefight after hearing the facts so plainly stated? Hernandez was being made to look like a petty bully.

Captain Granger came back through the radio. "Look, Commander Hernandez, I see you're a good man—a good American—but after Norfolk, it became every man for himself. We all need to do whatever we can in whatever way we can to make a difference. The Hatchet is crossing the Atlantic, and we will lend our help wherever it is needed, just like we did to save your ship, but we will make our own way and decide our own fate. It's survival now, don't you see? There's not going to be any great war because we've already lost. There's no more United States, there's just us—people. All that is left is resistance, and no resistance ever worked by following empty orders. It will only work by doing what needs to be done when it needs doing. Take your ship, and do whatever you can to help, but if you try to fight us, you're only helping the enemy."

That was it, the final nail. Hernandez saw the unease on the faces of his crew. They were waiting for an order they dreaded—to kill fellow Americans. Hernandez could no longer give that order, for it would end in disaster, but neither could he reverse course without losing face. He struggled in his own mind for several moments, a silence blanketing both ships. He needed to say something—something that the men could believe in. "I consider you a traitor to your country, Captain Granger, but I will not command my men to fire on fellow Americans. I disagree about the war being lost. It has only just begun. Your country requires your ship and your crew, but I can see that you have brainwashed them to abandon their beliefs—and even stand by while you deny the existence of the United States. I will not risk lives, but when America is victorious, men like you will be strung up for cowardice. If you have any honour at all, you will step down now, Captain Granger, but I don't expect that you will."

"The last thing anybody aboard my ship is guilty of is cowardice. I wish you a safe journey, Commander Hernandez. Do try to keep your men alive. We won't be there to rescue you next time."

Hernandez closed his eyes, locked his jaw, then turned away and removed himself from the railings. "Let's get the decks cleaned up. We depart for the mainland immediately."

Dead demons littered the decks, their exposed torsos like salt-encrusted jellyfish. The stench of death mixed with the briskness of the Ocean. Engines rumbled, and they pulled away from the Hatchet. The sound of its crew cheering carried across the water, contrasting with the glum silence aboard the Augusta.

Danza scratched at a bloodstain on his sleeve. "That was going to go badly whichever way you went about it."

"Are you trying to say that you warned me, Lieutenant?"

"I think it's pretty clear that I did, but you pulled it back at the end. The crew will recover eventually."

"Recover from what?" Hernandez glared at Danza. "They are sailors, not kittens. We have survived an attack, and will be ready for the next one. Johnson had no way of knowing what was coming, but I do."

"What exactly happened to Johnson? You were defending the rear of the ship with him, right?"

"Like I said, when the Hatchet fired on us, he got hit. I was lucky I didn't take a bullet too."

Danza sighed. "I suppose they couldn't help it, but it still smarts that they killed our commander."

"It is in the past now. Let us forget it."

"The men won't forget it. Granger defied us and sailed away scot free. That doesn't sit easily with me, and it won't sit easily with the men."

Hernandez stormed over to the railing and watched the now distant Hatchet. "What could I have done, Danza? What way out did I have?"

"You had no way out, I admit."

The sight of the retreating Coast Guard ship made Hernandez's blood boil. How he wished Granger stood beside him so he could knock the arrogant twerp—the traitorous twerp—on his ass.

"Granger won't be getting away scot-free," he told Danza. "This isn't over."

Danza raised an eyebrow. "Oh really? What are your orders, Commander?"

Hernandez told him. Danza rushed off to make it happen.

Ten minutes later, the Hatchet was almost out of view, but it would still be visible through the lens of a high-powered rifle—like the one Petty Officer Outerbridge currently held against his shoulder at the top of the Augusta's highest perch.

Hernandez picked up the intercom and hailed his sniper. "Outer-bridge, I want eyes on Commander Granger."

"Roger that." A few seconds of silence. "I have him. He's standing on deck."

"In your own time, Outerbridge. I want you to eliminate the com-mander." Hernandez saw the looks on the crew's face and decided to address their trepidation there and then. "The crew of the Hatchet helped us in our hour of need, I am aware. Firing upon them would have been wrong, yet Commander Granger is a traitor to our nation. He has assets at his disposal that can save the lives of the people back home, yet he puts his own selfish needs first. By removing him, com-mand of his ship will fall to the next senior officer, who we can only pray is more loyal to the United States of America. Granger is about to learn what happens to those who betray their country. We are sailors. We are soldiers. We are the men and women of the US Navy."

The crew stood silent and waited for the inevitable.

Kablow!

Kablow!

Kablow!

The sound of the .338 rounds exploding from the rifle barrel was like God cracking a whip. The crew flinched, but Hernandez did not. He had been eagerly awaiting the sound—the sound of him regaining authority. "Come in, Outerbridge. Give me your report."

"Target confirmed dead."

Hernandez swallowed. "Wonderful. You have eyes on Granger?"

"Negative, but I took the shot."

"I need confirmation, Outerbridge..."

"I... I can't see him, but I had a clear shot. The crew are panicking. They've all taken cover. I hit their commander, I'm sure. Their Lieutenant too."

Hernandez smiled. "Roger that. Danza, get me a line to The Hatchet."

Danza patched the call through to the other ship.

Hernandez spoke with newfound confidence. He had matched wits with a fellow commander and won. "Men and woman aboard the USCG Hatchet. Your senior officers are dead. Please put me in contact with whoever has inherited command. I wish you no harm, only that you follow the Augusta back to the coast where it will be added to the Navy's relief effort. You are no longer bound to fulfill whatever promises you made to Captain Granger. You are free." A brief pause. "Come in, come in, Hatchet. Whoever is most senior, please respond."

A voice crackled through the speaker. "Hernandez, this is the senior ranking member of the USCG Hatchet, Captain Guy Granger. You just killed a man worth ten of you, and I'm going to make you pay for it. You see, when this war is over, they will string men like you up. I will be the one to do it. As soon as I find my kids, I'm coming for you."

Hernandez wanted to reply, but his lips had pasted shut. He let go of the intercom and left it dangling by its cord. Shit!

2

"Hernandez, calm down," said Danza.

Hernandez spun on the man. "You do not address me as Hernandez. I am your commander. I will have that man strung up. You see if I don't."

"We could still pursue them," said Danza.

Hernandez groaned. "They are heading in the opposite direction and can match us for speed. It would be a waste of our time. We need to head back to the mainland."

"Would you still like us to plot a course for Jacksonville?"

"Yes, and see if we can hail anybody at Command. I need to report Granger's treachery."

Danza looked like he was going to add something more, but instead, he turned on his heel and headed off to do as requested.

Hernandez stood on deck, appraising the mess that was now his ship. Demon carcasses still littered the Augusta's decks, although they were gradually being tossed overboard by the men. The crew's own dead were lined up along the bow. The Augusta had lost at least fifty men, including Commander Johnson. His body lay beneath a blanket with all the others, no more remarkable now in death than the lowliest seaman recruit.

The situation was bleak, and coming into command in such a way was not how Hernandez had envisaged things, but it didn't change the fact he was now responsible for two hundred men and several hundred tons of hardware. His country needed him.

Outerbridge presented himself, the usual confidence of a man trained to kill now replaced by unease. His shoulders sagged.

"What the hell happened, Outerbridge?"

"I'm sorry, sir. I thought I had him. He was in my sights when I took the shot. Someone must have moved in line with him. The bullet would have taken several seconds to reach the target. It was a long—"

"Quiet," said Hernandez. "You had an order which you failed to carry out. Two nights in the brig. Present yourself immediately."

Outerbridge looked shocked, his blond eyebrows leaping away from his face. Yet, despite his obvious shock at the punishment, he saluted. "Yes, sir."

Hernandez took the time to walk the ship. He inserted himself into several fracas that needed dealing with, including a fight between two Ensigns who were exchanging fisticuffs over the body of one of the ship's helicopter pilots. The dead woman had apparently been a close friend to both of the men, and neither wanted to entrust her care to the other. Hernandez removed them both and had someone else dispose of the woman's corpse. He quickly moved on to other areas of the ship.

"Granger had the right idea," said a male Seaman recruit named Gleeson. "Norfolk was a bloodbath. We should all go back to land and find our families."

"We have a job to do," said a female Ensign named Cuervo. "If we scatter to the wind, then there really is no hope. Our families will be gone by the time we reach them."

"You don't know that," said someone else. "We have no idea what's happening back home. Norfolk is just one place. My family is in Ohio. They might be fine."

"Exactly," said Gleeson. "We should be finding out what's happening, not firing shots at the Coast Guard."

"That man was no longer a Coast Guard," said Hernandez, creeping up on them. "He abandoned his commission when he refused orders to return." The group of sailors flinched. Gleeson grew pale. It was to Gleeson, Hernandez addressed his question. "You believe Captain Granger was right to plot his own course?"

The Seaman recruit looked like a lamb before a wolf, but to his credit, he answered the question. "You heard what he said—there's no orders to follow. Every captain needs to make his own calls. He wasn't the enemy, but we fired on him like he was."

Hernandez turned to Ensign Cuervo. "Remove Seaman Gleeson to the brig."

Cuervo nodded shakily. "At once, sir."

When Hernandez turned around he was met by Lieutenant Danza.

"I gave you orders, Lieutenant."

"Yes sir, you did. It's as you thought. Command wants us back in Jacksonville."

"And Granger's treachery?"

Danza shrugged. "They had little to say about it."

"What do you mean?"

"I mean they have bigger fish to fry. A new fleet is being assembled, and its sole focus will be relieving the East Coast. One Coast Guard captain—"

"Granger is no longer a captain. He is a traitor."

Danza didn't seem to appreciate being interrupted, and he grunted. "Commander, do you want to take a breath?"

Hernandez felt a dark cloud descend upon him. He leaned closer to his lieutenant. "What did you just say?"

"I said take a goddamn breath. The ship is torn to shreds, and you've inherited command. It's a shock. You're under stress. Acting like a tyrant upon the high seas is not the way to go here. You're sending men to the brig when we're under-manned. This vendetta against Granger is pointless."

Hernandez grabbed Danza by the collar and pulled him off balance. "Any more insubordination from you and there'll be another man in the brig. I am being tough because the crew is on edge. They need to be brought in line."

Danza didn't try to break free of Hernandez's grasp, but neither did he cower. "You're losing it, Hernandez. Those men you think are so afraid fought to the death and survived. What they need is leading to the next battle with their confidence intact."

"Then do not undermine me, Danza. Johnson might have done things differently, but he's dead."

Danza shrugged himself free and straightened up his collar. "Yes, he is. If only the men had been there with him, perhaps he would still be in command."

"What do you mean by that?" Danza turned to walk away, but Hernandez grabbed him. "I said, what do you mean by that?"

Danza looked him in the eyes. "I mean, we only have your word about what happened. I knew Commander Johnson. He was a brave man, would have fought to the death, but I wonder if you were there fighting beside him just as hard, or running in the other direction. Why is he dead, and you're alive?"

Hernandez let out a long, slow breath as he met his lieutenant's defiant gaze. He realised the crew had gathered around as witnesses, and he was glad. "Three hours, Danza. That's how long you have to apologise to me in front of the entire crew. Three hours for you to learn your lesson and obey. If you don't, you'll spend the next six months in the brig, I promise you."

Danza locked his jaw, clenched his fists, but turned away in silence. Hernandez smiled.

3

Hernandez spent the rest of daylight in the bridge, contacting other ships in the area—of which there were few—and trying to find somebody in Command who knew what was going on. The only impression he got from anyone on the mainland was that 'things were bad'. The entire world was at war and there seemed to be no cohesive strategy to fight back. Naval Command had no clue what the Army or the Air Force was doing, and as for the President, no one had heard from him in hours. Washington had been penned in by a gate on each side and America's seat of power was crumbling to ruin.

Meanwhile, Hernandez continued to get his ship in order. He nipped any signs of dissent in the bud at once and had only grown more severe after considering Danza's words. The Lieutenant sought to make Hernandez doubt himself, the reason very clear. If Hernandez fell to pieces, it would be up to Danza to take command. The man was an ambitious shark.

Cuervo stood at the radar console, running constant scans for seabed activity. If there were any more gates at the bottom of the Atlantic, they would have plenty of warning. Johnson had run a tight ship, but Hernandez would run a tighter one. He didn't need sailors, he needed warriors. He needed Vikings. The Beretta on his hip would make sure he got them. The weak would be disposed of.

Hernandez checked his watch and saw that crunch time was almost upon them. When Danza subjugated himself in front of him, the remaining crew would fall firmly in line. Danza was a popular officer. The men would do as he did.

"Cuervo," Hernandez turned to his young Ensign and placed a hand on her shoulder. "You've performed well since the attack, and seeing as we are low on officers, I will be promoting you to acting lieutenant to serve alongside Officer Danza."

And report on his every action.

Cuervo looked shocked for a moment, but then she beamed. "T-Thank you, sir. I won't let you down."

"I'll make it official shortly. I am heading down to deck, and I would like you to join me."

"Of course."

Hernandez went and sipped a cup of water, realising that he had not hydrated himself in almost a day. Once he finished the cup, he had to refill it several more times. Once sufficiently replenished, he went down on deck to meet Danza. He was pleased to see the Lieutenant already waiting there for him. So were most the crew.

"Lieutenant Danza. I assume you have something to say to me?"

"I do."

Hernandez smiled, Crossed his arms and stood there waiting. He had directed the ship's spotlights to light up the deck so all eyes would be on Danza. "Then speak your piece, Lieutenant."

Danza hesitated, looked around at the crew surrounding him. What he was about to say was obviously difficult. Hernandez enjoyed every second of it. "Many of you have served with me for a while," began Danza, "so you know that I am an officer who does not necessarily follow the rules. The decisions I make are based on the situation, and I always try to do what's best for my crew. Commander Johnson was the same way, and if I can amount to half the officer he was, I will retire with full honours."

Hernandez tapped his foot. "Can we speed this up, please, Lieutenant?"

Danza nodded. "Protocol demands I fall inline under Lieutenant Hernandez's command, for he is the senior officer aboard. Those are the rules. It isn't best for my crew though. Today, we survived Armageddon, and I don't just mean aboard this ship. The world has fallen to ashes. We capable men and women of the US Navy are in a position to do something about that. Our country—the world, needs us, so the rules no longer apply. I will not follow the rules when they make no sense."

Hernandez scowled. Not only had Danza referred to him as 'Lieutenant', but it did not seem in any way like he was apologising. Every word out of the man's mouth seemed to take him further and further away from the word 'sorry'.

Hernandez tried to interrupt, but Danza waved a hand at him. "Just let me finish, Hernandez. All day, you've talked, and you've talked, and you've talked. At first, I thought you were losing it, but you're not that innocent. It's your ego. Your whole life you've wanted to be the man, but being the man isn't something you can seize. It's something you earn."

"I've heard quite enough. Will someone please escort Lieutenant Danza to the brig?"

Nobody moved.

Hernandez prodded Cuervo. "Do your duty, Lieutenant."

"Yes sir." She snapped off a salute and hurried towards Danza, but she was cut off by another member of the crew. Outerbridge stepped out of the crowd and blocked her.

Hernandez exploded. "Outerbridge! You were detained to the brig. You have defied a direct—"

"I released him," said Danza, "along with all the other innocent sailors you sent there. It is not a crime to refuse to pander to your ego."

"I am in command of this—"

Danza shook his head. "No, you're not. I've spoken to a portion of the crew, and they have all agreed to recognise me as Johnson's successor. The Augusta is under my command."

"Mutiny!"

Danza ignored the slur with a smile. "I am leading the Augusta to Jacksonville, where we will all do our very best to work together and help our nation. I will not be making decisions based on ego. I will do what is best for my crew and my country, and send only one man to the brig—you, Lieutenant Hernandez."

"How dare you? I have committed no crime. The command is rightfully mine."

"Perhaps, but until we ascertain the circumstances behind Commander Johnson's death, you are suspended from service. You will be contained to the brig for your own safety."

"Fuck you, Danza."

"You will address me as Commander."

Hernandez looked around at the men and woman on deck. Danza had not yet got to all of them, but a large enough portion seemed to be firmly behind him.

Hernandez pulled his Beretta out of its holster and pointed it at Danza. "The Augusta belongs to me!"

He pulled the trigger.

Richard Honeywell

"**G**LEN? GLEN, WHAT do you mean they're coming?" Richard shook his colleague, but he was unconscious. A quick examination exposed a ragged wound across his tummy, the skin grey and moist either side of a bloody furrow. It was bad.

"They're here, aren't they?" asked Aaron, standing over Richard and still wearing his chip shop apron. "The demons are coming."

Richard looked up at the boy and finally saw how scared he was. "Yes, I think so. Are you ready?"

Aaron looked like he might throw up all over his shoes, but he nodded.

"Then get your boys, get weapons, and get on the barricade." Richard placed Glen down on the pavement and stood up. He addressed everyone, almost shouting. "You hear that? The enemy is coming to kill us. Get ready to kill them first."

The seven newcomers still stood next to the barricade. Richard approached the one who had announced their arrival, a tall, middle-aged man wearing a leather jacket and carrying a cricket bat. "What happened to Glen?"

The man shook his head. "I don't know. We just found him lying on the side of the road. He said he'd been attacked by a demon."

Richard looked at the new group suspiciously. "Who are you people?"

"I work at the garage on Trotter Lane, and these guys work at the supermarket next door. We heard your friend shouting, saying he had a place we could all go to be safe. That sounded great to us, so we left to find where he was shouting from. Around the corner, we found him bleeding."

"So there was no demon? What about the officers who were with him?"

The man shook his head and looked like he wished he knew more.

Richard rubbed at his chin, then grimaced when he realised he had Glen's blood on him. "Thank you for bringing him back. You can get yourself a hot cup of tea at the church, but there might not be much time to relax. If the demons really have made it here from the city, then we have a fight ahead of us."

The man held up his baseball bat. "I'm ready, governor, don't worry. I'm Leonard, by the way."

"Good to meet you, Leonard. Get your guys ready."

Leonard nodded and took his six companions with him. Richard turned back around to face the disorganised chaos behind him. If he had not realised it before, he saw it clearly then. The people in the camp were just ordinary people panicking for their lives. Overcoming panic and acting courageously was not a normal response—it was either learned, in the cases of soldiers, firemen, etc, or occasionally built in, in the case of random heroes, but it was most certainly not the norm. The people in the camp were normal. They would not be courageous. They would not be brave—especially now the sun was going down. The dark sapped a man's courage.

He needed heroes, but until the battle began there was no way of recognising them from the cowards.

"Help me get him up." Richard looked aside to see Riaz struggling to get Glen up off the floor. It was wrong to leave their colleague there, so the two of them carried him towards the church. "You really think he was attacked by a demon?" asked Riaz, grunting.

"What else could have caused such awful wounds?"

"Many things, but I agree death is coming."

Richard moaned as he readjusted his grip on Glen. "Can I count on you?"

"I may not believe we have a chance, but I still believe it's my job to protect these people."

"Good, because they will be looking to you, Riaz."

Riaz said nothing. They struggled with Glen and got him to the church. Inside, Reverend Miles helped them take the man into the vestry where they set him down on a bench.

"I will tend to your friend," said Miles. "If the Adversary is on his way, you both must go. Lead us all to salvation."

Richard smiled, but did not mock. He liked the vicar, Christian or not. Before he went out to rally the troops, however, Richard went to find his family.

Jen held Dillon against her breast. He was sobbing and trembling. "We just heard," she said. "Someone ran in screaming that the monsters had come. I didn't know what to tell him."

Richard looked at his wife and wished he had eternity to spend with her. He reached out and rubbed Dillon's shoulder. "You remember what I said, sweetheart. You do whatever your mother tells you, okay? I will do everything I can to keep us all safe, but you need to stay inside."

"I can't let you go out there," said Jen, her eyes wide and full of tears.

"Jen, I wish you could stop me, but this isn't going to go away. We have people here that know what's coming. If we run now, we'll never stop running. Fighting is the only chance we have."

She nodded, and a tear spilled down her cheek. "Go."

Richard turned and ran. He exited the church as the first cry of terror rang out.

Fifty people manned the barricade. Aaron stood in the centre, and it was to him—a mere teenager—that Richard ran. "Aaron, what's happening?"

"They're here, boss. They're coming."

Richard wobbled and almost fell. Now that it was finally happening, all the talk seemed absurd. They had to run. Surely they couldn't stay.

"I had everyone link arms," said Aaron. "It was the only way we could all get up here without knocking each other off."

Richard nodded. "Good thinking, Aaron. Is there room up there for me?"

Aaron reached out his hand. Richard took it. Then he was up on the barricade, staring down the road with everybody else.

Death was indeed coming.

Just like news had promised, the enemy was a legion of burnt men. They shambled up the hill like zombies, their flesh peeling off in bloody scraps and littering the road. Leading the enemy's charge was a creature so burned that it was more skeleton than human. A foot taller than the other abominations, it cut a slender figure. Only the loosest slivers of muscle and sinew remained on its frame. Atop its shoulders sat a naked skull. The reason Richard knew it was the enemy leader was because it marched ahead of the line, several feet in front of the legion that followed.

"Oh God," someone cried. "God help me, please!"

Richard saw movement in the corner of his eye. People fell away from the barricade and ran towards the town. They were fleeing before the battle had even begun.

"Stand and fight! We must stand and fight!"

Aaron remained in place beside Richard and yelled to his friends. "Anyone runs, and I will find you and beat the shit out of you. Let's show these fuckers the real meaning of Hell."

Richard's heart lifted at the sound of the teenagers roaring defiantly.

Something sailed through the air, launching from the safe side of the barricade towards the incoming army. It smashed to pieces in the centre of the road and a fireball ignited. A dozen of the tightly-packed enemy went up in flames, their already burned flesh turning from glistening pink to charred black.

Richard looked back and saw one of Aaron's friends standing with a crate full of liquor bottles at his feet.

Aaron smirked. "You told us to be ready. Plenty of petrol going to waste in all these cars. Seemed a shame to waste it."

Richard shook his fist. "Good lad."

Aaron's friend lit another petrol bomb and launched it. Flames filled the road and took out more of the enemy. The rest of the barricade—those who had not run—followed suit and started lobbing bricks and chunks of concrete. Most did little to halt the progress of the legion.

"They're not going to stop," someone shouted. "This is insane."

More people abandoned the wall. Those remaining spread out, keeping the line as solid as they could. Aaron leapt down too and for a moment it looked like he was going to run, but he only went to help his friend with the petrol bombs. It was the best weapon they had. Together, the two of them launched rapidly, lighting and throwing one after the other. Fire filled the entire road for fifty metres. Diseased bodies combusted. Others marched through the inferno, limbs smouldering. The smell of burning flesh permeated the air.

Richard understood what Hell must be like.

The enemy leader, Skullface, reached the barricade first, and his proximity caused another route. Droves of people left the wall, leaving it unmanned in several areas.

Skullface moved right up to the barricade, but did not seek to climb it. He looked down at the ground and growled. The cast iron drainpipes from the church had worked. Demons could not pass iron.

The legion caught up to Skullface and paused at the barricade.

"They can't pass," said Richard triumphantly.

Skullface looked up at Richard and glared. Then he snatched out at a burnt man and seized it by the throat. The demon squirmed and fought, but was powerless as the taller monster tossed him at the barricade. It hit the iron drainpipe and exploded, sending chunks of meat everywhere. The concussive force threw a handful of people off the wall.

The iron drainpipe rolled away from the barricade.

Skullface leapt up and grabbed a brave young woman who had stood her ground. She froze as the creature towered over her but did not scream. It grabbed her by her brown hair and tossed her over his shoulder like a shopping bag. She flew twenty feet through the air and landed on her back in the middle of the road. An almighty wheeze escaped her impacted lungs. The enemy ripped her apart. The burnt creatures surrounded her and tore off her legs and arms, before shoving their skinless fingers into her torso until nothing remained but human mash.

Skullface grabbed a piece of the barricade and tossed it aside, exposing a gap for its comrades to infiltrate, then he hopped down on the other side and set upon anyone unlucky enough to be within reach. Two seconds was all it took to pull a screaming man's head from his shoulders.

The battle was lost. They never even had a chance.

"Fall back!" Richard shouted. "Fall back to the church."

Even as he said it, he hated himself. His family was at the church.

But he couldn't let everyone stand and die.

The barricade dissolved as bodies bled away from it. People scattered and raced for the church—although many kept on running long after they had passed it. Richard stopped to get Aaron. The lad was still lighting petrol bombs and tossing them. Tears and snot covered his face. "Aaron, we have to go."

"No, we have to stop them."

"We can't do it here. Come on."

Aaron's hands shook as he struggled to light another fuse. Richard grabbed the lad's hands and looked him in the eye. "I need you alive!"

Aaron nodded and allowed Richard to drag him away. Behind them, burned bodies clambered over the barricade. Their hungry moans echoed off the shop windows on either side of the road.

They found Riaz outside the church trying his best to organise the crowd of screaming terrified people. "Grab whatever you can. Stay together. Shoulder to shoulder. Help your neighbour."

Richard skidded on his heels trying to brake from his full on sprint. His colleague had to steady him.

"Still think this is the smart thing to do?" Riaz asked.

"What choice do we have? Are Jen and Dillon—"

"Still inside the church."

"Then I want to make sure the enemy stays on the outside."

"Oh my God!" somebody screamed. The crowd began to split apart.

"Stay together!" Riaz shouted at them again.

Nearby, Aaron's friends appeared around him. Each brandished knives—something Richard would have pulled them for once—just days ago, everything had been different.

He realised he brandished no weapon of his own, so he moved over to a public bin and wrestled off the top. The plastic lid would make a basic riot shield. He pulled the telescopic baton from his belt and whipped it open.

The enemy came.

People screamed louder, but this time nobody ran. What remained were the people who understood that there was nowhere to run. This was a problem they could not escape.

Skullface was nowhere in sight, and only burnt men attacked the church. An old man swung an axe at the first ones and scored an immediate kill, but his weapon lodged in its skull and left him defenceless. The next monster fell upon him easily. The old man's wife bellowed in anger and poked holes in the creature's back with a pair of scissors. The demon went down, but so did the old woman when the next demon grabbed her.

People were dying.

But at least they were taking the enemy down with them.

Richard rallied Aaron and his friends to a charge, and together they threw themselves at the enemy. Richard swung his baton over and over again until his shoulder went numb. The burnt men came apart like roasted chickens, their flesh barely clinging to the bone. They were easy to destroy, but their numbers were endless.

Aaron buried his knife in the eye socket of a creature that came at him from the side. As the thing died, it twisted and fell away, taking the knife with it. Aaron fought the next attacker with his bare hands, tossing it over his leg in a basic judo throw. Then he produced another blade from the back of his jeans and buried it in the thing's skull. He gave Richard a cheeky wink and got back to fighting.

Richard glanced back towards the church, trying to imagine what Jen and Dillon were doing inside—how scared they must be. It filled him with bone-shaking dread that the enemy moved so close to his family, but his spirit lifted because a crowd of people stood armed and ready. Richard and Aaron's display of courage had given hope to those watching, and Riaz rallied even further back. They were gaining a foothold.

In front of Richard, Aaron's group were joined by others—the front line swelling. They hacked and slashed at the burnt men, opening up their sinewy necks and disembowelling them.

Their confidence grew.

They were doing it.

They were standing their ground.

They could win this!

Then Richard heard the screams from inside the church. Suddenly, he realised that everything might already be lost.

2

As much as Richard had a duty to protect the people outside the church, his duty as a father and husband came first. He prayed the screams coming from inside were just fear, but the closer he got the more he became certain that something bad was going on inside God's house.

Riaz tried to grab Richard as he raced past, but Richard dodged him. "I have to check on Jen and Dillon," he cried out. "Keep fighting. I'll be back."

The sight of him running could shake the confidence of those still fighting, but he had no control over his body. His legs carried him into the church on their own volition. He flew through the heavy oak door and scanned left to right, taking in everything but seeing nothing. It was chaos. People clambered over wooden pews and barged Richard aside to escape. He let them go, not interested in their fear, only in Jen and Dillon.

"Jen! Dillon! Where are you?"

"Richard, help!"

Richard spotted his wife at the back of the church behind the altar. It was from that area that people seemed to flee. He did the opposite and raced towards it. What he saw confused him.

"Glen? What are you...?"

Glen was back on his feet, but in no way recovered from his wounds. In fact, his guts hung out the bottom of his shirt. Like the belly of a fish, he was pasty and pale. Reverend Miles cowered up against the chairs of the choir pit as the bleeding officer stalked towards him.

Jen waved her arms at Richard. "Help him!"

Did she mean Glen or Miles?

Richard decided it didn't matter and flung himself forwards. The first thing he thought when he grabbed Glen around the arms was: So cold. His colleague was the same temperature as the icy church. He was also strong, and when he threw back an elbow, he caught Richard right in the jaw. It dazzled his senses and sent him staggering backwards. His vision tilted, and he fell onto his backside.

Glen then turned back to Miles, grabbing the frightened holy man around the throat and dragging him away from the chairs. "Please," Miles begged. "You are injured, my son. You need to rest."

"There are no sons left in this world, preacher, only insect carcasses. The Red Lord will claim you all, and you will serve him with backs broken and eyes gouged. Your whimpers will stretch through eternity, and your Father will cower and hide."

Miles lifted his chin defiantly. "The Father watches over us all. He does not hide."

Glen snorted with laughter. He snapped Miles's neck with one hand and let the vicar's body slumped to the floor of his church.

Richard choked on his own words. "G-Glen, w-what have you done?"

Glen glowered at him and all became clear: this was no longer Glen. His eyes were black cauldrons of hate, and several of his teeth had fallen out.

Richard shuffled backwards, trying to get up without turning his back. "You're one of them."

Glen snorted with more laughter. "You are a worm."

Richard clambered up to his feet in time to dodge Glen's attempts to grab him. He stumbled over to his wife and pulled her away. "Where's Dillon?"

"In the vestry."

"Then let's get him."

They leapt down the steps before the altar and jinked into a small anti-chamber at the side of the church. Glen was right on their heels, but Richard had to know his son was okay.

Shirley sat up against the wall clutching her chest. She was dead.

Heart attack?

Dillon was cowering beneath an oak desk. When he spotted Richard his teary eyes sparkled with relief. "Dad!"

"It's okay, son. It's—"

Glen bundled into the back of him and sent him sprawling into Jen. She tumbled awkwardly with a pained screech. Seeing his wife hurt made Richard see red, and he spun on Glen with his telescopic baton held high above his head. The blow caught Glen's shoulder hard enough to push him back.

"Who are you?" Richard demanded.

"I am death," was all Glen said before launching himself at Richard.

This time Richard made firm contact with Glen's skull, the baton striking so hard that one of his eyeballs bulged from its socket. Glen slumped to his knees. Like an executioner, Richard brought the baton down again, aiming for the back of the neck.

The blow turned Glen off like a light, and he fell onto his face without a single sound or movement. Richard stood there for a moment, heaving like a rabid beast. His humanity came back to him a moment later, just when he feared it was gone forever, and he spun around to embrace his family.

Jen groped her ankle and hissed through her teeth. "I think... I think it's just sprained. I'll be okay."

"Dad?" Dillon came out from beneath the table. "Mrs Shirley..."

"It's okay, sweetheart." He gave Dillon the biggest hug ever and didn't want to let go, but they had to get out of there. No telling what was happening outside.

Jen limped along with his help as they exited the anti-chamber. The church had emptied, and Richard looked back sadly as they left Miles's body lying on the floor. The vicar had brought them all together and housed them. Without the man's hospitality, they might be dead.

Outside, Hell had not retreated. Fire still raged in the road and had started to lick at the barricade. People screamed everywhere. Bodies littered the pavement—human and otherwise.

Demon fought man and the fight was bloody. They spilled so much human blood that the floor was slick with it. So much chaos.

Richard trod on something that might have been a length of intestine. "We need to get out of here."

Jen shook her head, horrified by what she was seeing. "No, we have to help. That monster took Glen's body and killed Miles. We need to stay and fight these things, Richard."

"But Dillon?"

Dillon had his head buried in his mother's shoulder. With Jen's ankle, they would struggle to escape even if they tried. Their only hope might be to win this fight.

But it was impossible.

Ahead, Riaz came briefly into view. His shirt was torn open, and his baton dripped with blood. He was an animal, teeth bared as he cleaved open skulls with wild abandon. Yet it was hard to spot anybody else because burnt monsters filled every inch of Richard's vision. He shook his head. "I can't let us do this. We're leaving. We'll find a car and get somewhere. Soon there won't be anybody left."

Jen seemed to battle internally, her eyes red and brimming. "Okay, you're right. We have to get Dillon to safety."

Richard nodded, glad to have the decision made. "Come on, we'll head around the back of the post office. There'll be plenty of cars parked behind it. We'll think about how to get one started when we get there."

They began to move. Richard felt fish hooks in his heart as he fled the battle. Could he ever forgive himself? He looked at his terrified son and knew that he would. Still, he could not help himself but to take one last look back at the people he was deserting.

He spotted Aaron, and was glad the lad still lived, but none of his friends had made it. Richard saw them dead in a pile. Aaron sobbed madly as he stabbed and thrust at the enemy. The lad was determined to go down fighting.

What was he doing?

He had to go back. At least try to get those left alive out of there.

"Jen, keep heading for the post office. I'm going to try and—"

His wife's screams cut him off.

Richard spun around to see Jen in the clutches of a monster. She threw Dillon out of harm's way, even as Skullface reached down and gouged out her eyes. Her entire body shook, a seizure strong enough to snap her spine. Richard wailed as Skullface slid his fingers so far into his wife's eye sockets that the back of her skull broke apart.

Jen's arms flung out to her sides and clutched at thin air.

"Mummy!"

Richard grabbed Dillon and yanked him back. He glared at Skullface and screamed. "You fucking bastard!" He swung the baton with every fibre in his body. The steel connected with chalky white skull bone.

Snap!

It was not the sound of Skullface's cranium breaking, but that of the telescopic baton breaking in two. Richard stood there in shock as the slender monster before him smiled despite having no lips. Its smouldering eyes seemed ready to erupt into hellish infernos.

Jen's body slumped to the ground, her ruined skull thumping against the pavement. A jet of fluid shot from her left eye socket. Skullface stamped his foot and turned Jen's head to dust. The bellow of laughter that followed was mocking, tormenting.

Dillon wailed.

Richard was unarmed, but that didn't stop him from throwing himself at the creature that had just destroyed the love of his life. He hammered both fists against its rib cage so hard that his knuckles bled. The whole time Skullface just stood there laughing. Eventually, Richard's arms gave out, and he slumped to one knee. He glared up at his tormentor and spat. "You won't win."

Skullface stopped laughing. In a raspy voice like a swarm of bees, he said, "We have already won."

The abomination raised his bony hand into the air above Richard's head, ready to strike.

"Daddy!"

Richard closed his eyes. "Run, Dillon. Run wherever you can and hide."

"No!"

An almighty impact sent Richard onto his back, but when he opened his eyes he saw Leonard, the guy who had brought Glen back to the camp. The man still wore his leather jacket, but it was now ripped and slick with blood. The cricket bat he held in his hand was broken in two, a wide piece embedded in the side of Skullface's jaw.

The monster staggered, blasting out a ferocious roar.

Leonard grabbed Dillon and pulled him. Looking at Richard, he screamed, "Get up! Those of us left are getting the hell out of here."

Richard didn't argue. He scrambled to his feet and ran after the man who had just saved him. But it would all be for nothing. Dillon had just lost his mother.

Richard had just lost his wife.

Skullface was right. The demons had already won.

3

The entire area around the church was a bloodbath. Blood formed a river in the road, and the fires had claimed the buildings on either side. Demons swarmed everywhere.

Riaz fought up ahead, gathering those still breathing to his side. Aaron was there too, standing amidst only a dozen survivors—all that remained of nearly a hundred souls. He held a bloody knife in each hand and growled hysterically at the demons racing towards them.

Riaz spotted Richard and came running. "We have to go now. Richard, where's Jen? We have to move."

Richard flinched at the sound of his wife's name.

Riaz seemed to understand. "Shit, sorry."

"I need to get Dillon to safety."

Riaz nodded, and they moved in a group, gathering whoever was left.

"Where do we go?" asked Aaron. "Where?"

There were demons everywhere by now. Burnt men stalked every inch of the road and pavement. The only thing giving the survivors a chance was that the demons were occupied with ripping apart the wounded and dying. Dozens moaned on the ground, begging for help, but they were soon silenced by the tearing out of their throats.

"The newspaper," said Richard.

Riaz frowned. "What?"

"The reporters I spoke to last night, they were from The Slough Echo. It's nearby."

"Then let's go," said Leonard, jabbing his broken cricket bat into a burnt man's snarling face.

They altered course and headed across the high street and through an alleyway between two banks. It took them towards the college. The newspaper offices were nearby, housed in a mid-sized office block with giant printing presses visible through the ground-floor windows—Richard had taken Dillon to see them once. It would not withstand a siege, but if they got there without being seen…

They tore through the college car park and campus, Richard hopped an abandoned bicycle and stopping to make sure Dillon kept up. Unlike Aaron, all tears and emotion, Dillon was expressionless, his sunken eyes half closed.

"It'll be all right, sweetheart."

Dillon said nothing, but at least he kept on running.

Soon they reached the rear of the campus, heading across a grassy courtyard. The moon hung overhead and made the surface of the grass shimmer like shards of glass. The college structures were unlit rectangles against an inky black sheet.

Movement up ahead.

"Someone's there," said Riaz, pointing to a small shack that may have been a bike shelter. "Come on out."

They all halted in their tracks and stared apprehensively at the small structure ahead. There was most definitely movement coming from its rear edge. At first, it looked like it might be just one person hiding out, but then several shapes emerged from the shadows.

Eventually dozens.

Too many.

Aaron raised his knives up in front of him. "Demons."

Richard chewed at his bottom lip. Yes, demons, but not like before. These were not burnt men. These were some kind of animal shape—like apes.

Loosing an ear-piercing screech, the pack of creatures spilled out from the bike shed and raced towards Richard's group. By now, the survivors were used to fighting. No one backed away—not even Dillon.

Richard was still unarmed, so he kicked out at the first creature that came near. He caught it in the torso and sent it onto its back. Before it had time to right itself, Richard stamped on its skull—three times before it stopped moving.

Aaron stabbed and hacked with his knives. Leonard stabbed and swiped with his splintered cricket bat. Riaz swung his baton. The other survivors, who Richard knew only by face, fought bravely too, scraping with whatever they held on to.

But, one by one, the survivors fell. The apes were quick, and dodging them was difficult. A barrel-chested, bearded man beside Richard swung a hammer and missed. Off balance, he could not fight back as one of the snarling apes clawed at his neck and dug out a bundle of nerves, veins, and tendons. It looked like spaghetti.

More creatures emerged from the shadows between the buildings. More apes came.

Richard was sweating, his mouth hanging open as he fought for breath. He backed up against Dillon, keeping his son behind him. His fight was almost gone, but what could he do? The Church lay at his back along with certain death, but the way forward was no better. They were all going to die. Dillon would be alone as monsters feasted upon his flesh. The thought reignited Richard's fury and allowed him to fight on a while longer, but it couldn't last forever. His fellow survivors continued falling around him while the enemy continued to grow.

Riaz fell to one knee, bleeding from his shoulder. Leonard stumbled, looking ready to drop dead. Demon and human blood filled the chilly night air like a heavy mist. The smell of war was rancid.

"I'm done," said Aaron, now in possession of only a single knife. "I can't fight anymore."

They backed up against one another, forming a semi-circle with Dillon in the centre. Richard, Aaron, Riaz, and Leonard. All that was left of a hundred refugees from the church. Richard kicked out, but then fell to his knees. His head hung, exhausted. The next attack would kill him. He couldn't lift an arm.

They were done. Finished.

A creature reared up, prepared to pounce on its weakened prey.

Tat-tat-tat-tat-tat!

The ape's head disappeared from its shoulders. Several of its brethren fell too. Gunfire broke out and echoed off the tall buildings. The sound of salvation. Richard had been saved for a second time tonight.

"It's the fucking Army," cried Aaron.

But it was not the Army. Only a single rifle rang out.

Yet, the sudden attack at the demon's flanks had been enough to disorientate them. They broke apart in confusion, not knowing where the attack was coming from.

Tat-tat-tat.

More of the demons fell. Rifle shots perfectly aimed.

"Over there!" Riaz pointed. "Over there."

Richard looked up and saw three people across the road. Only one of them was a soldier, but his two companions were waving them over. Come on!

"Go!" said Richard, grabbing Dillon and getting them moving. While the demons were suppressed, the group was able to get a head start and got across the road without resistance. There, they were grabbed by the three strangers.

"Move!" said the soldier, lining up another barrage of well-placed shots.

They reached the T-junction at the end of the road. At the bottom of the hill lay the police station, where Richard assumed they might be headed, but instead the soldier led them along another side road—towards The Slough Echo.

"You're the soldier from last night," said Richard.

"Corporal Martin. You were the copper we spoke to?"

"Yes."

"Good to see you again."

"Likewise."

They carried on running, right up to the doors of the Echo which had been barricaded from the inside. A man waited there and moved furniture aside to let them through the door. He was severely injured, entire face glistening with fresh burns. One eye seared shut. Richard recognised the man from his clothes and what remained of his greying hair. It was one of the two reporters who had been in the jeep with Corporal Martin last night. What had happened to him?

"Some racket you made out there," the disfigured man said.

Corporal Martin grunted. "If I hadn't made noise, I wouldn't have got these folks in one piece."

Together, they shoved the barricade back in place and raced up a stairwell that filled the lobby. They went up several flights before they stopped.

The disfigured man appraised them then. "Are you all that's left?"

Richard nodded. "A lot of us ran when the battle began, but we're the only ones left who stayed and fought."

"Then you are worth ten of those who fled," Corporal Martin told them.

Richard sighed. "They were just scared. I knew it would happen. For a while, it looked like we might make it, but then..." Richard thought about Skullface and what the demon had done to Jen.

Corporal Martin patted him on the back. "Let's go inside."

They headed through a set of double doors and entered a busy office. It could be forgivable to think all was normal with the world if the newsroom was anything to go by. Reporters tapped away at keyboards while runners moved between desks with bundles of paper. Richard looked for the female reporter he had spoken to, but couldn't spot her.

An old woman came spilling out of an office and threw her arms out. "Welcome! I'm so glad to see someone else alive in this shit-stinking acid trip."

Leonard was the least shell-shocked, apparently, because he was the first to step forward and offer a handshake. "Thank you for rescuing us."

The woman shook his hand. "I'd been hoping for more of you. I'm Carol, and I run the Echo."

"H-How did you know about us?" asked Richard.

The old woman smiled. "Your colleague, Glen, came to us this morning. Said he was gathering up survivors to defend the town." She looked at each of them and then let her smile drop. "I take it he isn't amongst you? Shame, he promised me a drink after all this was over."

Richard was surprised to hear that Glen had been here. Obviously, it had been before he was... possessed... or whatever had happened to him. "Why did Glen come here?"

"He wanted us to post something on the website, telling people to head to the church. We did, but I admit it only got a few hits. Most of our traffic is coming from all over the globe, not so much of it local."

Riaz frowned. "Why is the world interested in a local newspaper?"

Carol grinned. "Because we are the last bastion of knowledge in this war. Yesterday, one of our reporters, Mina, set up a website sharing whatever we could find out about the demons. It's been helping people. Do you know that a few hours ago, someone closed one of those gates? Did you know that iron wards off the bastards? These are things we can use. Soon as we find them out, we share 'em on the net."

Aaron chuckled. "You're like the underground resistance or something."

Carol pinched the lad's cheek like he was eight. "That we are, lad. Can't let those buggers have it all their own way, can we?" She waved an arm at the office behind her. "Take a seat. I'll get you all a cuppa. You've already met Corporal Martin, and Tom and Annie."

Corporal Martin had already wandered off, but Tom and Annie nodded hello. They were obviously a couple because the tiny brunette leaned her head against the taller blond man as she spoke. "We went to the police station for help this morning, but no one was there. Corporal Martin found us and brought us here. Seemed like the least we could do was help bring you guys in."

Richard looked at her. "There was no one there?"

"No. We looked everywhere, but it was abandoned. The cells were all open, and it looked like maybe there'd been a scuffle. No one was around."

"Damn it," said Riaz.

Carol looked at Riaz. "Do you know if the police force is still intact? London fell last night, but we haven't been able to find out if there's still a force in place."

Riaz shrugged. "Last I heard, all local uniforms had headed to the city. I have no idea what forces in the other regions are doing."

"Same is true of the ambulance service," said a voice Richard recognised.

"Oliver? The paramedic from yesterday morning?"

The tall, shaven-headed man smiled. "Seems like forever ago, doesn't it? You never called."

"Sorry, things have been bad."

Oliver patted him on the shoulder. "For us all. I'm glad to see you again. I was planning to head home, but my ambulance got knocked off the road by some cheese dick in an Alfa Romeo. Pure luck someone spotted me from the windows of this place. I'm not used to standing around in an emergency doing nothing, but I don't know what else to do. I just wish I knew more."

Carol tucked a bunch of her greying blonde hair behind her ear. "No news is good news."

"Strange motto for a newspaper," said Leonard.

"And you'd be right. Anyway, enough doom and gloom. Who is this handsome young man we have here?" She was talking about Dillon and moved gently towards him, reached out to touch his face.

Dillon remained expressionless, but muttered, "Hello."

"You've had a tough time, huh, my lovely? Never mind, you're safe now."

"Mummy."

Carol was a smart enough woman to understand. She nodded compassionately. "She's in a better place now. If a person ever needed proof of Heaven, then Hell on earth is that. Must be a God and angels if there are demons, don't you think?"

Dillon nodded. A single tear spilled down his cheek, and his bottom lip quivered.

Carol touched his chin and lifted his head. "No need to be upset, my lovely. I have someone you should meet. Alice? Alice, where are you?"

A little girl appeared from underneath a desk. She had an unopened chocolate bar in her hand and a smudge of a previous one on her cheek. Her face was sullen, not innocent like a child's should be. "What is it, auntie Carol?"

"I want you to welcome our new friend…"

"Dillon," said Richard.

"Dillon. He's had a tough time, just like you, so I want the two of you to stick together, please."

Alice nodded. She looked at Dillon, but didn't gawp at his Down features. She offered out the chocolate bar. "I used to share with my brother, Kyle, but the monsters got him. I can share with you now, if you like?"

Tentatively, Dillon reached out and took the chocolate bar. "T-Thank you. I lost my mummy."

Alice nodded. "I bet you miss her. I miss my brother. We can miss them both together."

"Go on, you two," said Carol. "Go play in the fort Corporal Martin built for you."

Alice nodded and took Dillon by the hand. Richard felt his heart lurch at the sight of his traumatised son taking the little girl's hand and allowing himself to be led away. Even after all the bloodshed of the last couple of days, there was still kindness in the world.

How much longer could it last?

"How bad are things?" Richard asked Carol. The woman was a tough old bird, he could see it written into every crease of her face, but the question drew a dark veil across her face that seemed like it might suffocate her.

"As bad as they can be without being over. London and New York are both graveyards. Tokyo, Paris, Melbourne, Chicago, I could go on. The world is finished. We've been invaded, successfully. All we can do now is try to survive. There's a massive movement assembling in Turkey right now led by the Yanks. The Russians say they're holding their own, but who knows. Corporal Martin has been in touch with what's left of our Armed Forces here at home, and they're in the process of fortifying Portsmouth. Several battalions stationed abroad are on their way back. Humanity is still alive and kicking, but we're bleeding from every orifice."

Richard collapsed into a nearby chair and placed his hands on his knees. He vomited on the carpet. Afterwards, he wiped his mouth and apologised.

Carol shrugged. "You know how much blood and puke I've seen lately?"

"Not as much as we have. I watched my wife get her head crushed by a seven-foot skeleton. What the Hell are these things?"

"Demons. Did you ever think they were anything else? Those gates lead straight to Hell, I would bank my pension on it. We are at war with Lucifer's legions."

Riaz snorted. "You can't verify that."

Carol raised an eyebrow. "Want a bet?"

"How?"

"I can verify it because we captured one of the bastards alive and have him locked in a cupboard."

They all laughed, except for Carol who never changed her expression.

"What? You're telling the truth?" said Aaron.

Carol smirked. "David, show them."

The disfigured man appeared and nodded to the door behind him. "Right this way, ladies and gentlemen."

They went back out into the hallway where David opened a door to a broom closet. Inside, tied to a chair, were the remains of a human being. It blinked at them when they turned on the light.

Vamps

VAMPS DUCKED BEHIND an abandoned tour bus and tried to understand what he was seeing. After escaping the warehouse, they had found themselves on Oxford Street outside the Selfridges building.

Where it all began. Where the London Gate had opened and spilled evil upon the city.

And the gate was still open, its glow lighting up the night made it seem like day.

"I can't believe what I'm seeing," said Mass. "Now that we're looking right at it…"

Vamps nodded. "I know, Mass. I know."

"Come on, you pussies," said Pusher, already moving along the side of the bus with his two guys. "Time to get the fuck out of here."

But Vamps didn't move. The gate was a hundred metres further down Oxford Street, but even at that distance, he could see the huddled masses of human beings cowering before the shimmering lens. Demons moved everywhere, lining the street, but the section of road directly before the gate was filled only with frightened people—chained up like the ones Vamps had seen Prime Minister Windsor hand over.

What were the demons doing? Why were they keeping people alive?

"We can't leave all these people," said Vamps. "They need our help."

Pusher stopped moving and looked back. "Are you fucking kidding me? We need to run. Look at your ginger muppet. He's lost the plot."

Vamps looked at Ginge and rubbed his friend's wide back. He had not said a word since Ravy had died on the floor of their cell. "He's fine. He'll be fine."

Pusher sniggered. "Yeah, whatever, mate. He'll get you sodding killed. Unless you leg it right now."

Vamps looked back at the people huddled in front of the gate. He winced when he saw one of the demons step forward to grab a young girl—a child—and hoist her up against the shimmering lens.

"Mass, we have to help them, right? Mass?"

"I dunno, man. What can we do? There are a hundred of them monsters there."

The gate pulsed, and the little girl screamed. The demon holding her pulled out her arm and held it straight. Something glinted in the light and streaked across the poor girl's flesh. She screamed again and blood jetted out of her wrist. She tried to struggle, but the demon held her in place. Eventually, her struggles weakened, and the only thing holding her on her feet was the demon.

The gate pulsed faster. A bolt of lightning shot out, struck the girl in her chest. She bucked and seized, but then stood straight and shoved aside the demon holding her. The little girl turned around, wickedness glowing in her eyes.

"I think they just possessed her," said Vamps, feeling sick. "She's... she's one of them now. What the fuck?! That's why they have all those people chained up! They want to possess them!"

"Then we don't have no choice," said Mass.

Vamps looked at his friend.

"We have to help those people."

Vamps grabbed his friend's hand. They pulled each other close and enjoyed the last moment of peace they might ever get as they were probably about to throw away their lives.

They had no choice.

Vamps turned to get Ginge, to try one more time to talk his friend back to reality, but he was taken by surprise when Pusher grabbed

Ginge by the back of the shirt and tossed him into the road. Ginge tripped over his own feet and sprawled against the tarmac. Instinctively, both Vamps and Mass ran to gather him back up, but as they did, Pusher yelled at the top of his lungs, "Hey bitches, enjoy Hell."

The shout was loud enough to alert the demons at the gate.

Pusher and his two guys legged it into an alleyway and were gone from sight in seconds.

Vamps and Mass tried to pick up Ginge, but he was a dead weight, not even trying to help them by standing. No matter what they did, they could not get him moving. But no way were they leaving him.

Vamps looked at Mass, who looked back at him. Both of them were scared, but neither was about to leave the other. They were family, and that was how brothers on the street lived and died.

"I got your back," said Mass.

Vamps nodded. "And I got yours, brother."

They managed to get Ginge to his feet just as the demons surrounded them. At least Vamps had been able to hide his grandfather's browning under his t-shirt before they grabbed him.

2

Witnessing a mass of demons racing through the night towards you is terrifying, it doesn't matter who you are or how tough you might be. That was why Vamps found himself shaking for the first time in his life.

The burnt men were accompanied by their ape-like companions, and other demons more human—more like greying zombies. There were also a couple of flesh-and-blood human beings, but their eyes were pure Hell. They were possessed.

"You want to fight?" Mass asked, holding Ginge against his big chest so that their friend didn't see what was coming.

Vamps shook his head. "Not yet. We fight now, we die. Maybe later."

"Later we'll probably be dead too."

"But not for certain. We fight now and it's certain."

Mass let his body relax just as the demons fell upon them. Vamps swore as a burnt man clobbered him around the back of the head and shoved him. Before he had chance to shake it off, he was grabbed on either side and restrained. One of the ape-like creatures backhanded him with one of its long, bony arms. Vamps saw stars and went limp as they dragged him away, but turned his head enough to see that Mass and Ginge were being brought along too. Least they were still together.

Being this close to the demons—with them actually touching him—made it hard to breathe. The air was like spoiled fish on a barbecue.

What lay ahead was worse.

Further up Oxford Street, the imposing gate shimmered in all its wretched glory. Before it huddled a mass of frightened people, as many children as adults. Their fear was intoxicating. It made Vamps want to throw up.

"Sssit down," one the demons hissed. Vamps was about to oblige, but the thing hit him in the back of the shoulders. It knocked the wind from his lungs, and he ended up panting on his hands and knees. Mass and Ginge got clobbered too, but Ginge didn't cry out. He was too far gone to even register pain.

Vamps reached out and touched Ginge's arm. "Ginge, man. Please!"

One of the demons kicked Vamps in the backside. "Quiet!"

That the demons could speak was frightening. Vamps had considered them monsters until now, but they were more intelligent than that—monsters with an agenda, enemy soldiers that could be cruel and vicious all on their own. They were so confident of their own strength that most of the prisoners weren't even secured. Their fear kept them in place.

Vamps shuffled up beside his friends and kept his mouth shut. He still had to believe there would be an opening—not just to escape, but to help some of these people. Pusher may have screwed them over, but Vamps was right where he had been intending to be—sat in the road in the heart of the city with his family beside him. If he was going to die, better it be here. If he was going to live, better to fight here.

The demons grabbed a young man—perhaps thirty—and shoved him towards the gate. His screaming face was awash with snot and tears. "Please, I have a family. I have children. I'm a school teacher."

A burnt man whacked the man in the kidneys and shut him up. Then sliced open his wrist. "You are nothing."

The gate shimmered and popped.

Another lightning bolt.

It struck the man the same way it had struck the girl. Only a few seconds passed before he turned around and smiled at his comrades. "My brothers!" The school teacher now spoke with a German accent. "My brothers, thank you. I am back in this world of eternal struggle, and I am ready to fight!"

The demons continued their work, shoving people up against the gate and bleeding them. All manner of accents materialised. Vamps heard people change their speech to German, Spanish, French, and many tongues unrecognisable.

Who was possessing these people, and why had they not been able to escape through the gates like the other demons?

The latest possessed soul spoke with an Arabic accent or similar. The young woman in broken spectacles looked bizarre as she spouted off fiercely. "Ha! I stand in their graveyards as I swore to do one day. I topple their towers and ruin their greatest city. I stab fear into their hearts. But I knew nothing of true terror. Now, I will bring this degenerate world to its knees. The Red Lord will reign."

Mass looked at Vamps and raised an eyebrow. "Man, I think that's Bin Laden."

Vamps said nothing to that. It was absurd. So why did he believe it might be true?

The huddle of frightened people grew smaller with each sacrifice, and the buffer between the gate and Vamps reduced. He wanted to help, yet for thirty minutes he sat and did nothing whilst people had their bodies taken over. Soon he, Mass, and Ginge would suffer the same fate. So why wasn't he doing something?

Because he had absolutely no idea what to do.

He looked at Mass. "I think it's time to fight."

"Really? Shall I take the forty demons on my right, and you take the fifty on your left?"

"Maybe these other people will join us if we start something."

Mass scanned the trembling, white-faced people. "I don't think so, blud."

Vamp sighed, nodded, sighed again. "Then I guess this is it. The Brixton Boys' last stand."

Mass sighed too. "Time to die?"

"I think so. You got my back?"

Mass punched his palm. "Till the grave, Jamal."

The mention of his birth name almost wrecked Vamps. Thoughts of his old dear—the only person who called him Jamal—and the friends he had known and lost, made him want to weep. But it also made him angry. Angry that these fucking demons thought they deserved another shot at the world after screwing up the first time round. They belonged in Hell. They had no right to be here.

Vamps nodded at Mass. "Let's do this."

"Quiet!" One of the zombie-like demons marched towards them, looking like a middle-aged postal worker with jaundice. Before the demon struck him, Vamps leapt up and head-butted the fucker right in the face. Mass leapt up and grabbed him around the neck before he fell.

Snap!

Mass let the dead demon fall to the ground where its face fell unnaturally to the side on a broken neck.

All Hell broke loose as the remaining survivors screamed and cowered. Some leapt up to join the fight, but not enough. This was a fight they would all die fighting.

Vamps was okay with that.

He pulled out his Browning and popped the nearest burnt man in the head. Then he swivelled and aimed another shot into an ape's face. The next trigger pull brought the echoing click of an empty chamber, so he took down the third demon by smashing the old wooden butt into its face. The scrap of skull between its eyes crumpled and blood filled both eyes.

"Lights out, motherfucker!"

Vamps turned and saw Mass perform a double leg take down, not on a demon but on a gun toting human who was working with the demons. One of Windsors' men. He knocked the wind out of the son-of-a-bitch and took his pistol. He shoved the muzzle in the guy's mouth and pulled the trigger without pause. It was messy.

Vamps thought of the rapist he had shot, and froze for a second. Everything around him moved in slow motion, and he wondered if he was paralysed. All sound merged into a single, high-pitched buzz. The only smell was blood.

He was in Hell.

Then he was back.

Back in a world where killing was no longer avoidable.

Mass leapt up and continued firing shots, rounds flying all over the place and striking demons in the kneecaps and arms. One bullet even hit a kid, but there was no time for guilt. These people were dead anyway unless Vamps and Mass somehow pulled off a scene to rival Sparta.

Vamps remembered Ginge and spun around to get him. Surprisingly, the big lad was on his feet. Vamps grabbed him by both arms and looked into his eyes. "Help us, Ginge. Help us get the fuck out of this."

Ginge stared straight through him. He turned away like he'd just remembered he'd needed to be somewhere. Vamps cursed.

The three or four men who had leapt up to join the fight were now dead—torn to pieces. It had seemed like only thirty-seconds since they had first jumped up. That was how quick it was between a man living and dying in this new world.

But Vamps was still alive, and so were his friends.

Vamps' focus had still been on Ginge, which led to him being blindsided by a burnt man, but Mass was there to grab the monster in a rear naked choke and pull it away. Vamps stamped on one of its knees to make the struggle a little less strenuous. Mass broke another neck and threw the demon to the ground, but he was tired and panting.

Vamps was tired too.

A hundred demons surrounded them—a giant net closing in. The enemy had stopped rushing in so carelessly though, now approaching slowly and methodically. Vamps smirked that a legion from Hell was being cautious around him and Mass. It was something he could hold on to if this was the moment of his death. He had died as one hard-as-nails motherfucker.

They were about to rush back into the fray when something blasted down Oxford Street. Windows either side of the road that were not already broken now shattered into a million pieces. The demons stopped their attack and stared upwards. Mass and Vamps exchanged glances and realised that something was behind them. The blasting roar had come from further down the road.

"Should you go first or should I?" asked Vamps.

Mass swallowed. "I'll go."

"Okay."

Slowly, Mass turned around to face the other way. Once he had, his eyes almost popped out of his head. "Fuck me."

Vamps swallowed and turned around too. His eyes went even wider than his friend's. "I was hoping I'd imagined that thing."

The giant stared down at them both, a huge monster glaring at a pair of ants.

Hernandez

THE SHOT ECHOED off the deck, but the sound it made as it struck Danza was muted. Nothing more than a soft thud. The look on Danza's face was also muted—in fact, he seemed more confused than anything else.

Then the Lieutenant fell to one knee. A rosette of blood bloomed in the centre of his chest. His breaths wheezed, like air escaping from a tyre.

Hernandez clenched his jaw and made sure Danza looked at him as he spoke. Dusk cast a shadow across his face—or maybe it was the man's light fading. "You forget yourself, Lieutenant."

Danza opened his mouth, but instead of words, only blood spilled out. The man fell onto his belly and died like a fish. Hernandez let his weapon rest by his side, but spun to address his crew. "You all forget yourselves! When Commander Johnson fell, the Augusta became mine. I will not tolerate mutiny—not when the world itself is at stake. I seek only to aid my country. As Navy men and women, you all vowed to do the same. So I ask you, what exactly is the problem? Why heed the words of a weasel like the one who lies dead at my feet?"

Silence. Nobody dared answer the question.

Hernandez re-holstered his weapon and allowed his anger to subside. "Good, then I expect you all to follow orders from now on. Without exception." He turned to Cuervo, who smiled nervously yet affectionately. "Lieutenant Cuervo is my second-in-command. You will all obey her as you obey me."

"She's just an Ensign," someone muttered.

Hernandez scanned the crowd. "Right now, she is the only one I trust to carry out my orders. Dismissed."

Hernandez turned on his heel to leave, but before he did, he motioned for Cuervo to follow him. She followed along without complaint, but there was something about the way she glanced at him that suggested she feared him. That was good.

As they walked in silence, it occurred to Hernandez that he didn't know where he was heading. Then it came to him, and he knew exactly where to go.

Johnson's cabin was his now, more spacious than any other on board. The man's things lay everywhere, and Hernandez was quick to hide away the former commander's family pictures in a drawer.

"Would you like me to store all of Commander Johnson's things for you?"

Hernandez looked at Cuervo and smiled. "You are a senior officer now, Lieutenant. You don't tidy up. Have someone else do it later. I just wanted to come here and take a look for now."

She looked at him and smiled, then downwards like she was suddenly embarrassed.

"What is it, Cuervo? You can speak freely."

"I thought what you did was brave. Dealing with Danza the way you did. I can't believe he was about to stage a mutiny at a time like this."

"You don't mind that I killed him?"

She shook her head. "I don't think the rules apply anymore. I didn't enjoy it, but I think it had to happen. Only the strong will survive now."

He took a step towards her. "Or those who align themselves with such."

She looked at the metre of carpet between them then back up at him. She opened her mouth to speak, but he cut her off with a kiss—a kiss unlike any he had ever given before. It was powerful and confident. He was powerful and confident.

He was the commander of this ship.

There was no hesitation as he ripped off Cuervo's shirt. He wanted her, and she was his.

And for the next two hours, they made Commander Johnson's bed their own.

2

The knock at the Captain's door woke Hernandez's body first, his mind second. He quickly filled with anger. Cuervo was naked beside him and radiated the most heavenly warmth, and the feel of her bare feet rubbing against his shin was enough to renew his erection.

The unannounced visitor at the door better have a good reason for disturbing him.

"Wait there!" Hernandez grunted and put on his uniform. Cuervo did the same, which was a shrewd move. Hernandez did not care whether his men knew he was screwing the Lieutenant, but Cuervo would already have a hard time trying to gain their respect. No reason to give the crew ammunition for their slurs.

Before Hernandez got his shoes on, the door burst open, and Outerbridge stepped through. Other men stood with him.

"What is the meaning of this?" Hernandez demanded. He marched up to the ship's disgraced sniper and raised his fist in the man's face.

Outerbridge head-butted him ferociously.

Cuervo yelped.

Hernandez staggered backwards. He righted himself on the bed, hands falling upon dampened sheets, and then tried to face his attacker. But tears filled his eyes and blood clogged his sinuses. He could see nothing but his own pain.

Outerbridge had struck him. The wretched slug. How dare he? How dare—

Hernandez was grabbed by both arms and yanked across the room, any argument he was about to present abruptly halted by an elbow across the jaw. They dragged him through the corridors while a dozen men and women jeered. What the hell is going on?

They took him out on deck and threw him unceremoniously to the ground. He made it back up to his knees before something froze him stiff. "D-Danza?"

Danza looked like death, sweaty and pale in the moonlight that had risen overhead since Hernandez had last been outside. The crew had placed him into a wheelchair, and the ship's doctor stood beside him. When he spoke, he sounded winded, and in pain. "When you shoot a man, Hernandez, you should try to avoid the breast bone. It's the best piece of armour a man has." He moved his trembling hand over the centre of his chest and winced. "I might just get to live. Which is more than I can say for you."

Hernandez snarled. "You have no right."

"As you had no right to play executioner. You are not fit for command, Hernandez, or to even have a place aboard this ship. We are proud men and women of the US Navy, and your presence shames us. You are a self-serving coward. And a murderer."

"I am no such thing. You live!"

Danza laughed even though it pained him. "Did you shoot Johnson the way you shot me?"

"Johnson was a fool who didn't know when to run."

"He was a brave man worthy of command. You are a coward worthy only of death."

Hernandez wanted to keel over and vomit, but he would not give his rival the satisfaction. "Then get it over with."

Danza nodded. He reached gingerly to his side and pulled out his service pistol. When he pointed it at Hernandez he frowned. "If any person on this ship objects to the execution of former officer Hernandez, please say so now. I do not intend to run this ship as an unquestioned king."

Nobody spoke up in Hernandez's defence.

"Cowards," Hernandez snarled at them. "I am your commander!"

Danza lowered his pistol and placed it down across his knees. He seemed to think for a moment. "On second thought, it takes far greater virtue to release one's enemy than to kill him. I will not stain the Augusta with any more blood, and truthfully, you do not deserve to die upon its decks. Outerbridge, I think we should put this piece of sludge in a lifeboat and let the sea take him. Maybe it will give him some time to think about his many mistakes."

Outerbridge laughed. He reached down and grabbed Hernandez around the collar and yanked him off his knees.

"You can't do this," Hernandez cried. "It's illegal! This is my ship!"

"I'll tell you what," said Danza. "Apologise to me, right here and now, and I'll let you live out the rest of your days in the brig."

"What?"

"I said apologise."

Hernandez clenched his fists. "I apologise for nothing." He swung a punch at Outerbridge, and the sniper fell, but another crewman took his place, and Hernandez was beaten back down to his knees.

"Very well," said Danza. "Take him."

Outerbridge got up and grabbed Hernandez by the collar again, this time even more roughly. Someone stamped on the former officer's ankle, making him remember he was barefooted. It added to his humiliation in some way. Outerbridge forced his arm behind his back and manhandled him into one of the ship's lifeboats. Before he could try to climb out, the man punched him hard in the face, assuring his nose was broken.

Hernandez sobbed, but stopped himself. He turned the outpouring into a growl. "I will kill you all."

Outerbridge sniggered. "No, you won't. Better you turn your mind to fishing. Maybe then you'll make it through the week. Oh, and one other thing, take your whore with you."

"No, please. No."

Cuervo appeared at the edge of the boat and then was thrown head over heels to join Hernandez. Her head cracked loudly as it struck one of the bolts fastening the bench to the floor. Her cries stopped and transformed into meek sobs. Instinctively, Hernandez reached out and touched her. An entire crew, and she was the only one on his side. Now she had been pulled down with him.

Danza did not appear, probably too weak to leave his wheelchair, but his voice came over the railings clear enough. "I wish you luck, Hernandez. You always wanted to be commander of your own ship. I have given you your wish. May we never meet again."

The winch started up, and the lifeboat lowered towards the water.

Soon the Atlantic would take him.

Rick Bastion

RICK AND DANIEL followed along undetected for more than an hour. Dawn now nibbled at the horizon, and the prospect of daylight changed things significantly. It was one thing creeping around behind a column of demons in the dark, but in daylight?

"We need to fall back further," said Daniel weakly. The Fallen Angel was growing increasingly short of breath. His injuries were not healing, and he needed to rest. If they stopped, though, the demons would move on and disappear. Keith, Maddy, and Diane might be gone forever—if they were even amongst the poor huddled masses being moved along like cattle.

"We can't fall back anymore," said Rick. "We'll lose sight of them."

Even now, the demons were several hundred yards ahead. The motorway stretched on in a straight line for miles, which aided visibility, but the sheer amount of stalled traffic made it hard to pursue. The easiest thing to follow was the noise—the moans and cries of the captives a beacon for Rick and Daniel to lock onto.

Daniel slinked through a gap between a lorry and a caravan. "Once the sun is fully up, it will only take one of those demons to take a look back over his shoulder to spot us."

"We'll keep low, move behind cars. I have to know if Maddy and the others are with them. I can't leave them."

"In the case of your brother, that might be the exact thing you should do."

"You know, for a former angel you're not very Christian."

"Jesus was before my time."

Rick stopped for a second. "But he did exist?"

"There are lots of things in this universe that existed and exist. Reality stretches further than your eyes see."

"What do you mean?"

"I mean that what is happening here is just a drop in the ocean. Even God is tiny in the grand scheme of things. He's a soldier, like everyone else."

"A soldier? Daniel, what are you talking about?"

"Never mind. It would be hard for you to understand."

Rick blinked a few times. He was tired, and his eyes were getting fuzzy. How much longer could he keep going along the motorway? Safety lay to the south not north. Should he turn back?

Could he?

No.

"We have to keep going, Daniel. I—"

"Shh. Something's happening up ahead."

Rick squinted. "What?"

"Look! There's a gate further down."

Rick's stomach filled with lead as he spotted the shimmering lens on the horizon. It was about a mile down the road, tiny at this range but bright enough to light up the dim grey of dawn around it.

"Is this bad?" he asked Daniel.

"It's what I suspected."

Rick looked at him and waited for something more.

Daniel shook his head. "It's a prison break."

"What do you mean?"

"Let's get up in those hills ahead. We need to get a good look at things before we decide what to do."

"So there is something we can do?"

"That's the good thing about being human, isn't it? There's always something you can do. Even if it's stupid."

They climbed the barrier at the edge of the motorway and clambered through the ditch. They pushed through the hedges, and once in the nearby fields, stayed hidden from sight of the motorway. Rick could only just see the fringes of glimmering light through the trees, but they hurried through the long grass until they were right in line with it.

Daniel and Rick peered through the bushes.

Demons amassed outside the twenty-foot gate, and seeing one up close made Rick's skin tighten. It was like standing next to a hungry lion—something in his body tingled at being so close to something so dangerous.

The legion of demons arrived and gathered around the gate, shoving their chained captives to the ground.

"How many of these gates are there?" Rick asked Daniel in a whispered tone.

"Six-hundred and sixty-six."

"Six-six-six. Like the number of the beast?"

"No, like the number of seals God placed upon the earth to keep it safe. One seal for each adversary."

Rick was struggling to understand. "What adversaries? I thought Lucifer was God's adversary."

Daniel chuckled quietly. "Lucifer is a naughty child. The six hundred and sixty six Adversaries are something else entirely. They are equal to God—cut from the same celestial cloth. Each of them yearns for power, and that power exists within life. The life that fills each plant, every moth, and billions of human beings on every single plane of existence. The more worlds conquered by the Adversaries, the stronger they get, and the weaker God becomes."

"I don't understand any of what you just said."

"How could you, Rick? God sacrificed his power to bind his kin. God was the strongest of the Adversaries—the six hundred and sixty seventh—and all the others envied and resented him. A fight brewed, one that threatened the very fabric of existence, so God used his vast power to castrate the Adversaries, himself included. God rendered their powers inert, preventing their ability to act upon the earths.

In doing so, God left you all to fend for yourselves. That is why the prayers of men go unanswered."

"He did it to protect us?"

"To protect everything. This was even before the time of Angels."

"So what's happening now? Who opened the gates?"

"The Black Ram."

Rick laughed. "Are you winding me up? This sounds like a bad novel."

Daniel shrugged. "I suppose it does. The Black Ram is a man—just a man—but he has existed almost since the beginning of time. He has learned to move between the worlds and has assembled a secret society known as the Black Strand. It is they who have put into motion the destruction, not only of this planet, but of many. Each world that falls weakens God, for his power is derived from us. Inside the heart of every man and animal is His essence. When you kill a man, you kill part of God. To kill billions would weaken Him substantially. He is at war; without an army."

"What about the angels?"

"Ineffectual. The seals prevent them from acting upon the earth also."

"But the seals on this world are broken. The Fallen Angels are here, so why not the good angels?"

Using the word 'good' to describe the other angels but not Daniel appeared to hurt him. He closed his eyes for a moment. "I don't know why Heaven's angels are not here. I can only imagine it's because they have their hands full. This is not God's only battle."

Rick was going to ask more questions, but the sound of screaming cut him off. He peered through the bushes and saw that the demons were grabbing people off the ground and shoving them towards the gate. A woman screeched like a bomb siren as a demon slit open her wrists.

"They're using them as vessels," said Daniel. "The very worst souls in Hell are relieved of physical form and doomed to burn in the darkest, most painful pits of the Abyss. Matter cannot exist in the Abyss—only pain and torment. These wicked souls could not pass through the gates like the others, for they lacked the freedom to move."

"They had no bodies," said Rick, hating the fact that he understood.

Daniel nodded. "The only way to bring them here is to give them bodies—vessels. Draining them of blood weakens them and reduces the amount of iron in their bodies."

A bolt of lightning shot from the gate and hit the screaming woman. When she turned around, her eyes were smouldering black stones. A crooked grin distorted her face.

"The worst men and women in history," said Daniel. "Coming home."

The possessed woman grabbed a small boy from the floor and shoved him, screaming, towards the gate. She opened his throat with her teeth. The gate began to vibrate and shimmer.

"Leave him alone," someone shouted.

Rick moved his head to see past a bunch of branches and saw a woman leap up and run to help the boy.

It was Maddy.

Daniel grabbed Rick. "Wait."

"We can't. She's in danger."

A burnt man leapt in front of Maddy and backhanded her across the face. She fell to the ground, clutching her cheek. Another bolt of lightning shot from the gate and hit the boy. A few seconds later he threw his arms around the woman who had bit him and hugged her. "Mummy."

Rick glanced at Daniel. "Who the hell are they?"

"Carmilla and Edward Stokes."

"Who?"

"Carmilla was a doctor who lived near White Chapel. Her twelve year old son wanted to be a surgeon. Carmilla wanted to teach him."

"White Chapel? You mean he... they were Jack the Ripper?"

Daniel nodded. "Yes. Carmilla used to hire prostitutes, explaining that she wanted to make her son a man. She would sedate them with tainted sherry, and then little Edward would get to work."

A demon dragged Maddy and threw her down in her place in line. A man and a woman took hold of her and cradled her as she moaned. Keith and Diane.

Rick felt his stomach trying to escape through his throat. The sight of Maddy's tears made him feel worthless. "We have to go help them."

"We try now," said Daniel, "we die now."

"You don't know that."

Daniel sighed. "Rick, of all the things you've learned about me, surely the one thing you've realised is that I know more than you do. I'm telling you, we go out there and we won't get to walk away."

Rick grabbed a branch and clutched it tightly, thorns digging into his palm. He used the pain to help him concentrate. "There're enough people down there to overthrow the demons. We have to fight. The longer we wait, the more people who will get possessed."

"If we do this, I won't be able to help you anymore."

Rick stared at Daniel, trying to work out what he was saying. "Why?"

"Just decide if you really want to do this."

"I'm sure. Maddy, Diane, and my brother are down there. I won't sit by and watch them get possessed."

Daniel nodded. He looked sad. "Okay then."

The Fallen Angel burst through the hedges and leapt down into the ditch at the side of the motorway. The demons saw him and attacked at once. Daniel waved an arm like he was swatting a fly, and a force unseen hit the incoming demons like a wave of hot air. Their flesh turned to ash. Skin flew from their bones. Withered skeletons collapsed to the ground.

Rick broke from the hedges and clambered into the ditch to help. He was unarmed, so he moved away from battle and towards the captives. When Keith and the others saw him, they looked gobsmacked. "Rick," said his brother. "You came to rescue us?"

Rick looked at Maddy as he spoke. "Of course I did. Now get up and help."

The captives were restrained with rope, not chains, so they were able to shove their binds off easily. Some ran immediately, but most were too shocked to make a decision. The gate towered over them all.

"Get up and fight," Rick bellowed at them. "Fight now or die as cowards. You are not animals. Do not let these monsters treat you like you are."

Perhaps it was Rick's anger that caused the captives to rise, but rise they did—two thirds of them. None held weapons, but each threw themselves at the enemy like barbarians, beating with fists and clawing with fingernails. Many fell quickly, but most caught the burnt men by surprise.

Rick grabbed a demon and tossed it into the central reservation. He stamped its skull against the safety barrier until there was nothing left. Meanwhile, Daniel cut a swath through the enemy camp, waving his arm and searing demon flesh from bone. The invisible heat waves turned the grass brown at the edges of the road and cracked the windscreen of an overturned Jeep. No demon could get within two metres of the Fallen Angel. He was a force of nature.

But he was growing weaker by the second.

Rick went to help, but heat blazed around Daniel. It was impossible to get close. More demons fell within the Fallen Angel's cocoon of heat, like lambs in a nuclear blast. Daniel's expression was grim. Sweat swamped his face. His arms trembled. He slumped to his knees and the heat disappeared.

The demons recovered.

Rick moved in front of the gate and cried out. "Everyone, fight!"

There were now only a fraction of the demons remaining, Daniel having dismantled half himself. The captives were so inspired by the sudden victory that they fell upon the demons three to one. They ripped the burnt men limb from limb.

Adrenaline surged through Rick, and he spun around to fight the first demon that came near. He found a little boy standing before him. The little boy now possessed by Edward Stokes.

With a snarl, the black-eyed child lunged. Rick was off balance and stumbled to the ground when Edward struck him. He found himself on his back with the young boy tearing at his face like a wolverine. He tried to defend himself, but could not protect his face and fight at the same time.

"I'll slice you into pieces, you whore," Edward screamed. He opened a wound on Rick's forehead and dug into it with his fingernails. Rick bellowed in agony.

"Get off him, you little brat!" Maddy grabbed Edward's hair and yanked him backwards. The little boy kicked and screamed.

Rick scrambled to his feet, but didn't know what to do. Edward might be a demon, but he was inhabiting the body of an innocent child. Was there a way to save him? An exorcism?

Maddy struggled to hold onto the thrashing monster. "Rick, help!"

"What do I do?"

"Just do... something."

Rick was rooted to the spot. As much as he knew the boy before him was a demon now, he could not get past the fact it had once been a little boy. "I-I can't."

The fearful look on Maddy's face hurt Rick, and left him unprepared when someone shoved him aside. "For fuck sake, Rick," said Keith. "Can't you do anything?"

Keith moved in front of Edward as the boy slipped free of Maddy's grasp. He clutched a tyre iron, and he brought it down on the demon's skull before it had chance to evade. One blow was enough. Edward fell to the floor dead—his tiny skull shattered.

Rick's jaw dropped as he looked at his brother, but Keith seemed only angry about what he had been forced to do. Between them, Maddy stood with a face full of conflict. It was something that needed to be done, but to do so with so little hesitation...

Maybe Keith understood what living demanded now more than they did.

"My boy! What have you done?" Rick spotted Carmilla racing towards Keith, hysterical eyes like bubbling oil slicks.

Rick snatched the tyre iron away from his brother and pushed him aside. He brought the heavy length of metal down with perfect timing and split the woman's skull in two. He held up the tyre iron and allowed his brother to take it back. "We need to help, Daniel."

Keith grinned, and with exuberant tone he said, "With what? The battle is won."

Rick looked around. He saw no demon left alive, only a road covered in blood and bone. Of the captives, perhaps eighty still lived. They had truly won, but would they have done so without a Fallen Angel fighting for their cause?

Daniel was slumped up against an overturned jeep. Its tyres had blistered and melted like chocolate overspilling a pan. Rick hurried over to him. "Daniel, we did it. We rescued all these people."

Daniel smiled. "Not bad for a disgraced angel, huh?"

"You're good, Daniel. One mistake you made thousands of years ago doesn't make you who you are. You're good."

"Thank you."

"Are you going to be okay?"

He laughed, but it reduced to a spluttering cough. "I think I'm beyond the point of being okay, Rick. This body was not meant for such feats. It is already dead. Help me up."

Rick nodded. "If you're sure."

"Yes. Let me bask in victory. It might be my last chance."

Rick strained to lift the angel to his feet. "You're a halo-half-full kind of angel, aren't you?"

The survivors had now given way to shock and relief, clinging together for comfort. They hugged and kissed one another, family, friends, and strangers.

But they were not yet safe. Before them towered a portal to a place beyond nightmares. The gate shimmered and spat angrily.

"How do we destroy it?" Rick asked Daniel, who was limping gingerly and clutching himself.

"Ha, you don't want to know."

"But there is a way?" said Keith, hurrying over and looking ready for more fighting.

Daniel nodded. "Yes."

"Then tell us."

"How about a little thanks, first? Me and your brother just sprung you from a death camp."

Keith snorted. "We would have been fine. I was figuring things out."

"What happened to you?" Rick asked his brother.

"We waited at the car lot," said Maddy, joining them along with Diane. Diane said, "They came out of nowhere and took us. We thought we were dead, but they just grabbed us."

"They carried us down the road and put us with everyone else," said Maddy. "All these people. They were using them. Possessing their bodies. Rick, if you hadn't come..."

"It was Daniel," admitted Rick. "I couldn't have done anything without him."

Diane moved over to Daniel and hugged him. "Thank you."

The Fallen Angel winced in pain, but seemed touched by the gesture. He patted the girl on the back. "Don't mention it, love."

"How do we close the gate?" Keith demanded. "More demons might come through at any moment."

Daniel nodded. "You're right. But to close the gate will take something I'm not sure you will want to give."

Keith got in Daniel's face, like the Fallen Angel hadn't just dispatched fifty demons. "Just tell us."

"Keith!" Maddy chided. "Calm down."

Rick felt the hairs on the back of his neck twitch. Things had grown tense, but it wasn't from the argument in front of him.

Sweep.

Daniel's shoulders sagged as he endured Keith getting in his face. "To close the gate. To close it—"

"Yes?" said Keith impatiently.

"—you have to—" Daniel stopped mid-sentence. His eyes narrowed.

Keith clenched his fists. "Tell us, for crying out loud."

Daniel stood in silence, his eyes boring into Keith. Keith grew angry and grabbed him, but yelped when the angel slumped forwards into his arms.

Blood exploded from Daniel's mouth.

Rick ran to him. But it was too late. The possessed human body had been torn open, its back flayed and split apart. Spine and nerves peeked out between pink muscle.

Keith leapt aside and let Daniel fall to the ground.

Sweep.

Rick glanced around, but saw nothing. Something had torn Daniel apart, yet there was nothing there.

Sweep.

Rick dove to the ground beside Daniel. Blood spilled from the angel's mouth, yet he somehow managed to summon words. "Does being human always hurt this much?"

Rick stroked his friend's face. "It never stops hurting."

Daniel closed his eyes, and for a moment it looked like he was gone, but then his consciousness returned, and he seized Rick by the arm, pulled him close. "You can't do this without my help."

"Then live."

"I cannot."

"Then we're doomed."

"No."

Rick began to sweat from his shoulder blades and suddenly wished he was unclothed. He tried to pull back his arm, to stand up and get some air, but Daniel held onto him tightly. Where the angel's fingers touched his flesh, skin burned. Rick cried out—his entire arm on fire. The heat travelled upwards, into his shoulder and to his head.

"Daniel, please, stop!"

"In a moment."

"You're killing me."

"No, I am giving you life."

The pain reached a zenith, and Rick thought his head might explode, but then Daniel lost consciousness and released his grip. The pain disappeared. Rick couldn't breathe, and for a moment, he thought he might asphyxiate. Then his breath returned to him, and he gasped until his lungs hurt.

Sweep.

"What the fuck happened to Daniel?" Keith demanded, dodging around anxiously with his tyre iron.

Rick looked at his friend and sighed. "He's gone. Wherever he is, I hope God finally forgives him."

Sweep.

"The Caretaker is here, isn't he?" said Maddy.

Rick stood up defiantly. "Yes, and this time we can't run."

"What do we do?" asked Diane.

"We make the most of the chance Daniel gave us. We fight. We stay together, and we fight."

Rick looked around at the eighty-odd survivors and knew most of them might die in the next five minutes, but at least now they had a chance of living. Only one thing stood in their way.

Sweep.

2

Sweep.

"Where is he?" Diane whimpered. "I can't see him."

Keith growled. "How do we fight something we can't see?"

Sweep.

Rick instinctively moved to shield Maddy. The Caretaker was amongst them, had killed Daniel—their only hope. A great beast hunted.

Someone in the crowd screamed.

An older man fell to the floor, his spine broken in two and poking out of his back.

The survivors panicked.

Rick searched for The Caretaker, glimpsed the creature for a split second but then lost him again. A faceless skull flitting through the crowd.

Keith clutched his tyre iron. "I'm going to cave his skull in. Where are you? Show yourself!"

Diane backed up against the central barrier and yelped when she bumped into it.

Rick held a hand up to her. "Just stay calm."

Another person in the crowd screamed and fell down dead.

"What's happening?" someone shouted.

The crowd broke apart.

"Stay together," Rick shouted. "Our only chance is to stay together."

"What do you expect them to do?" asked Keith. "They're dying."

"None of us can make it alone."

More people screamed and died, backs broken, skulls crushed.

Rick raised his fist. "It's me you want. I looked upon you and saw your wretched form. Show yourself."

Another scream, another grizzly death.

Panic reigned. People fled.

"Stay together," Rick bellowed again. In anger, he flung out his fist. The overturned jeep at the side of the road leapt off the ground and tumbled over the central barrier. Several people tumbled to the ground too, as if pushed.

Rick gasped, looked at his shaking hand. Keith and the others stared at him. The survivors were stunned to silence, even as more of them fell. The Caretaker preyed on them from the edges of vision.

Rick felt faint. His mind filled with thoughts and understanding not his own. What had Daniel done to him? What had he been given?

He'd been given knowledge.

Rick knew how to goad the Caretaker.

He held up his hand and bit into his palm. The pain wracked his entire body, but he clenched his jaw and bore into it until the deed was done. Blood spurted down his wrist, spattered the road with a pitter pat.

Keith covered his mouth with revulsion. "Rick, what the hell are you doing?"

Rick ignored his brother and raised his bleeding hand. "Blood. It sets your teeth on edge, doesn't it? It stains the ground and soils the earth. It is unclean."

Something shimmered within the crowd.

Rick clenched his fist, pumping more blood from the wound. "I defile the ground, and you cower in the shadows, a frightened slave. A worthless slave."

The air turned black and colour drained from the world. Then, with a flash, a figure appeared before Rick. The Caretaker snarled without a mouth. Its skinned skull was a map of purple throbbing veins, and when it reached out to Rick, the air itself retreated.

Rick stepped back, away from the foul creature's grasp. He brought up his own hand and surprised himself once more with the power he wielded. A gust of flame emanated from his bleeding palm and blanketed The Caretaker. The grotesque mockery of an old man staggered backwards, flailing its arms and legs. Only deterred for a moment, it lashed out and sent Rick flying off his feet. He landed on the bonnet of a BMW saloon and bounced off onto the road. Pain stunned him, yet he was able to rise. Thoughts swirled through his head like fireflies. He threw up both arms in front of him and sent another arc of flames across the sizzling tarmac.

The Caretaker was gone.

Maddy shouted. "Rick! Behind you."

Rick twirled, but couldn't dodge The Caretaker's razor sharp talon. It entered his guts and travelled sideways through his torso, gutting him like a fish. Blood and shit covered the ground.

The Caretaker let out a keening sound and shook. Its hand went to its face in a mock expression of horror.

More knowledge coming to him, like secrets unlocked from cabinets, Rick reached into his guts and flung his blood and guts at his enemy. The Caretaker squealed. Blood covered its featureless face, and it clawed at itself madly. Talons cleaved flesh. Torrents of black pus burst from a dozen wounds.

Rick climbed to his feet, guts still falling out onto the floor. He leapt forward and grabbed The Caretaker's bleeding skull. Numb spikes of ice shot up his wrists. He reached inside himself and tried to find the parts of Daniel that now existed inside of him. "I have the power of God inside me, you ugly fuck. Go back to Hell!"

Possessing strength he had never dreamed of, Rick crushed the Caretaker's skull beneath his fingertips as if it were an over-ripe watermelon. Black pus and mould erupted as if the foulest boil in existence had just been squeezed. The old man's body shook, trembled, and became nothing. The Caretaker collapsed inwards and turned to dust. A sudden wind blew and took his remains.

Maddy rushed forward and caught Rick as he fell. "Rick, are you okay?"

"D-Daniel. He... He is still with me."

Maddy lowered him to the ground and nodded. "He did something to you."

"To help us."

"Yes."

"My stomach... It's bad."

Maddy shook her head. "No."

"Liar."

"No."

Rick looked down at his stomach. His shirt was bloody and torn, yet when he pawed at himself, he found only clear, unbroken flesh. "But...?"

"You healed," said Diane, hurrying over with tears in her eyes. "You can't die."

Keith huffed. "Everything dies."

"Including The Caretaker," said Rick, filled with relief now they were safe for a while. He really wanted to rest.

"Is he really gone?" asked Maddy.

Rick searched his mind for answers and knew that The Caretaker was once again sweeping the hallways of Hell. More knowledge came to him in a steady stream. "They're frightened," he said.

"Who is?" Keith frowned.

"All of them, the demons. They are afraid of being sent back to Hell. This is their one and only shot. We can win this war. We can fight back. If not, then they wouldn't be afraid. They know there's a chance for us."

Those who had not fled gathered round, listening intently. His words were met with whispers and sobs—perhaps hope.

Maddy smiled and nodded. "As long as we keep fighting, we can beat them."

Rick stood up, and without a word, he walked towards the shimmering gate.

Keith called out to him. "Rick, what are you doing? Get away from there."

Rick faced the shimmering tapestry of light and tried to see through. Voices whispered to him in a thousand languages. Eyes watched him. Eyes full of fear.

He reached out his hand—

"Rick!"

—and touched the gate.

There was no explosion—no fireworks or noise—it simply stopped being there. Like a snapping eyelid, the gate blinked out of existence. All bodies of dead demons littering the ground disappeared as well. The evil was gone, along with any memory of it.

Rick turned to face the astonished crowd. "We have work to do."

Richard Honeywell

THE DEMON KNOWN as Andras was a sorry sight. David, who was no picture himself with grievous wounds still healing, admitted to sawing off the demon's legs and arms before cauterising the blood vessels with flames from the building's kitchen. Although hellish in nature, Andras inhabited a human body, and felt the pain to go along with it.

"Why did you do this?" Richard asked David, surprised it didn't sicken him more. Seeing his wife's head reduced to mush had altered him, stripped a part of him away—the human part.

David huffed. "For information. Plus the bastard killed Mina."

Richard groaned. So that was what happened to her.

"He doesn't have long," David went on, "and once he dies he'll return to the pit he came from. He claims to be a Lord of Hell, a former angel, yet he acquired a human body for means of subterfuge. Soon as he escapes us, he will share all he knows with his brethren."

"And what does he know? What information do they even need? We've lost."

David glared at Richard through his one remaining eye—the other burned away—and said, "We have lost nothing except the first move. They hit us, now we hit back. Soldiers in Syria closed a gate, we have a Lord in our captivity... Things are bad, but we still have fight left in us. We've even been getting news of some kid who took on one of the giants in Tokyo and lived to tell about it. Human spirit is what will see us through."

Richard glanced at the mutilated body in the cupboard and sniffed. "Not sure there's much humanity left in us anymore."

"Some of us give up a part of ourselves so that others don't have to."

Andras spat at them. "You chatter like monkeys."

David backhanded the demon. "And you mewl like a dying kitten. Your brothers are at war while you sit wounded in a closet. How shameful."

"Then release me, and we will see where the shame lies."

David smirked, a ruinous gesture on his mangled face.

"What do you want?" Richard asked the demon. "Why are you doing this?"

"To take what is ours. We are the exalted ones, held down unjustly by mankind. You are unworthy of this earth, of such freedoms."

"You might be right," said Richard, "but you don't deserve it either."

Andras's head slumped through weakness, but he fought to lift it again. "Regardless, we will take it. The Red Lord will rule, and humanity will be reduced to pigs in shit."

"And you, lowly farmers," said David.

Richard stopped David from striking the demon again. He moved close and stared Andras in his eyes. "You think this earth is so wonderful? It is filled with pain and hatred, no different to the Hell you came from. You are welcomed to this earth. Leave your gates open because you might want to return before long."

Andras sneered, his teeth broken and cragged. "Return is not an option. We must take this earth and flourish, or fail and die."

Richard raised an eyebrow. "You must? You said you must take it. What happens if you fail?"

Andras writhed furiously. "We will not fail! The Red Lord will take this place in his fist and squeeze all life from it."

"Why?"

"Because it is his will. Every life taken will weaken God's grip on the Heavens until we storm his kingdom and make him kneel."

David flinched. "You want war against God?"

"Not for the first time, pig. Lucifer led us in glorious pursuit, yet he cowers and hides now as the Red Lord leads us anew. Every human death tips the balance in our favour."

David nodded. "So our extermination has a purpose? You need to kill us to... what, unlock Heaven?"

Andras locked his jaw and said nothing else.

David removed himself and Richard from the closet and closed the door. "You made him angry, Richard. Good work. His ego has been our greatest asset. He might be a Lord, but he speaks before he thinks. This war isn't about us. It's about God. Maybe that's important."

Richard sighed. "I don't care. I need to go check on my son."

He left David in the hallway and went back into the news office. The lights were off, conserving the last of the power that came from a generator. No one could say when the main grid had failed, but the town centre beyond the windows of the fourth floor were blanketed in darkness.

Dillon sat in a corner of the office with the young girl, Alice. They were reading comic strips in the back of old copies of The Slough Echo. "Dillon is nice," said Alice. "He tells me jokes."

Richard chuckled. "Really? He doesn't tell me any." Dillon looked away shyly. He had little experience of girls, young or old. "Alice, would you mind if I spoke to Dillon alone for a few minutes?"

The little girl nodded and got up. Richard thanked her and sat beside his son.

Dillon kept his head lowered.

"Dillon, what happened to mummy... It was something no child should ever have to see."

"She's gone forever, isn't she?"

"Yes."

"Are you going to get the bad man who did it?"

Richard thought about Skullface—a seven-foot skeleton. "I don't think I can, Dillon. All we can think about right now is staying safe."

"But you're a policeman."

"My job doesn't matter anymore."

Dillon looked up, tears raining down his cheeks. "Yes it does! You look after people when they need help. Mummy needed help, and now she's gone. You have to get the bad man!"

"Dillon..."

"No, you need to still be a policeman. I want Alice to come back."

Richard looked at his son and realised he was getting overwrought. "Okay, sweetheart. I'll go and get her."

He went back over to get Alice who was speaking with Corporal Martin. "Hi Alice, Dillon would like to play again when you have a moment."

Corporal Martin nodded to her. "Go on."

She went back to join Dillon. Martin nodded to Richard. "Learn anything from our prisoner?"

"Not a lot. Something about a war on God. David seemed to understand more than me."

The soldier rubbed at his chin. "I'll speak with Portsmouth, see if they've heard anything similar."

"The Army still exists?"

"Just about. There're a dozen soldiers heading here, as we speak, to help protect what we're doing—all they could spare. Any help we can get though at this point, you know?"

"You really think you're helping by running a website?"

"Hey, I wasn't a believer either, but we're just about the last news site still running. The big companies got hit when London and New York were attacked. The Seattle Post is about the only other paper making regular updates, but in the UK we're it—the last bastion of news. People are hiding out in their homes, logging on with their phones. We can't help for much longer, but we've done enough to galvanise a few people into action. Case and point is the gate that closed in Syria. Portsmouth had discovered that it was a British Army Sergeant who managed it. One of the men he was fighting with went through it. The news we spread about it has given hope to people all over the world."

Richard lifted his chin and made sure he was hearing correctly. "Somebody went into the gate?"

"Apparently, that's how it was closed. Demons can come out, but a human going in short circuits it."

"So we can close the gates?"

The corporal laughed. "Yeah, if we commit suicide."

Richard looked back at his son and nodded. "I understand."

"I just hope," the corporal went on, "that someone closes the London gate soon. Andras doesn't have long left, and once his human body gives in, his soul will return to Hell. He'll reemerge in his proper form—a bloody giant—and well, this'll be the first place he comes for retribution."

"A giant?"

"Yes, have you not seen them? There's only three in the UK, but they're unkillable. They are leading the demons, forming armies ready to finish this war before it begins. The giants were angels once."

"And Andras too?"

"Yes."

Richard shook his head. "How do you know all this?"

"Andras himself mostly. He killed Mina, the reporter who was with me when we first met."

"I remember her."

"Andras tried to call home—I won't go into how he did that—and David overheard him. He's spilled even more information from the monster since. There are ways to win this war, Richard, we just have to find them."

"Like closing the gate in London?"

"The gate will allow the demons reinforcements. There are over a hundred gates in this country, but the one in London is the one that threatens us most directly."

Richard looked back at Dillon again. His son was playing with Alice again and seemed to have forgotten his tears. Alice stroked his hair as they read more comics. The young girl seemed to understand that, despite Dillon being older, she was truly the elder of the two. She was a good girl, and Richard wondered what had become of her parents.

"I'll pass through the gate," he said.

Corporal Martin gave him a look and then laughed. "What are you talking about?"

Richard stared the man in the eyes to convey that he was not joking. "Those soldiers on their way here. Have them take me into the city, and I will pass through that gate. I'll give my life if it means you will all be safer here. If it keeps my son alive."

"Don't be absurd. Rich—"

"Somebody has to do it, don't they?"

"Yes, but not fathers with sons to look after. Not those with a choice."

"None of us has a choice anymore. All we can do is try to make life hard for these bastards. I will pass through the gate. I've already made my mind up."

"And what about your son?"

Richard watched Dillon for a few more seconds. "My son is damaged. All I can do now is try to give him enough time to heal. If I can do something to keep more mothers from being taken away from their sons... I want to do this."

"I say let him." Leonard walked over to them. "I only met Richard this morning, but he kept us all alive. If he wants to do this, I'll help get him there."

"Me too," said Riaz.

"And me," added the paramedic, Oliver.

"Sod it, I'm in," Aaron added from the corner of the office.

Richard looked around and realised several people had woken up and been listening. Their support was unexpected, yet welcome.

Corporal Martin laughed. "This war doesn't need a Fellowship of the Ring. We don't need heroes, we need strategy and planning."

Rick shook his head. "We need both. Every war has its heroes and planners, and I'm no planner."

Corporal Martin sighed. "Look, Richard. You're a free man. All I ask is that you sleep on it. If in the morning you are still set on a suicide mission, we'll work something out."

Richard nodded, satisfied. "I won't change my mind."

And he was certain he wouldn't, which was something he found absurd. Was he really willing to give his life? He looked once again at his son—forever innocent, courtesy of his Downs. Yes, he was willing.

"Thank you for getting us this far," said Aaron.

Richard patted the lad on the shoulder. "You got yourself this far. Bravery is not something you're short of."

"Ha! I've pissed myself three times today."

"So have I."

"You really sure you want to go into the city?"

Richard nodded. "What happened today showed me what a losing battle we're fighting. If I can do something to hit back, then I'm sure."

Aaron sighed. "I'll be ready when you are."

"No, I want you to stay here and watch Dillon."

"Me? What about your partner."

"Riaz isn't my partner. Anyway, I want you to stay here because you're tough, and you believe in sticking by your friends. Dillon will look up to you, and you're too young to accompany me on a suicide trip. You can do more good here."

Aaron looked like he was about to argue, but didn't. "I'll keep an eye on him."

Richard pulled the lad into a hug. Aaron resisted for a moment, but then hugged back. It was a gesture the lad was obviously unused to, but one he soon embraced. "You're a good lad, Aaron. Stay alive and keep Dillon with you."

"Richard?" The voice that called his name was that of a woman, familiar yet... pained.

Everyone in the office turned towards the door, but it was Richard who reacted most hysterically. He flew across the room towards his wife, arms outstretched, eyes and mouth wide open in shock. "Jennifer!"

David came out of nowhere and grabbed Richard six feet before his wife. "Open your eyes, Richard."

"Get off me!"

"Mummy?" Dillon got up of the floor, but Alice held him back.

"Stay here, Dillon. That's not your mummy."

Richard looked at his wife—saw the misshaped curve of her flattened skull, left eye dangling down her cheek—and realised she was still dead. Whatever this was, it was not Jen.

"What do you want?" David demanded of the ghoul at their door.

Her teeth chattered madly for a second, and then she spoke. "I just want to see my husband. Richard, I'm hurt. I need you!"

Richard snarled at the thing abusing his wife's corpse. "Jen would have asked for Dillon before she ever asked for me. She was a mother. You monsters took her from us."

The crooked mouth smirked, and her single eye scanned the room. "You are all going to die. Andras will crush you all." She reached down and picked something up off the ground before tossing it into the middle of the room.

Andras's head.

"Shit!" said David. "Shit! Shit! Shit!"

The mockery of Jen cackled. "He is coming."

Bang!

Jen's head exploded for a second time. All eyes turned to the back of the room where Corporal Martin held a smoking semi-auto. Richard screamed out in pain. He did not attack the soldier, for he knew he had done nothing to harm his wife. Jen had been dead the moment Skullface took her head between his hands.

So, instead, he fell to the floor and cursed God. Dillon hurried over and dropped to the floor beside him, and they cried together.

2

Morning broke, allowing Richard to look out of the office windows at the silent town of Slough. Somewhere out there a horde of demons lurked, but how many humans too? Would they fight back, or die like dogs in the street?

Pigs, Andras had called them.

They had found Andras's decapitated torso in the cupboard moments after the thing dressed as Jen had arrived. The creature's purpose had been to free Andras from his mortal coil—using the carcass of a loved one had been a perverse bonus. The demons enjoyed causing pain.

Dillon slept in a side office with Alice and Carol. The older woman was the head of the newspaper, but she was also the mother of the group. Richard felt safe leaving Dillon in her care. Many others in the office slept too. It'd been a long night, and the morning promised only more hardship. Smoky tendrils rose behind a dozen buildings on the horizon. The world was on fire, becoming a new Hell for mankind to endure.

Corporal Martin appeared beside Richard, and for a while, the two of them stood there looking out at what was now a battleground. Martin spoke first. "The extra soldiers will be here within the hour. You still want an escort to the city?"

"No. I'm staying."

Martin nodded. "What changed your mind?"

"My wife. Not what appeared last night pretending to be her. I mean my actual wife. Jen would never forgive me for leaving Dillon. These bastards think they can murder us and wear our bodies for sport. They think they can escape the punishment of Hell by brute force and we'll stand back and let them? No, I won't have it. There might not be any laws left, but there are still rules. You don't take what isn't yours. You don't kill to get what you want. I'm a police officer, and as long as I still live I will protect people by enforcing the rules. Way I look at it, what we're up against is no more than a bunch of escaped prisoners. It's time to start sending them back."

"Glad to have you on board. I'm sure if we all put our heads together we can figure out what to do next. That London gate still needs closing, so let's just hope there's someone still alive out there, and that they have the balls to do what needs to be done. You were right about us needing heroes."

Richard nodded. "We have heroes. Everyone left alive will be one in the days ahead. It was you who was right, Corporal Martin—we need a plan."

"Do you have one?"

"Yes," said Richard. "I just might."

Vamps

THE GIANT ROARED, and kicked a city bus so hard that it skidded from one side of the road to the other. At the same time, a black Mercedes hurtled down the road, heading towards the gate. When it screeched to a halt, two bodyguards and Prime Minister Windsor stepped out.

Vamps spat at the sight of the man.

Windsor looked excited as he hurried along the road. His bodyguards struggled to keep up with the long-legged man, and they didn't seem to know whether to walk fast or break into a run.

The PM stopped before the giant and looked up. "Lord Amon, it is a pleasure beyond words."

The giant looked down at the tiny man and sneered. "For you, I imagine it is. Have you done as asked?"

Windsor nodded enthusiastically. "Yes, yes. I have brought you flesh as required. Hundreds more are en route."

"Excellent, then your head need not part from your shoulders."

The smile on Windsor's face wavered. "I am yours to command."

"As are all." The giant glared at Vamps and Mass who were still frozen in place. "Regain control of affairs, Prime Minister, lest affairs take control of you."

Windsor nodded to his bodyguards who seized Vamps and Mass and dragged them towards the gate. Mass blinked rapidly, as if he didn't trust his sight. He didn't seem to realise he was being dragged backwards. "That thing is talking, yo! A giant and the motherfuckin' Prime Minister are having a conversation. When are we gunna wake up?"

"I don't think this is a nightmare," said Vamps, not daring take his eyes off the giant.

They were thrown back with the other terrified survivors, who had fallen to silence in the presence of the giant. Lord Amon, Windsor had called it. Upper-class fucks.

The giant stomped over to the gate, making the ground shake and the road crack. "Make haste," he bellowed. "My brothers seek liberty to see the sun rise to the sky and moon to follow."

The demons before the gate reformed and resumed their gathering of people. A catatonic woman was placed before the shimmering gate and stood there like an ironing board as they sliced open her wrists. Once the lightning hit her, she was animated once more and clapped her hands gleefully.

Then the demons grabbed Ginge.

Vamps leapt up but was smashed in the guts by a burnt man. He fell back to the ground, wheezing and gasping, clawing at the ground to get back up.

Mass shouted to their friend. "Gingerbread! Ginge, don't let them take you."

Ginge was still someplace else, his stare far off in the distance. He was completely obliging as a demon led him towards his fate.

Vamps caught his breath and cried out. "Ginge... Ginge, you need to wake up! These bastards killed Ravy, and now they are going to use your body like a puppet. Brixton Boys don't lay down for nobody!"

Ginge stopped. His weight was substantial enough that the burnt man dragging him was forced to stop too.

Mass and Vamps exchanged glances.

"Ginge, wake up!"

"Will you shut them up?" John Windsor shouted, watching from beside his Mercedes.

Another demon went to its colleague's aid and doubled up on Ginge, dragging him by each arm.

Mass cried out again, but a demon kicked him in the mouth. A burnt man stalked towards Vamps too, so he had only one final chance to say goodbye to his friend. "Ginge, we need you, man. Don't go. We're your brothers!"

Ginge stopped again, even with two demons trying to drag him. They struggled with his arms, but he would not move.

"Get him moving," Windsor bellowed.

One of the demons raised a twisted hand and slapped Ginge across the face. Ginge did not flinch. What he did do was turn his head slowly to face the one who had struck him.

The demon snarled. "Move it!"

Ginge grabbed the demon like it was a child and lifted it over his head. He tossed it on top of the other one at his side and then let out a roar to rival any monster.

Windsor stepped away from his Mercedes and flung out an arm. "Get him in front of the gate now!"

Ginge punched a demon in the face as it went to grab him, then spun around and booted one of the ones he'd tossed to the ground. Half a dozen burnt men tried to bring him down, but he was a wild bear, shoving and clubbing at all within reach. The whole time he roared.

Vamps leapt up and grabbed the burnt man that had been planning to silence him. Mass jumped up too, and between them they snapped the demon's neck. They took down two more before the demons even realised that they were under attack. Ginge's freak out held most of their attention.

Vamps looked at the other survivors and yelled at them to join the fight. None did. They might have done something before, but not in the presence of the giant.

Lord Amon stood silently by as the chaos ensued, watching with what might have been amusement. Vamps shuddered under the demon's glare, but got back to fighting. He and Mass punched and kicked and wished for something more than their own limbs to fight with. The burnt men were supple, and easy to take in a fight, but there were so many—and they never backed down.

Mass nailed one of the ape-creatures with a spinning back kick that made Vamps laugh at the audacity of it. Ginge grabbed a burnt man by the arm and flung him into the air like an athlete throwing a hammer. Vamps raced towards the PM.

If he only had a short amount of time, best make it count. Go for the high-value target.

Windsor's attention was on the gate. He didn't see Vamps coming.

Vamps clenched his fists and prepared to launch himself at the worm who had once led the country before betraying it.

"Where you going, mate?"

Vamps collided with the barrel chest of a bodyguard. He bounced off and ducked just in time to avoid a right hook. The other bodyguard came up on Vamp's right.

Windsor backed off towards his Mercedes. "Take care of him."

Vamps spun out of the way as another punch sought his face. He moved himself beside the bodyguard on his right and stamped down on the bigger man's knee, making him scream like a baby and go down clutching himself. The other bodyguard threw himself at Vamps and lifted him off the ground. Vamps drove the point of his elbow into the top of the man's skull and they both fell to the ground. The bodyguard got the upper position and began raining down blows. Vamps covered up, but was locked in place between the heavy man's knees.

What would Mass do in such a position?

Vamps opened his arms, which caused him to take a few unmet punches. He ignored the rattling of his teeth and reached up to grab his attacker's head and neck. Then he pulled up his left leg and slid it around behind his attacker's shoulders. The man struggled to straighten up so he could rain down more blows, but Vamps held the back of his neck with both hands and snaked his left leg around enough to clamp down on it with his right. Now, between his thighs, he had the man's head, neck, and left arm trapped.

Vamps squeezed his thighs together with all his strength.

The bodyguard pawed at him with his trapped arm and beat at his ribs with the other. His face reddened. Spittle escaped his mouth. He fought, struggled, tried to stand.

Then his body went limp.

Vamps held the triangle choke in place for a few more seconds, making sure the man was truly unconscious, then let go and pushed the chump aside. Mass would have been proud.

John Windsor aimed a revolver at Vamp's chest and cocked the hammer. "I think you've had enough fun. Time for you to fall in line."

Vamps rolled aside just as Windsor pulled the trigger. A chunk of road leapt up into the air, and so did Vamps, pouncing at the PM and knocking the revolver aside. Another gunshot went off, but he ignored it and head-butted the Prime Minister. Blood exploded across the man's cragged face and stained his thick moustache.

"You thug!"

"Fuck you, you blue-blood motherfucker." Vamps grabbed Windsor's throat and squeezed.

"ENOUGH!"

The bellow shook the ground and distracted Vamps enough for Windsor to bring up a knee into his groin. Agony exploded in his pelvis, and he doubled over, the ground rising to meet him. There he lay, looking back towards the gate.

Lord Amon held Ginge in his hand, twenty feet above the road. Ginge struggled and beat at the massive hand around his waist, but it was clear he could not breathe.

Mass had been beaten down and lay bleeding on the floor, a burnt man standing over him. A gunshot rang out somewhere.

It was over.

Vamps struggled to catch his breath as his testicles buzzed with agony. He reached out a hand to the giant holding his friend and begged. "P-please…"

Lord Amon stared at Vamps and grinned. Then he opened his hand and let Gingerbread fall.

Vamps cried out, wishing to defy gravity with pure willpower. Ginge's body shattered against the road, then Lord Amon lifted his foot and stepped on him.

2

Vamps screamed in a mixture of rage and grief. The pain in his heart was so intense that he was almost unaware of hands grasping him and pulling him to his feet. He was shoved back towards the gate where he was met by a bloody Mass.

Despite his condition, Mass was grinning. "I took out nearly a dozen, buster. Not a bad last stand."

Vamps bit down on his grief to give his one remaining friend a response. "Is that all, you pussy? I stuck the nut on the Prime Minister."

"Quiet, both of you," said the demon with dreadlocks who had helped capture them. "Your bodies will be given to dogs to copulate with."

Mass laughed. "Haven't you heard, mate? All dogs go to Heaven."

The demon walloped Mass across the face. He shook it off, but remained silent. Vamps looked at him and exchanged a glance of understanding. Neither would beg for life. Both would die with their balls intact.

"Resume duty and have the deed done," Lord Amon demanded.

"And make it hurt," the Prime Minister added.

"Prime Minister?" A group of suited bodyguards appeared from a side road. With them was Pusher, both his eyes blackened and swollen. He limped along with his hands cable-tied together. The flesh of his cheeks beneath the bruising was pale.

Windsor grinned ear to ear. "Ah, another escapee from the cages. Wonderful. You see, Lord Amon? I may have run into a complication or two, but I deliver in the end."

Lord Amon stood impassively, staring down at the Prime Minister with little interest. "Late result, poor result. Your noise irritates."

Windsor cleared his throat, spat a mouthful of blood caused by his broken nose, and stepped back submissively. He nodded to the bodyguards holding Pusher. "Get him in line with the other two. Sooner we show these people what happens to trouble-makers, the better."

They shoved Pusher into line beside Vamps, who sneered at the man who had left Ginge to the wolves. "Fuckin' backstabber."

"I have a son to think about. I left him with my sister, and she spends most her time on smack. I need to get back—"

"Don't pretend you have honour," said Mass. "Our friend is dead because you used him to escape. We live through this, I'm gunna kill you."

Pusher ignored Mass and waved his hand to get Windsor's attention. "Prime Minister. It was me who helped you capture these two and their friend. I'm on board with what you got going. Just let me go, and I'm your man for life, yo. I swear down."

Windsor glanced nervously up at Lord Amon, but then strode up beside Pusher. "Why would I want an untrustworthy snake in my midst? One who is mortally injured, no less."

Vamps glanced down and noticed for the first time that Pusher was badly hurt. The back of his shirt bloomed with blood, and it leaked down the back of his jeans in a steady trickle. The front of his shirt was clean. If one of the Prime Minister's men had shot him, the bullet had not passed through. Vamps was pretty sure that was bad.

"I'll be okay," said Pusher. "I eat bullets for breakfast."

"We cannot take a dying man," said the dreadlocked demon. "Our brothers need living vessels. Dispose of him."

Windsor looked Pusher in the eye. "Any last words?"

Pusher slumped to his knees. "I'll do anything. Please..."

"You shame yourself." Windsor raised the revolver he had pointed at Vamps and pulled back the hammer.

Pusher wept.

Vamps looked at the drug-dealing scumbag and actually felt pity. Pusher was just living by the rules of the street. The city made him, not something deeply embedded like the abominations coming through the gates. Windsor was doing what all men in power did—playing with the lives of the vulnerable for his own gain.

Windsor closed one eye and aimed. His finger tensed against the trigger.

"Please," Pusher begged.

Vamps placed his foot against Pusher and kicked out.

Windsor pulled the trigger. Pusher fell aside just in time, and the bullet flew out of Windsor's gun and hit the ground. As the Prime Minister cursed, he adjusted his aim at Vamps, but Mass rammed a shoulder into the PM and knocked him to the ground. The smoking revolver fell from his hand and bounced off the curb.

Vamps kicked out and caught the PM beneath the chin. A tooth flew into the air like an escaping fairy.

The demons closed in once more as Mass tumbled to the ground with the dreadlocked demon. Vamps focused his attention on the PM, but Windsor scuttled backwards behind a wall of demons ready to protect him as if he were one of their own. Vamps cursed the man, but knew he'd wasted yet another chance to end the maggot.

Pusher climbed to his feet, still weak and bleeding. He held out a hand to Vamps. "You saved me, blud. I dodged a bullet because of you. We need to get the hell out of here, or I'll never get to repay the favour."

Vamps felt the gate at his back, its surface shimmering and popping like hot soup. He saw the light reflecting in Pusher's eyes. Their hands met and the two of them shook hands for the first time. "I wasn't about to stand around and let that crooked fuck kill you," said Vamps. "Not when I wanted to end you myself."

Vamps yanked Pusher's hand and threw him towards the gate. Fear sparked in his eyes as he stumbled into the shifting net of colour and disappeared. He'd not even had time to scream, devoured by the gate like a stone falling into a pond.

Silence filled the air, as if all sound had been sucked into some far away funnel. Then the gate emitted a high-pitched whine. The lens shimmered wildly, the colours growing angry in hue—reds, blacks, and purples.

Mass grabbed Vamps and shoved him away. "I think you broke it!"

The two of them ran, shouting for anyone still living to do the same. For once, the crowd of captives listened and got up from the floor to run. The demons, however, stood around in stunned confusion, watching the gate fearfully.

They were terrified.

The high-pitched whining grew louder. The upper windows of the Selfridges building shattered and rained upon the street. Lord Amon bellowed, then turned and ran at great speed. Vamps enjoyed watching the giant run in terror, but his main thoughts were on getting away himself.

The gate exploded, bathing the whole of Central London in its furious glow.

.

Guy Granger

GUY GRANGER STOOD upon the bow of the USCG Hatchet and watched the south-western tip of the United Kingdom appear on the horizon. Never before had he sailed the English Channel, but he embraced it now as home waters for his children, Alice and Kyle, lay only a hundred miles inland.

"We can reach Portsmouth in a few hours, Captain," said Lieutenant Tosco at his right side.

"Who knows what we'll find," said the retired captain, Skip, to Guy's left.

Guy nodded. "We will find the world changed, as we have everywhere these last few days, but if my children are safe, then it is familiar enough for me."

"What will you do at Portsmouth?" asked Tosco unsubtly. The thought of gaining command of the Hatchet glowed green in his eyes.

"I don't yet know, but if I depart, I may need to return to the Hatchet once I have Alice and Kyle."

"We need to join the fight," said Tosco. "Back home ideally."

"This is the fight, Lieutenant. Alice and Kyle are children. Is saving them not the very essence of the fight we have before us?"

"There are many children besides your own who need help."

"And we shall help them, but before we reach Portsmouth, it would be unwise to plan."

"Agreed," said Skip. "We've been hearing the United Kingdom has a force assembling there. Who knows what aid they might offer us, or we them."

"We are not here to help the United Kingdom," said Tosco. "We serve the United States."

"Way I see it right now," said Skip, "we serve the human race."

Tosco went to speak again, but Guy cut him off. He knew a quest to save his children was selfish, but he didn't care. As captain of the ship, he had earned the right. Their time for being heroes would come later. For now, Alice and Kyle needed him to be their dad. He hadn't always been there, but he would be there when it counted.

He would be there for them soon.

They sailed in silence for the next hour, day breaking fully and giving the men on deck a brief respite to enjoy the sunshine. The day was mild, and run through with a gentle breeze, but it gave one cause to hope. Humanity might have fallen, but the day still displaced night as it was supposed to. The world still turned.

The south coast reeled along like a spool of rope pulled before them. Portsmouth would be upon them soon, and their fates decided. Tosco and Skip left to attend duties, but Guy remained upon the bow alone, looking out at a country not his own and praying that it still cared for his children.

The Hatchet listed starboard and then back, then rose up on an errant wave.

More waves followed. The ship tilted to and fro.

The English Channel was not the high seas, and such rough conditions were unexpected. Guy was about to hail the Bridge when a great booming roar skated across the water. The Hatchet leapt up on another massive wave, and Guy had to hold onto a railing to avoid going overboard.

Inland, the sky lit up with light bright enough to eclipse the sun. The explosion was massive, unparalleled by anything Guy had ever witnessed, and it came from the direction of London.

Alice. Kyle.

Hernandez

HERNANDEZ HELD CUERVO across his lap, stroking her damp hair. Her bloody scalp had matted, yet the sea clung to their skin with every spray of every wave and kept them wet. She had not spoken in more than an hour, and in the three preceding, had only mumbled incoherently. The young officer had followed Hernandez loyally and been rewarded with betrayal. He would see her wounds healed with willpower alone if he could.

He had always assumed his death would be upon the oceans, it was a noble, traditional death in a way, but to be marooned in the abyss like a Caribbean pirate... Dehydration would set in eventually—the salt water around him a cruel mockery—and then he would lose his mind. By the time he died he would have no idea who he was. Everything he had been would be a fever dream. He wondered about his ma, and if she was still alive. She would never see him again either way. Fury filled his veins. At his mutinous crew, yes, but more so in another direction. Granger.

Hernandez's downfall had begun the moment that lowly Coast Guard captain undermined him. It had forced him to enact strict rule or lose immediate control to that smug toad, Danza. Trying to win over the crew after his encounter with the Hatchet had been a losing task. Granger had sabotaged Hernandez's legacy. The Augusta was rightfully his after Johnson's death, but he had lost it.

Oh, how he would love to wrap his hands around Granger's neck. If his boat had sails, he would find wind and seek the man out. England, he said. Going to England to find his kids. When the man's country burns, he seeks only to fulfill his own needs.

The sun began to peek above the horizon, and told him he was facing east. If there was a God, he was taking Hernandez towards his desires. As if to confirm it, a beacon lit up a small patch of the retreating darkness.

A boat.

Hernandez shook Cuervo in his arms. "Wake up. We're saved. Wake up, Cuervo."

The woman remained still in his arms. And cold. When had she grown so cold?

"Cuervo?" Gently, he rolled her over in his arms and gazed into her face. All life had left her. It pained him that he was unsure exactly when it had happened. A woman died in his arms, and he hadn't noticed.

The boat would not see Hernandez in his tiny dinghy. Not unless he did something about it. He reached inside the waterproof container at the front of the boat and rooted around. From its contents, he found the small orange stick he was looking for and yanked off the end. The flare ignited, chasing away the darkness around the boat.

A horn blared out.

They saw him.

Hernandez took another item from the storage compartment, one he might need.

The boat took almost an hour to move close enough to collect him from his floating prison, and the origin of his rescuers brought irony along with them. It led Hernandez to unexplained laughing, which the English fishermen probably thought was madness of dehydration, or grief over the dead woman in his boat. But the laughter came because Hernandez was suddenly sure that his downfall would be amended with vengeance.

The captain of the small fishing hauler was an amiable man named Thomas, yet he did not appreciate being held at knifepoint. The long blade was the last item Hernandez had taken from the storage container, and it gave him back the authority Granger had taken from him. "Where were you men heading?" he demanded of the frightened skipper.

"Nowhere. We were planning to live off our catch and stay on the ocean until it's safe."

Hernandez pressed the knife closer to his windpipe. "You fool. The oceans are no safer than anywhere else."

The skipper seemed surprised. "Really? Then where should we go?"

Hernandez removed the knife from the man's throat and smiled. "I'm sorry, it's been a long couple of days. My exhaustion is making me mad. My ship was attacked by creatures from the ocean bed. It is not safe to be out here. We must make for land."

The skipper rubbed at his throat, but nodded and seemed willing to forgive. "Okay, fine, but where?"

Hernandez grinned wider. "Home. I want you to take me home."

"America?"

"Not my home, friend. I want you to take me to yours. Take me to England. I have someone there I need to see. I take it you know the way?"

The skipper nodded and once again seemed afraid of Hernandez.

He had reason to be. Hernandez had a score to settle, and anyone who tried to get in his way would pay dearly. Oh, yes. He was done playing by the rules.

Vamps

VAMPS OPENED HIS eyes and saw only light, but slowly, gradually, like grains of sand through an open fist, his vision returned. The world had filled with smoke and dust, a choking atmosphere that clawed its way into his lungs and made him choke. It was only the sound of his friend cursing blindly that told Vamps he was still alive.

"Fucking 'ell," said Mass. "My fuckin 'ed."

Vamps rolled onto his side and found his muscle-bound friend lying beside him. "You dead, man?"

"Nah, man."

"Good."

They lay there in silence for a few moments, trying to catch a breath against the cloying dust. At one point, Vamps turned his head and looked to the end of the road. He thought he saw Lord Amon disappearing into a side street, but strangest of all was that he was almost certain he saw a second giant stomping along beside him.

Two giants?

"V-Vamps?" The voice was not Mass, yet it was from a friend.

Vamps sat up, possessing more strength than he realised. "Gingerbread?"

Mass tried to get up with him, but his leg was busted, and he cried out. Vamps bid him to remain and searched the rubble for their friend. "Ginge, where are you?"

"O-over here."

Vamps clambered over the front end of a ruined Volvo and found his friend lying beneath a pile of bricks and concrete. Oxford Street had fallen down. "Ginge, you're alive?"

"I'm hungry."

Vamps laughed. "You always are."

The relief of seeing his friend was the greatest elation Vamps had ever felt. They had lost Ravy, but three brothers still remained. They had each other.

But the elation quickly faded when Vamps moved away some of the bricks and concrete from Ginge. He didn't mean to, but he sucked in air anxiously.

"What is it?" asked Ginge. "Is... Is it bad?"

Both of Ginge's legs were broken beyond repair, pointing in odd directions. His stomach was also twisted and hung oddly to one side. "Can you move?"

"I don't know. Can I?"

Vamps watched, but his friend remained still. Not a single finger moved. A tear traced its way through the dirt on Vamp's face and spilled onto his lap. "You're fine, mate. Just a couple of bruises. We'll get a few beers in you, and you'll walk it off."

"I'd rather have a snickers."

"I'll go get you one. You just rest, okay?"

Ginge was quiet for a moment, but then asked a question. "What happened, Vamps?"

"I don't know. The gate exploded."

"Oh. I thought it might have all been a dream."

Vamps looked around for the demons, but they had somehow perished in the explosion. Had the gate taken all those who had passed through it? Were the demons somehow bound to the gates? Lord Amon might still be present, but there was no way his underlings could have all hidden away so quickly.

Even the bodies of their dead had disappeared.

He patted Ginge on the arm. "It wasn't a dream, mate. It was a nightmare, but it's over now."

"Good. Because it was getting old."

Vamps laughed. "Yeah, it really was, wasn't it? If you hadn't kicked ass there at the end, we wouldn't have made it. You were a gangster."

Ginge smiled. "I w-was, wasn't I? Did I make you... proud? Did I..." His lips stopped moving and his eyes seemed to change. Whatever life he had clung to left him.

Vamps ran a hand affectionately over his friend's face. "Yeah, Ginge, you made me proud. I hope that before I join you, I can make you proud too."

Something in the rubble moved a hundred metres away, disturbing Vamps' final moments with his brother. John fucking Windsor.

The Prime Minister clambered out of a pile of metal and brick and dusted himself off. He was covered in as much blood as masonry, but his limbs were intact. When he saw Vamps sat up and looking at him, his eyes went wide, but he did not approach. Instead, he scurried away. Some of his men were still alive too, shocked and stunned, but still of service. They gathered up the PM, and together they built a quick retreat. Vamps considered chasing after them, but he was too tired, and he was not yet ready to leave his friend.

Something else moved in the rubble. Something closer.

"Is Ginge okay?" Mass shouted out from where he still lay.

Vamps stood up, looked at his friend and shook his head.

Mass swore loudly, then went silent. Vamps wasn't sure, but he thought his last remaining friend might have been weeping. But it was the movement in the rubble that was of most concern. Vamps was quite certain the demons were gone, but did danger still remain? Somehow, throwing Pusher through the gate had blown it up. There were other human survivors, Vamps realised now. They lay amongst the rubble, too afraid to move. Yet something did move.

A man.

While he was trapped beneath the rubble, he was not covered in either blood or dust. He was unhurt. Wearing ragged robes more suited to the Middle East than London, the man was able to stand up straight and face Vamps.

"Who are you?" Vamps demanded, examining the strange Arabic gentleman standing in the rubble before him.

The man looked around with confusion, seeming not to know where he was. All the same, he glanced at Vamps and gave an answer. "My name is Aymun, my friend, and it is good that I am here."

Vamps frowned. "Why?"

"Because I know how to kill the giants."

Rick Bastion

WEARY AND ILL, the survivors marched along the motorway. This time they headed south and were accompanied by no demons. They had freed themselves from slavery, and the memory of it spurred them on. Whether any semblance of safety still existed in Portsmouth, none of them knew, but having a destination kept them focused.

In total, there were fifty-seven of them. By no means an army, but at least a seed of one. As the demons had travelled the lands gathering up lost souls, so too would Rick and his companions, collecting bodies like a rolling stone collecting moss. Their numbers would swell.

For the last hour, since setting off from where Rick had closed the gate, Keith and the others had kept their distance from him. He was no longer the man they had known. He was something else—perhaps no longer even human. Daniel had left a part of himself inside Rick—had changed his very soul—and that unnerved the others, yet Rick knew that the dying angel had bestowed a gift. Daniel had been good, there was no doubt in his mind, and whatever he had done to Rick was to help them all.

Rick had no idea of his new powers, but he had dispatched The Caretaker and closed a gate. He could do things no other human could, and for that reason, he knew that he was important. His destiny was no longer his own. His body belonged to the people around him, and his power must be set towards good purpose. No longer could he think only of himself or those closest to him. It was time to start resisting. It was time to fight back on a grander scale. Looking back at the weary crowd behind him, Rick knew that the war had only just begun. And he had become a leader.

Yet leaders could lose battles as well as win them, and his decisions would get people killed. The only question would be how many and for what?

Rick had never felt so alone, not even in the alcohol-fuelled exile of his former life. His brother could barely look at him now, and Maddy— the one person who actually made him feel anything—was afraid of him. Would he ever be close to another again?

The road ahead was long and the end was unknown, but Rick was ready for whatever lay ahead. He hoped others would be ready too. The first line of a favourite song rang through his head and the lyrics were ominous.

All our times have come.

Here, but now they're gone.

Win or lose, things had changed forever, and so had every soul left alive.

Hell had come to earth, and its Legions scoured the earth. The reaper had come.

But Rick no longer feared him.

GET BOOK 3

EXTINCTION

SUMMER 2017, ONLY ON AMAZON

ABOUT THE AUTHOR

Iain Rob Wright is from the English town of Redditch, where he worked for many years as a mobile telephone salesman. After publishing his debut novel, THE FINAL WINTER, in 2011 to great success, he quit his job and became a full time writer. He now has over a dozen novels, and in 2013 he co-wrote a book with bestselling author, J.A.Konrath.

WWW.IAINROBWRIGHT.COM

Printed in Great Britain
by Amazon